Coming Home (Welcome to Chance – Book Six)

ELSA KURT

COMING HOME

Dedication

To my husband, always.

Contents

Acknowledgments

Writing the Welcome to Chance series has been such a true joy for me. As pleased as I am with the accomplishment, I find this a bittersweet moment. Saying farewell to the characters who've become so real to me is, in some ways, like leaving home.

I've had so much support and encouragement along this journey, and I'm deeply grateful to all who have contributed their insights, encouragement, advice, and praise (and critiques!). I'd like to again thank my very own Brightsiders – Annie and Bobby C. You two make my heart so happy. Thanks again to the monstrously talented and generous Dan Tracey, who wrote *You Don't Know My Heart* especially for the book. And thank you to Jane Lovett, Redhead Band, & the whole Open Mic crew.

These stories would not have been told without my readers asking for more. Is this truly the end of our time in Chance? I can't say for certain. I guess we'll all have to wait and see…

1 Feather Anne

Feather Anne debarked the private plane and stepped onto the tarmac. She hitched her battered backpack higher on her shoulder. Her gaze swept the runway, surrounding field, and stopped on the airport building. Home. She was *home*. For the first time since... since when? Eleven and a half months of touring, promoting, recording, pretending. Hours upon hours of rehearsing, performing, hopping on busses and planes, and doing it all over again.

Only twice since making it into the top five finalists on the Greatest American Singer had she visited Chance, and both were for publicity. Hardly relaxing homecomings. But now that was all over; her obligations fulfilled. She was free... unless she signed the contract John St. James had waved under her nose every day for the past two weeks.

No use thinking about that now, though. John gave her one month, and she planned on stretching it to the last minute. Her phone buzzed and Feather Anne grinned at the caller ID.

"Hi, Mae."

"Feather Anne? Where are you? I called your hotel room, and they said you'd checked out."

Feather Anne sighed. So much for the element of surprise. The driver hired by the record company pulled up, and as she climbed into the backseat, she huffed into the receiver, "Well, it was *supposed* to be a surprise, but... I'm home." She sang the last word.

"Home? Here? In Chance? But..."

"Calm down, crazy pants. I'm at the airport, leaving now. I'll be there in about forty-five minutes. You at the café or home?"

"Oh, my God," Mae squealed into the phone. "Oh, but why didn't you tell me? I could have picked you up, and—"

"Don't be silly. I have a driver."

"I forgot; my baby sister is a big-shot star." She mimicked Feather Anne. "I have a driver, la-de-dah."

Feather Anne snorted. "Oh, shut up. And listen, don't make a big fuss, okay?"

"Yeah, yeah. No fuss, whatever." Mae's tone

was too agreeable.

"Mae," said Feather Anne as threateningly as possible. "I mean it. I just want to slip into town quietly; no banners, or cameras, or—"

"Okay, fine. But I can't help if everyone is excited to see you."

In the background, Feather Anne heard the familiar voices of the Brightsiders and Rosabelle. They called out their hellos and *hurry home* orders. Feather Anne said, "Tell them hi for me. I take it you're at the café, then?"

"Oh, sorry, yes. Melina's on her honeymoon, so I'll be here until at least four. You'll come straight here, right?"

"Yes, of course. What about the twins?"

"Afterschool book club until three-forty-five, then Gina is picking them up for me and bringing them here."

"How about I have the driver bring *me* to pick them up instead?"

"They'd love that. I'll text Gina and let her know. See you soon, brat."

"See you soon, sis."

"Hey," said Mae. "Everything okay? I thought you still had another two weeks."

"Yeah, no. Everything is fine. Just homesick."

"Yeah, well, we've missed you, too. Like crazy."

After they'd said goodbye, Feather Anne rested

against the seat, the phone to her chest and her gaze out the window. She looked at the screen again, her finger hovering over the text icon. Two unread messages. Was she ready to read either?

"Nope." Feather Anne set the phone on the seat beside her and closed her eyes. *Later*. She'd deal with it later.

The quiet lasted thirty seconds before her phone—face down—vibrated against the seat. Who would it be this time? John St. James? Mae again? Another name floated underneath the others, but she refused to let it surface.

It won't be him. He doesn't know I'm back. He wouldn't care even if he did.

Feather Anne told herself this, not believing it. It'd be so much easier to not care. But it would also be a lie. *She* cared. She cared so much it left a hollow ache in her heart. She flipped the phone over with a sigh. John St. James.

"Hey, John. I landed. Safe and sound." She'd forgotten to call him.

"There she is. Listen, no pressure, but Entertainment Tonight wants to do a segment on your big homecoming. Killer, right?"

"*No*, John. You said I'd have this time to myself," said Feather Anne. She glared down at the hole in her jeans and picked at the threads holding it together.

"Yeah, I know, but—"

"But nothing. You *said*." She hated the whine in her tone almost as much as she hated the cajoling in his.

"Hang on. I'm putting Claire on the phone."

"No, I don't want—"

"Sweetie, hi. It's Claire. Listen. This is an exceptional opportunity for you. You should do it."

Claire Benoit—the publicist hired by the Greatest American Singer to manage the top five while under contract with the show—had a fake, saccharine sweet voice. It made Feather Anne's teeth hurt. When Claire got on the line, it meant it was an order, not a request. John St. James had a knack for giving all the dirty work to his staff, leaving him to play the role of martyr, hero, or sympathizer when the occasion called for it.

Feather Anne deflated. No sense fighting it, they'd win for as long as they had her under contract.

"When are they coming?"

"One sec, sweetie," said Claire.

A rustling and muffled words followed, then John came back on the line. "That's my girl. They'll be there Thursday. Claire's flying in to be with you."

"Thursday? That's in two days. I thought—wait, why is Claire coming? Doesn't Shayna need her for—"

"Relax, kid. Shayna's got a few years on you; she's an old pro," said John.

"Yeah, okay, but *she* was the winner of the

show. Doesn't she, like, take priority or whatever?"

It relieved Feather Anne when Shayna won the coveted title of the Greatest American Singer. All the pressure would be on her, *not* Feather Anne and Nick. Second place was no bad deal, anyhow. Option to sign a recording contract, a new car for each of them, commercial deals, and a damn good chunk of change to stick in the bank were all fine with her.

John hedged. "Listen, between me and you? She's not cut out for this. The limelight, the pressure—it's getting to her."

Feather Anne's head jerked back in surprise. She, Shayna and Nick—along with the other finalists—had grown close over the tour. Never had Shayna showed any struggles. Nothing more than the usual griping they all did. Long hours, traveling, rehearsing, missing family… they all felt it.

"She didn't say anything to me," said Feather Anne. Her crash course in everything music business made her wary.

"Kid, don't bust my balls, huh? Why are you questioning it? This is a good thing for you. Potentially, I mean."

Feather Anne's suspicions were just. John St. James and the rest of the suits had something planned, and they would rope her into whatever it was. Before she levied more questions at him, John jumped in again.

"Okay, listen, I gotta go. You enjoy your family

time, huh? We'll be in touch."

"Wait, I—" Feather Anne shouted into the phone, but the line had already disconnected.

Damn you, John St. James.

The driver caught her eye, and she smiled. "We voted for you," he said. "My entire family."

"Yeah? That's cool. Thanks."

With his eyes on the road, he added, "We thought you and Nick should've won. Shayna's great, but…" He shrugged and met her eyes. "We all hoped you and Nick would say if you're a couple."

The driver—seeing Feather Anne's stony expression—must have understood he'd overstepped and apologized.

"It's all good… sorry, what's your name?"

"Brian."

"Well, thanks again, Brian."

She never got used to that part. People—total strangers—talking to her about… about *her*. Like they were invested or knew her. Asking personal questions, offering their opinions on everything from what she wore to whether her and Nick were a couple. That the hashtag #featherannesflock trended on Twitter and adolescent girls showed up at the shows wearing feather earrings and t-shirts with her and Nick's faces on them still freaked her out. Everyone kept telling her to enjoy it while it lasted, but there'd been no time to process anything, let alone enjoy it.

Now John wanted her to sign a solo recording contract. Did *she* want that? Someone else's hand in her art? They'd already taken the song she wrote—a mellow acoustic—and turned it into some techno-pop trash. If *that* was their "vision" for her music, then she had no interest. Could she walk away from the opportunity of a lifetime, though? Because that's what everyone called it: an *opportunity of a lifetime*. Her one in a million shot.

Feather Anne's shoulders had crept back up by her ears and Brian the driver's eyes kept darting up to the rearview mirror to look at her. She forced her shoulders back down and fixed her gaze on the passing scenery. The routine was all too familiar. It happened everywhere she went. The glances and stares, the whispers. The girls nudging and shoving each other to be the first to ask for an autograph. The guys who gawked but never had the nerve to approach. The guys who *did* have the nerve. Thank God for security.

"You're gonna miss all this," said John St. James at the airport.

They'd needed security to get through the terminal when the travelers spotted the paparazzi trailing John, Claire, and Feather Anne. What would've happened if she'd insisted on flying commercial? She shuddered and realized what an absolute diva she sounded like.

The first sign marking her as home was a literal

one.

"Could you slow down for a sec?"

Brian checked the rearview for traffic and slowed down. Feather Anne clicked a photo of the Welcome to Chance sign. A grin spread across her face and her hand drifted up to the compass tied with a leather string around her neck. The last gift from William had carried her through some of her roughest days on the road. A reminder of where she came from and where she always had a place. *Home.*

2 Mae

Brianna slipped her credit card from her designer wallet and handed it to Mae. "Was that Feather Anne?"

Mae—unable to contain her excitement—leaned toward Brianna and said, "She's on her way home right now." Then she clamped a hand over her mouth. "Shoot. I'm not supposed to tell anyone."

"I'm hardly *anyone*, Mae," said Brianna with a sniff.

"No, right. Of course, you're not. I mean, just don't tell anyone else."

The clarification mollified Brianna, and their fragile friendship survived another day. Mae sidled away when Brianna's phone rang, but returned a few minutes later to find her still there.

"Oh, I'm sorry, Brianna. Was there something else you wanted?"

"Yes. The banana cream pie—boxed, to go—and to plan a welcome home party for Feather Anne."

Mae's mouth opened and closed. "I-oh. Well, I don't know, Brianna. Feather Anne was pretty insistent about not making a fuss. So—"

"Nonsense. Chance's famed daughter returns to the nest, and we do nothing to commemorate the occasion?"

"Oh, now, it's not like she hasn't been home at *all*."

"Yes, but that was with cameras and hysteria, and all the craziness. This will be family and friends, no groupies or hashtag Byrd Feathers, or whatever it is they call themselves." Brianna waved a disdainful hand at the notion of Feather Anne's rabid fan base.

Mae laughed. "I think its hashtag Feather Anne's Flock. Something like that. Okay, the family and friends thing; she'll be okay with that, I think."

"Excellent. It's settled then. I've already spoken to the country club; we can use the ballroom. I'll design, you cater, yes?"

"I-I—wait. That was fast. When did you speak to the country club?" Mae sputtered.

"While you were in back doing… whatever it is you do. You know what they say, Mae. If you want something done, ask a busy person to do it."

"Yeah, I think I've—"

"Well, I'm off. I can't wait around for the little waif to get here. I'll text her from the car. Thanks for the pie. Here, keep the change."

In rapid succession, Brianna slapped a twenty-dollar bill on the counter, snatched the boxed pie under her arm, and breezed out the door. Mae watched her take the sunglasses off her head and place them on her face. When Brianna turned back to the café, Mae almost ran in back to avoid her, but she didn't move fast enough.

"Did you forget something?" Mae tilted her head.

"No. Yes. I—how are you? I mean, you know. How *are* you?"

Mae's brow creased, and she faltered. "Oh, I-I'm fine. Really. Thank you."

Brianna looked as if she might say more but changed her mind. "Right. Good. Okay, then. I'll email you the details tonight. Hug the brat for me."

This time she really left. Although her perfume lingered. Mae sighed and glanced at the calendar. The one-year anniversary of William's death loomed. She didn't need the calendar to tell her though. It was in everyone's over-bright smiles and gentle gazes. They all asked how she was the same way Brianna had. How *are* you? How are you *doing*? *Are* you doing all right, Mae?

They meant well. Mae couldn't be angry or too frustrated with them, but it didn't mean she welcomed their sad eyes and soft tones. In fact, she longed to yell, "Act *normal*, damn it." Especially when they did it around Evvie and TK. The Huxley-Grants were not victims. They did not need pity or special attention, or to be treated different. What they needed to do was live a happy, fulfilling life. The way William would have wanted them to do.

The only ones who understood were Feather Anne and Katrina. And both of them were halfway around the world most of the time. But not for long. A glance at the clock told her Feather Anne would arrive with the twins any—

"Hey, sis. How about you quit daydreaming and say hello." Feather Anne—looking taller, thinner, and more beautiful than ever—smirked at her older sister. Evvie and TK had glued themselves to her thighs and hardly acknowledged their mother.

Mae dropped the cake server and dashed around the counter, joining her children in squeezing the stuffing out of Feather Anne. The handful of diners left in the café applauded and someone called out, "Welcome home, superstar."

Feather Anne extracted herself from Mae's smother-hold to see who it was. Her face lit up, and she walked across the café, dragging the twins with her.

"Mr. B.! Man, you're a sight for sore eyes," said Feather Anne.

Her voice wobbled at the end, and the man who'd been like a surrogate grandfather to her patted her cheek. His eyes were red-rimmed, as were everyone else's by then. "It's good to have you home, dear."

"Wait. Where's Mrs. B.?" She looked around the café, then back at Mae.

"Georgie is next door, doing her Ti Chi class with Lotus. She'll be here any minute," said Charles.

Mae shooed the twins away and touched her arm. "Hungry?"

"Starving," replied Feather Anne.

"Sit. I'll make your favorites."

Mae left Feather Anne with Charles Brightsider and hurried back to the kitchen. She gathered ingredients and prepped the stovetop with absent attention—the kind that comes from long practice of a skill—and focused her thoughts on Feather Anne. The girl looked way too thin and her gray eyes seemed wary as they panned over the café. Like she expected an attack at any moment. This was the price for fame, it would seem.

When Mae returned with Feather Anne's salmon burger and a pile of sweet potato fries, she overheard Charles asking her if she planned on coming to the open mic. "It's tomorrow," he said as Mae set the plate before her sister.

"Oh," said Mae, "she's probably tired of performing—"

"No," said Feather Anne. "It's not that, really. I love the performing part. But… I don't want the entire night to be about me, you know? It, uh, tends to become a circus. I'd hate to take away from any of the local talent."

Mae studied her sister. Who *was* this introspective, reserved girl? Where had that devil may care attitude and fireball energy gone? The old Feather Anne would have attacked that burger with borderline savage glee and devoured the sweet potato fries in a blink. *This* Feather Anne plucked the bun off the burger and set it aside and used her fork to push the fries around the plate.

Ignoring the other conversation for a moment, Mae said, "I thought you were hungry?"

"I am," assured Feather Anne. She speared and ate a fry to prove her point. "Don't be a mother hen, Mae. And stop looking at me like that."

"What?" Mae threw her hands up, palms out. "I'm not looking at you like anything."

"Oh, look, there's my lovely bride," said Charles in a loud voice.

Mae and Feather Anne each gave the sly old man a knowing look. But the distraction technique had its base in fact; Georgie Brightsider, in a pale-yellow track suit and her purse slung over her arm, walked across the café, arms outstretched to welcome Feather Anne.

The girl sprang up and went to the woman, accepted the hug in her classic, awkward way. This made Mae smile. *There's our girl.* Maybe time at home was all she needed to reset and get grounded again.

Charles must have read her thoughts. He patted her hand and said, "Give her a bit of time. She'll settle back in."

Later, after everyone left, and the sign switched to CLOSED, Mae, Feather Anne, and the twins sat in a booth and rolled silverware into napkins. TK gave a long, detail rich report on all he'd been up to since Feather Anne had last seen him. To her credit, Feather Anne seemed genuinely interested and amused by her nephew.

When he finished, Feather Anne praised him and said, "You remind me so much of your Dad, you know that?"

Without batting an eye, TK said, "Yeah, Mommy says that, too. And that I'm handsome like him. Next week is Daddy's heaven birthday. We're going to the park to have a… what's it called again, Mommy?"

"A memorial," said Mae. She smiled at her earnest, smart boy.

"I'm making the cake," piped in Evvie.

Mae corrected her. "You and Gigi are making a cake together. Remember what I told you?"

Evvie—like a miniature Feather Anne—rolled her eyes. "No baking without an adult. I *know*."

Feather Anne tried and failed to suppress a laugh. "Do I want to know?"

"Go on, tell your Auntie Feather Anne what you did, miss."

After some cajoling, the little raven haired, gray-eyed child explained that she'd been trying to make cupcakes for a surprise and spilled the entire bowl of batter on the counter. Mae added that the batter also splattered onto the backsplash, over the stovetop, and onto the floor. Evvie had tripled the recipe.

Feather Anne, still smirking, questioned Mae. "Oh, boy. On whose watch did that happen?"

"Who do you think?" Mae quirked an eyebrow at her sister.

In unison, they said, "Chris."

Still laughing, Feather Anne asked, "So what time is their Gigi and Pop getting back from their camping trip?"

Mae looked up at the clock. "Sometime tonight. I told them you were home. Sorry."

Feather Anne shrugged. "It's all good. I planned on texting Gina when we got home."

"You're not mad anymore about the interview?"

During the height of the Greatest American Singer frenzy—or *Feather Anne and Nick* frenzy—reporters had often shown up in Chance looking to interview anyone who knew either of the two. The town—at least those who *did* know Feather Anne and Nick—banded together and shut down the interviews. One persistent and sneaky reporter conned Gina into hiring her at the bakery and proceeded to mine personal information and even family photos of Feather Anne growing up.

When the story published, the reporter made it look like Gina had knowingly given the woman the information. Lawsuits were threatened, and the reporter gave a public apology and retracted the story, but as far as Feather Anne cared, the damage was done. She'd been livid with Gina for being so gullible and naïve, and Mae had to act as a go between for weeks. It relieved her to see a thaw in Feather Anne's cold grudge.

"No, I guess not. She seems to have learned her lesson. So, this memorial… is it just for—"

"It's for all of us, and anyone who'd like to join." Mae reassured her sister. She'd noticed the compass, still worn around her neck just as it had been throughout the tour. "Your tribute to him last week was beautiful, by the way."

At the last show of the finalist tour, Feather Anne had taken the stage solo to sing the song she'd auditioned with—Wild Horses—and dedicated it to William. When she couldn't finish the lyrics through her tears, the crowd sang for her. It was a beautiful, moving moment, but knowing Feather Anne as she did, she suspected her sister had been furious with herself for letting her emotions show in such a public way.

"Damn cell phone cameras." She made no further comment.

Mae let it go to tackle another touchy subject. "And… have you and Nick spoken since—"

"Nope. According to Twitter, he's in Nashville, working on his big, new album."

She said *big, new album* in a snarky, sneering tone, so Mae inferred all she needed to know about that situation. The next minefield she considered tiptoeing into was whether Feather Anne had spoken to Brandon. Before she could form the question, her phone buzzed on the table. Both she and Feather Anne looked down at it.

"Brianna? Why is Brianna Baker calling *you*?" Feather Anne's incredulous expression turned suspicious.

"It's nothing," said Mae, two octaves too high.

"*Mae*. Why is Brianna calling you? Does this have something to do with Brandon, because I—"

"No, no. She wants to throw a welcome home party for you, and I couldn't say no." Mae let out the breath she'd been holding.

Feather Anne dropped her head on the table, making Evvie and TK giggle. Without lifting her head, she felt around the table for the buzzing phone, grabbed it, and held it up to Mae. She knew as well as anyone: no one said no to Brianna Baker.

Mae took the phone and answered. "Brianna, hi." She looked at Feather Anne and said, "Yes, she's here," paused for Brianna's reply, then said, "Good. Yes, she looks good." A series of *mhm*'s, *okay*'s, and *sounds good* followed each subsequent pause. When she ended the call, she gave Feather Anne a guilty smile.

"Spill it. What have you gotten me into?"

Mae placated. "Now, it's not so bad, really. Saturday evening, friends and family only. Fifty people, tops. Ultra-casual."

"Hmph," replied Feather Anne. After a few minutes of sulking and rolling silverware, she said, "So, fill me in on the latest gossip. What have I missed?"

Mae thought for a moment. "Hmm, let's see. You know the Rosabelle and Miles are expecting their third—gender unknown—any time now?"

"No way? That's awesome," said Feather Anne.

"Yep. And Charlotte and Joel adopted a little girl from Guatemala. She's one-and-a-half and her name is Belinda."

"So, that makes Benjamin, Brooklynn, and Belinda? Cute."

"Very. Who else? Now, you saw for yourself the Brightsiders are doing amazing. Active as ever. And Lotus and Dylan are great—wait until you see Petal, you're going to die—and who am I forgetting? Oh, the Villeneuves! Did you know Marisol was an attorney, too? Well, she started practicing again and she and Pedro share an office building."

"Wow, but yeah, I think I remember her mentioning it when I used to babysit for them. So, no one else to update me on? No one at all?"

Mae unrolled and re-rolled a silverware set but didn't look up. "Yep. I think so."

"Mhm. Okay, so you have said nothing about Bruce."

"I didn't? Huh. Well, nothing much to say. I mean, not that I know of. I hardly see him." Mae tried to sound nonchalant. By the way Feather Anne stared at her, she'd failed. Mae amended. "We're both just super busy, I guess."

Truth be told, Bruce's ghosting hurt Mae's feelings after the funeral. She tried to be understanding and even appreciated his... what was it? Respect for William? Yes, that... but she suspected it had more to do with his fear of saying or doing anything that might offend her and jeopardize their friendship. Ironic, now that they barely had a friendship to speak of.

Before Feather Anne could grill her further, she dropped her own loaded question. "Have you talked to Brandon at all?"

"Nope," said Feather Anne. "Last I knew, he got his scholarship at UCONN and he was living the college dream."

Mae cocked her head at her sister. "You... don't know?"

Feather Anne's head jerked up, and the color drained from her face. "What? Something happened to him?"

Mae's expression softened. The reaction showed more than friendly concern and proved to her that her sister's feelings still ran deep for her old boyfriend. "He's fine, Feather Anne. But he tore his ACL again, and they revoked the scholarship. He's working for Ricky at the auto body shop."

Feather Anne swallowed. "Oh."

"What do you say we get out of here, huh? Go home?"

Feather Anne rallied and offered Mae a terse smile. "Yeah, that sounds good."

3 Bruce

"Yo, old man. Aren't you scared you're gonna throw your back out?"

Bruce heaved the log onto the pile he'd made and faced Feather Anne. "Old man, huh? That's how you greet me after four months? Get over here, you little shit."

Feather Anne shuffled forward and let Bruce pull her into a bear hug. She pretended she hated it, but he knew better. After he set her back down, he tossed a pair of work gloves her way. She slipped them on without batting an eye and that minor act relieved him to no end. *She's still Feather Anne. They didn't change her. Thank fricking God.*

He watched from the corner of his eye as she hoisted one of the smaller logs—still a good size and heft—and carried it over to the rest. They worked in silence for a good fifteen minutes. When they'd cleared the remaining logs from around the fresh stump, they sat on the ground and wiped the sweat from their brows.

"Place looks good." Feather Anne thrust her chin at the restored Victorian and the grounds. "You clearing all the trees, though?"

"Nah. Just these guys closest to the house. The storm last month had them swaying too close for comfort."

"Good. I like the trees."

"Mhm. So, we gonna talk about the elephant in the… yard?" Bruce lifted an eyebrow at Feather Anne.

She reciprocated. "Which one?"

Puzzled, Bruce frowned at her. Then he realized what—or rather, who—she referred to. *Mae.* Her name in his head still shot a physical pain through his heart. He ignored it, and Feather Anne's retort. "You know who I'm talking about. Nick. What's going on with you two?"

Feather Anne picked up a jagged piece of bark and picked at it. She didn't look at Bruce. "Nothing. He baled, I stayed. End of story. It's all good." Her shrug suggested indifference, but the way she massacred the bark said otherwise.

"He said he asked you to join him."

Bruce kept his tone neutral. He wasn't taking sides; he just wanted to hear her version of things. Nick leaving the finalist tour after the first night caused a significant amount of drama in the public eye and he could only assume privately as well. So far, neither Nick nor Feather Anne had addressed it in any capacity.

"Yeah. As an afterthought." Feather Anne sneered. "*Some* people believe in honoring a commitment, let alone a contract, but not Nick Amendola." She threw the fragment of bark left in her hand.

"But it's *all good*, huh?" Bruce tried not to smirk.

"Anyhow. What's the deal with you and Mae? She says she's hardly seen you since..." She trailed off.

William's funeral.

He'd slipped and said something stupid that day, took it back as best he could, and they'd seemed okay. Only, Bruce was far from okay. He'd more or less made a move on a woman *at her husband's funeral.* A man who'd been nothing but a gracious friend to Bruce, and that's how he'd repaid the friendship.

He sickened himself. Feather Anne didn't need to know any of it. Unless Mae already told her. His heart stuttered at the thought. But one glance at her open, blameless expression told him otherwise.

Bruce cleared his throat. "Yeah, well... you know. Been real busy with—"

"*Busy*? Seriously? That's what you're going with? You've been too *busy*. Don't bullshit me, old man. It's because you're still in love with her and you're trying to be, like, all respectful and shit. Am I right?"

Bruce had just tilted his water bottle to his lips for a swig. He coughed and the liquid splashed onto his face and shirt. "Jesus, kid. Don't hold back, huh?"

"Don't avoid the question, huh?"

Bruce tipped his water bottle at her as if to say *touché*. He stalled for an answer appropriate for Mae's kid sister. Lying wouldn't do. Bruce's love for Mae had become wallpaper—something seen but ignored after time—to almost everyone in Chance. Maybe he exaggerated, but not by much.

"Feather Anne, it is what it is, you know? It's better this way."

"Better for who? I can tell you it's not better for Mae. She misses you. She *needs* you in her life, Bruce."

Bruce shook his head.

Feather Anne emphasized. "She *does*."

His mouth spoke against his will. "She say that?"

"She didn't have to. I can tell. Just go see her."

"Yeah, okay," said Bruce.

"I mean it," said Feather Anne.

Bruce pointed at her. "Make you a deal, sport. You talk to Nick, and I'll talk to Mae. Deal?"

Feather Anne rolled her eyes. "When he gets back from Nashville."

If she thought she had a long time before that happened, she was mistaken. "Good. His flight comes in tomorrow."

"Tomorrow? Shit," groaned Feather Anne. "You played me, old man."

"Not at all. I figured maybe you knew already." He shrugged, feigning innocence.

She stood and dusted off her jeans. "Well, I gotta motor. Brianna wants to meet for lunch and—"

"No one keeps Brianna Baker waiting. Yeah, I know. Go on, get lost then. Hey, your old job is here if you want it. Unless you're too much of a superstar for all this blue-collar work, that is."

Feather Anne chuckled. "I'll keep it in mind. Thanks. My people will get in touch with your people."

Bruce waved her off with a laugh. He grabbed his work gloves and the ones she'd left on the stump and brought them inside; a grin still on his face. *Smartass kid. Good to have her home. When my boy arrives, it'll feel like old times again. Almost like old times.* The smile faltered. So much had changed in a year. Bruce reconsidered. No, not a lot had changed, but one major thing that made his entire world feel unbalanced. Maybe Feather Anne was right. Enough time had gone by; he could trust himself not to be a fool around Mae. Couldn't he?

4 Rosabelle

Miles plucked a bagel slice off Rosabelle's plate and clamped it between his teeth. She tried to yank it back but—with the tiny passenger in her belly—was too slow. He jerked his head back and waggled his eyebrows.

"Did you just take food from a pregnant woman? You must have a death wish, Hannaford." Rosabelle's eyes held menace, but her smirk held a trace of humor.

"Sorry, babe. Here, you want it back?" He held it out.

"Ew. No, not after you've slobbered all over it," said Rosabelle. She crinkled her nose in disdain.

"You didn't seem to mind my—"

"Not in front of the children, Miles."

Miles looked at the girls with his eyes crossed and Fiona and Poppy giggled. Amusement and reproach replaced the menace.

"Don't get them started," she said. "And I packed your breakfast to go. Right on the counter. Now beat it."

Rosabelle turned her cheek up for a kiss. Miles' face hovered beside hers until she turned it to look at him. The second she did, he kissed her on the mouth. This elicited more giggles from the girls and Fiona clapped and sang, "Daddy kiss Mommy, Mommy kiss Daddy."

Miles wagged a thumb at the girls and said to Rosabelle, "You're raising a couple of voyeurs, Mrs. Hannaford. For shame."

"Ha," snorted Rosabelle. "Enjoy their approval now; in a few years they'll be saying *ew, that's disgusting* when we kiss in front of them."

"In that case…" Miles finished the sentence by smothering Rosabelle with kisses until she squealed for him to stop.

He did—eventually—and stood up as if no silliness had occurred. "Remember, I'll be out of the office the first half of the morning for my D.A.D.s meeting, then I have two closings and a late commercial showing."

"Got it. And *I'll* be teaching my art class at ten, bringing the girls to kid's yoga at eleven-thirty, then meeting up with Mae and the girls at one. You're not the only one with a big day ahead, buddy."

Miles snatched up his lunch tote and keys. "Hey, speaking of Mae, I'm hearing buzz around town that Feather Anne is back. You see her yet?"

"No. She's been lying low until the party; doesn't want a fuss."

"Party? We invited?" Miles stopped at the door.

"Yes, of course. Although, fair warning, Brianna is throwing it."

Miles mocked choking, gripping his throat and rolling his eyes up. This sent the girls into another fit of giggles. Miles shrugged an apology and left Rosabelle to settle them down again. She didn't mind; not really. Having her life—*their* life—back on track again had restored her sense of security.

Neither shied from acknowledging it had been a rough year. The roughest they'd faced, even compared to Rosabelle's near-paralyzing accident. They never gave up on each other, though. That was their superpower, as Miles called it. But when they discovered she was pregnant again—a surprise—she feared the stress might trigger his depression. Instead, it fueled the fire he'd lit under himself to stay grounded.

Around the same time—maybe even because of the pregnancy—Miles started a support group for dads with depression, calling it Dads and Depression, D.A.D.s for short. According to Miles, the percentage of men—fathers, specifically—battling and masking depression because of societal beliefs staggered him and he wanted to do something about it. With the help of his therapist, they created the group and have been going strong for the past four months.

"Hel-*lo*," sang Ruth Waterman as she tip-toed into the kitchen. "Are my beautiful granddaughters ready for their Bubbe?"

"Good morning to you, too, Mom," said Rosabelle. "Geesh, I see how I rate these days."

Ruth patted her daughter's head as she breezed by to smother her granddaughters with hugs and kisses. "Now, now. Hugs and kisses to you, too." She looked up from her grandchild sandwich to say, "Is that what you're wearing?"

Rosabelle sighed as she heaved herself from the chair. "No, Mother. I'll be changing out of my robe, and slippers, thank you. Where's Dad? I thought he was coming with you?"

"Your father is home, putting together the table from IKEA he insisted on buying yesterday."

"Another project, huh?" Rosabelle smirked. Since they'd stopped traveling the country in their RV and settled back in Chance again, Stephen Waterman had found a lengthy series of hobbies that all ended with a garage full of half-finished projects.

Ruth raised a hand to ward off the subject. "Don't get me started. Anyhow, you go get ready for your class and I'll take my precious angels with me."

"Thanks, Mom. Meet you back here at eleven?"

"Or, I could just bring them to yoga, and you can relax for a bit," said Ruth.

The way she said it sounded more like an order than an offer. "I'm fine, Mom. It's not like it's my first rodeo, so—"

"All the more reason to rest when you can. If your husband's minor episode taught us anything, it's to take time for self-care."

Rosabelle's eyebrows crept up, and she suppressed a smirk. "Self-care, huh?"

"Yes, self-care. Your mother is more enlightened than you think, missy. Now go. I'll bring the girls back in the afternoon."

She kissed her girls goodbye and shuffled out of the kitchen and up the stairs. Sunny followed behind with his tennis ball lodged in his mouth. When Ruth, Poppy, and Fiona left minutes later, the house fell silent. Rosabelle knew she should cherish the quiet, but she'd become used to the chaos of their life and the absence seemed *wrong*.

"Who'd have thought it, huh, Sunny? The introvert craving noise and people?"

Sunny picked his head up and thumped his bushy tail on the floor. His big head tilted left, then right, and he whined around the ball still clamped between his jaws. His round, brown eyes watched her; he was on high alert for any sign of an impending game of fetch.

"Not right now, buddy. I've got to get dressed for my class."

As if he understood, Sunny plopped his head back onto his paws and let the ball roll from his mouth to the carpet. Rosabelle pulled out her favorite painting clothes—baggy overalls and a t-shirt that were not so baggy anymore—and twisted her hair into a loose bun.

Twenty minutes later, she stared up at the community center building where a hand printed sign on the door read, "**All New Classes Use Doors On Left**," with an arrow pointing left in case there was any confusion on which way was 'left.'

Her art career had stalled after the birth of their second child and life impeded pursuing it with the same tenacity she'd had before. Sure, plenty of women managed the tightrope balance of career and home life, but Rosabelle didn't *want* to be a tightrope walker. She wanted a peaceful life, a calm life. So, she gave up one passion for another and told herself maybe someday she'd pick up where she left off. For now, teaching art once a week and painting for the sheer pleasure of it in her studio would do. She rested her hand over her belly. With this little one added to the mix, it *had* to do… for now.

5 Pedro

At about the same time as Rosabelle Hannaford pulled up to the community center, Pedro and Marisol Villeneuve unlocked the doors to their law office across town. They bickered good-naturedly over who would put on the coffee in the kitchenette, then over who'd pick up the kids from school and daycare.

"Mi amor, I told you last night I have a late client," said Pedro.

"And I told *you* my sister is arriving, so you must pick them up so I can get her from the airport."

"And what is little Effie's latest drama," asked Pedro, holding the door open for his wife with a chivalrous sweep of his hand to usher her in.

"No drama," said Marisol with a hint of defensiveness.

"So, I am to believe Ophelia hopped on a jet from whatever island she was on this month to come to Connecticut to see her family for no reason?" He quirked a dark eyebrow at his wife.

She tossed her briefcase onto a chair and allowed, "Okay, maybe a little drama. She broke up with Jason. I guess they had a big fight and, well, she's coming home."

"To our house, you mean."

Marisol conceded. "Yes, but it's like a home to her. Especially with Mami and Papi no longer in our childhood home."

"I'm sure they have room for her in their condominium in Clearwater. Why doesn't she go there?"

This was the wrong thing to say if he'd any hope of diffusing their quarrel. Marisol crossed her arms over her chest and leaned against the door frame. Now her eyebrow curved at him. "Are you saying to me, *mi amor*, that you do not want my only sister— my baby sister—to come visit with me, her big sister who misses her, and her nieces and nephew who adore her?"

If Pedro wanted to sleep in their bed and not on the couch that night, he needed to backpedal fast. "I am not saying that. I would never say such a thing. I just thought maybe she would want some quality time with your parents, too." He smiled widely.

A changed expression came over Marisol's face; one Pedro liked less than the previous. Before he could contemplate what the look meant, she said, "You are so right, *mi cariño*. She would love to spend time with them. I'll book their flight right now."

Pedro's smile faltered. "Wait, what? Book their flight to where? Here? Connecticut? Now?"

She patted his cheek with a sly smile. "Yes, here. Connecticut. Now. And they, too, will stay with us."

Gloriana, their office manager, walked in, said good morning, and glanced from one Attorney Villeneuve to the other Attorney Villeneuve. She looked down and side-stepped through them to get to her desk. If she sensed any discordance between the couple, she pretended to not notice and instead started right in on business.

"Let's see. Mrs. V., you have an immigration hearing for Miguel Hernández at ten, and a new client consultation at one. Oh, and a Helen Dunquest asked to see you at four. Mr. V., you have meetings from nine to twelve-thirty, then two hearings. And your five o'clock had to reschedule. She'll be in tomorrow at two."

"See? Our problems are solved. You'll finish in plenty of time to pick up the children."

Marisol arched both eyebrows, a dare to her husband to contradict her. He did not.

Several hours and clients later, the Villeneuves reconvened in their office. They gathered their briefcases and papers, discussed their plans for the evening, and locked up. Pedro—with the caution of a man approaching a coiled rattlesnake—broached Marisol's sister.

"So, your sister... her flight is on time, yes?"

"It is," replied Marisol.

"Excellent. And do we know how long she'll be staying?" Pedro kept a neutral tone.

Marisol did as well. "No, we do not. A week, maybe two. Maybe more, depending how things go here."

"Things? What things?" Pedro suspected he knew what things and hoped Marisol would prove him wrong.

"Well," began Marisol. "I'm not sure. But... she asked about Bruce."

Pedro's head dropped. "Mari, mi amor, please do not encourage her. This has the markings of a disaster all over it."

"Maybe a little tryst would do them both good." She shrugged, but the doubt in her own voice betrayed her.

He stopped mid-stride and touched his wife's arm. "She is on the rebound and will get back together with Jason Marsdale the minute he sends her an expensive gift and an apology. Bruce Grady is in love with Mae. Plus, they've already gone down this road once before. With disastrous results."

"Disaster, doom, gloom, says my husband. Where is your sense of adventure, of-of chance? Besides, they're all adults. Their choices are their own." Marisol walked to her car, parked beside Pedro's. "Make dinner reservations for tonight, please."

Pedro sighed and unlocked the driver's side door. "Yes, my lovely wife. But when this all goes wrong, don't get mad when I say I told you so."

Marisol made a *hmph* sound and blew him a kiss. "See you shortly, mi amor."

6 Brianna

Brianna Baker watched her brother in brief side glances that flicked away whenever he looked up from his phone. From beside him at the kitchen table, Ricky Baker watched his wife. When she made eye contact with him, he gave her the *don't say anything* look. She pretended not to know what the look meant. Then she said the something Ricky had warned her against.

"So, have you talked to Feather Anne since she's been home?" Brianna knew the answer, but wanted to hear it from him.

"Nope," said Brandon.

"You haven't called or texted her?" Again, Brianna knew the answer.

"Nope," said Brandon. Then, likely knowing his sister wouldn't let it go, he added, "She hasn't called or texted *me*, so..." He let the sentence hang.

Brianna threw the sponge in the sink and took the lecture stance. Ricky and Brandon sank down in their chairs. "You know, Brandon, you're just being childish. Both of you are. I know for a fact she'd like to hear from you." Before he could give a rebuttal, she went on, louder this time, "And I know you miss her. So, stop being an ass and call her. Better yet, go see her. *Before* the party."

"Who says I'm going to the party?" His tone was defiant, but he also didn't dare look up at Brianna.

"Oh, you're going," said Brianna.

Ricky, who'd sat quiet throughout, spoke up. "All right, you two. This doesn't have to be a battle. Bri, babe, let the guy decide what to——" Brianna's icy glare stopped him, and he raised his hands in surrender. To Brandon, he said, "Sorry, man. I tried."

He gulped the last of his coffee and stood. "Well, I'll leave you to it. Bran, see you at the shop. Call you later, babe."

He mouthed one more *sorry* to his brother-in-law and winked at his wife before closing the door between him and them.

Brandon raked back his now long—long for him—hair and blew out a gust of air through his mouth. "Bri, let it go, huh? Whatever Feather Anne and I had, it's over. It's *been* over. She's got her big career and a rock star boyfriend, and I've got—" he spread his hands wide, "this."

The bitterness in his expression broke Brianna's heart. It had been a painful year for her kid brother, and she couldn't for the life of her figure out how to make it better. All her hopes rested now on Feather Anne, fair or unfair. Maybe they could rekindle their relationship. Or at least their friendship. And maybe—even she could concede—maybe their time *had* passed, and they'd outgrown each other. Still…

"You won't know anything unless you two talk, Brandon. Even if it's only closure. Don't you want at least that?"

"Bri, I know you mean well, but please don't start on all that therapy crap."

"Therapy *crap*?" Brianna stared at him and considered taking the sponge out of the sink and whipping it at his head.

Oblivious of her thoughts, Brandon continued. "Yeah, you know. *Talk things out.* Get *closure.*" He used air quotes and mimicked—what she could only assume to be—her.

"It's not *therapy crap*, jackass. It's called being an adult. Which is what you are now, buddy. So try acting like one."

Brandon pushed away from the table as if he were ninety years old and Brianna had just asked him to run a marathon. "I appreciate what you're trying to do, sis. But, Jesus, don't you ever tire of micro-managing everyone's life?"

He grabbed his keys and left before she could reply, so she yelled at the closed door. "Yeah, well, who's using *therapy crap* words, now?" Under her breath, she muttered, "Micro-managing. I'll give you micro-managing, you little shit."

From behind her came Mrs. Teccio's voice, full of reproach. "Missy Brianna, why you having the fighting with your brother, eh?"

Instead of answering, Brianna huffed at her, then said, "I swear your accent is heavier every time you come back from Italy. Next time, maybe you won't speak any English at all."

Her long-time housekeeper-come-nanny shook a fist at her and laughed. "You wish."

Brianna laughed then, too. "Only sometimes. But then I remember you're the only one who ever listens to me." She took off the half-apron she'd put on to protect her skirt and handed it to the rightful owner. "Well, I'm off to deal with a Bridezilla and finalize the details for Feather Anne's party at the hall. The children got off to ballet and karate all right?"

"All is good. Now go. I see you later, alligator," said Mrs. Teccio with a grin. "This Americano enough for you, eh?" Making it seem like an afterthought, she added, "And you no more Michael-manage Brandon, no?"

Brianna grimaced and said, "It's mic—you know what? Never mind. Don't worry, Mrs. T. I will not *Michael manage* Brandon anymore. He's on his own." She brushed her hands together to show she'd wiped him off her slate.

"Uh-huh," said the older woman, not bothering to hide her smirk. "Okay, you go. I stay. Bye-bye." She all but shooed Brianna from her own kitchen.

Brianna allowed it with good nature; they both knew Mrs. Teccio could say or do close to anything without fear of reproach from anyone in the Baker household, least of all from Brianna. The woman was the closest thing to a mother—an active in her life mother—she'd ever known.

"Cheeky woman," scolded Brianna as she found herself out the door, purse and keys in hand. *Cheeky?* Where'd *that* phase come from?

She pondered the entire ride across town. When had she heard anyone use such a term? At the light on Orchard, she remembered they were repaving the far end of the road, so she turned onto Robin's Lane to bypass the traffic. Brianna paid little attention to the cottage-like ranches that dominated the street until she came to Mae's. She slowed, admiring the clematis vines that climbed the porch railings and the bursts of purple, orange, and red blooms in her hanging planters. Her well-manicured front lawn stretched out and sloped to the road, and the driveway curved. *It* needed repairing. But the rest seemed well-maintained for a woman all on her own.

Although, she wasn't *really* on her own. Surely, her lapdog, Bruce Grady, helped her out. It was an uncharitable thought, but William Grant's sudden death must've felt like a stroke of wonderful fortune for the lovesick puppy. She'd never say that aloud to anyone but her closest friends, who would gasp and call her awful but smirk, too. Elise, maybe not. Brittany, definitely. Charlotte's face would pinch in disapproval, and Katie would admonish her and call her fresh or something.

It came to her then. *Cheeky woman.* William Grant had said that to her once. *Called* her that. They'd crossed paths at Mae's Café and he overheard her say something—God knew what—and he wagged a finger at her, grinned, and said, "Cheeky woman, you." She remembered thinking he looked and smelled delicious and understood Mae's attraction to the man. She'd blushed. Brianna Baker had *blushed.* Brianna had no comeback and had stammered something idiotic, much to her friend's delight.

How long ago had that been? It felt like only a year, but…

"It was seven years ago. Cassidy was an infant," said Brianna to the empty SUV. "But today is significant, too. Why?"

She pulled over and stopped, heedless of where she was, and opened the calendar app on her phone. There it was in bold type. **September 20th. Anv. – W. Grant**. Brianna looked up and breathed, "It's the one-year anniversary of William's death. Jesus." Movement to her left—outside her driver's window—caught her eye and her head swiveled to see Mae strolling toward her car, a puzzled but friendly expression on her still too damn perfect face.

How was it that grief had only made her prettier? Another uncharitable thought. *Cheeky woman*. Would he have called Brianna that had he heard her thoughts? No. Even the divine William Grant would've thought her a bitch.

Brianna collected herself and powered down the window. "Mae, hello. Good morning." That was stupid. It *wasn't* a good morning. Not for the Grant family. Christ. Now the children were outside, staring at her.

Mae smiled and said, "Are you joining us for the memorial? It's at the park, actually. Not here. You can follow—"

"Oh, no," exclaimed Brianna, perhaps too emphatically judging by Mae's rapid doe-eyed blinking. She adjusted her tone. "No, I-I wanted to know if you needed anything for the…" *Think damn it. Think.* "For the—"

Mae inserted, "For the luncheon after the memorial?"

There she is. Ever helpful Mae.

"Yes. That. Exactly. Is there anything you need for the luncheon?" Brianna concentrated on finding the balance between a helpful tone and a sympathetic expression. One that Mae couldn't see, because Brianna's sunglasses covered her eyes and half her face. She raised them and tried again. "This must be such a grueling day for you, sweetie."

To her immense credit, Mae smiled a surprisingly peaceful smile. "I thought it would be, too. But I woke up this morning feeling… I can't explain it exactly. Just… like everything is all right. Like William is watching over us alongside my dad, and they're smiling. Anyhow, the more the merrier. If you can't join us at the park, please come by the café for the luncheon. Charlotte and Katie will be there, too."

"You're very sweet. I—"

"William was fond of you, you know. He called you—"

"Cheeky," finished Brianna. A lump lodged in her throat. She coughed it away and surprised herself by adding, "I'll be there."

Mae reached through the window and touched Brianna's arm. "Good. We'll see you soon."

Brianna watched Mae pick her way up the driveway in her patent leather Mary-Janes and wished she could pull off such a girly shoe. She observed her wrap an arm around the slight shoulders of her children and pull them in for a hug. When Mae glanced up and gave a short wave, Brianna nodded once, replaced her dark sunglasses on her face and pulled away from the curb.

Her dread at attending the luncheon—the sad faces, the potential for tears—soon shaped into an alternative plan. Brianna was a problem solver. And her looming problem of late revolved around her kid brother and Feather Anne. She gave the wake-up command for her phone.

"Call Ricky."

On the second ring, he answered. "Hey, babe. What's up?"

"Block off lunch for you and Brandon. We're going to the memorial luncheon for William Grant. Meet me there and for fuck's sake, make sure Brandon combs his hair." She supposed he had a response, but there were more calls to make and tasks to manage, so she disconnected and moved on. She had two hours before the gathering. Plenty of time.

7 Mae

Ten people gathered under a massive oak tree in Center Park. Its branches reached out over the pond and shaded the bench with names and hearts carved across every available surface. Mae and William had spent many sunny days under that tree, first as a couple, then as a family.

On this autumn day, the leaves had turned to their copper-yellow hue and contrasted against the cloudless azure sky. Mae, gazing up through those branches, felt her chest swell with gratitude, and yes, sorrow.

Feather Anne took her hand and said, "It's a very William kind of day, isn't it?"

Mae closed her eyes, felt the warm dampness of her lashes as they touched her cheeks, and smiled. "Yes, it is." She squeezed Feather Anne's hand and looked at her. "How are you doing?"

Feather Anne, for once not offering a famous eye roll, said matter-of-factly, "Sad, but happy, too. It's stupid, but I feel like William is watching over me. Us, all of us. But it's like—every time I've had doubts or fears along this whole music thing—I think about what William would say, and it, like, gives me clarity, or something." She looked down and away. "That's dumb, huh?"

Mae rested her head on her sister's shoulder. "Not at all. I feel that way, too, so there must be something to it, right?"

She felt Feather Anne's body tense and followed her gaze. There was a man standing across from them on the other side of the pond. He looked back at them. Mae understood why she'd frozen. The man— from their distance—could easily have been William. Same hairstyle, same built, even the same clothing William wore. A navy-blue V-neck sweater over a white button-down shirt, tan dress slacks.

A breeze ruffled the man's hair, and he raked it down just the way William used to. Mae's body felt liquid, her knees like rubber, but she took a step forward. She'd have walked straight through the pond. Feather Anne grabbed her arm.

"He looks just like—it can't be, but—" Feather Anne's sounded awestruck.

Her voice, her *words* brought Mae to her senses. "It's not him, sweetheart. Just our wishful thinking."

Still, they watched the man turn and walk down the path until he rounded the bend. Georgie Brightsider called their attention. "Hello, my lovelies. Shall we start?"

Mae filled her lungs, exhaled, and said, "Yes, let's." They gathered onto the blankets Mae had spread out in an informal circle, with Evvie and TK flanking her, and Feather Anne beside Evvie. She thanked everyone for coming and just as she explained her wish for everyone to write a memory of William to add to their memory jar, Bruce came up behind her.

He'd shoved his hands deep in his pockets and his shoulders hunched, like he feared Mae would send him away. Instead, she reached a hand up to him. Bruce stared at it a moment, then unfurled and released the fisted hand from his pocket. He let Mae pull him down to sit beside TK.

"We've been doing this all year, and it's finally dawned on me to ask you, the people who also knew and loved William, to add your memories to ours so that when we're feeling sad, or just want to hold him close, we can reach inside the jar for comfort." Adding a sentiment light years beyond his age, TK added, "And to keep our Daddy alive in our minds."

Oh, my sweet boy. Looking at you keeps your father alive for me. Mae caressed her son's hair and smiled down at him.

"You two hand out the pens and paper, please." She handed the ivory sheets and pens to her children, saving one of each for herself.

For the next hour, they wrote in companionship. More than once, someone burst out with laughter and had to share the memory aloud. The children shared some of their favorite memories, and Feather Anne recalled the first time she'd met William.

"I still have my first library card," she said at the end.

Bruce cleared his throat. "I, uh, remember the first time I met William, I wasn't too keen on him being around… Chance so much. Didn't make any bones about it, either. But William was nothing but gracious and patient. Can't help but respect and admire a man like that." He glanced up, but not at Mae. "Anyhow, I grew to like William very much. You could even say I loved him for how happy he made Mae, and Feather Anne, and for bringing these two little monsters into the world. I loved William because he let me stay in the lives of my favorite people." He sniffed. "And because he was my friend."

Feather Anne linked her arms around his beefy bicep and hugged. He tipped his head to hers, and they sat this way until it was time to go. Mae tried to catch his eye, and when he looked at her, she mouthed, "Thank you."

He nodded, but the smile he offered appeared solemn. Her eyes traveled to him several times as they packed up to leave. How she longed to hug her dear, sweet friend. Mae had missed him almost as much as she missed her husband.

She frowned at the thought. No, that couldn't be true, or even right. The comparison felt wrong, traitorous even. To miss her friend nearly as much as her dead husband? Mae shook her head against it. But when Bruce turned to face her, the force of her need to run to him and bury her face in his chest knocked the breath from her lungs.

He took a step toward her and she knew his ache and sense of loss matched hers. The look on his face was proof enough. But then Katrina called his name and beckoned him over to her and James. The magnet drawing them together severed.

Mae scooped the folded blanket against her chest and walked towards the parking lot at the top of the hill where the scattering of cars waited. The sun, higher in the sky now, reflected off the windshield of the car facing her. Mae squinted and shielded her eyes.

A figure stood beside the car, but because she'd looked at the bright orb on the windshield, black spots dotted her vision. She blinked hard to clear them, and when she looked again, the figure had disappeared.

The man from across the pond.

"Don't be ridiculous," said Mae.

"What's that, dear?"

Mae twisted around to see Georgie Brightsider behind her.

"Oh, it's nothing. I thought I… never mind. Take my arm. This hill is steep."

"That was a lovely memorial, Mae. Charles and I are so very proud of you, you know. Our strong girl."

Georgie patted Mae's hand, and the pair navigated the hill together. At the top, Mae scanned the lot. Georgie watched her. "Mae? Is everything all right, dear? You seem… out of sorts."

Mae tried to give the older woman a reassuring smile. "I'm fine. It's just… it's just the day, I suppose. I feel like I'm seeing William everywhere. To be expected." She shrugged it off.

Georgie tapped her chin, a thoughtful look on her face. "Funny you say that. Charles and I thought we'd both gone senile yesterday."

Mae tilted her head and waited for the explanation. Charles joined them, his breath coming heavier than Mae liked. "What's that you two are saying?"

"Don't speak until you've caught your breath, Charles. I was about to tell Mae about our senior moment yesterday."

"Senior mo—oh, that's right. Yes, it was…"

"I told you, catch your breath. I'll tell her," said Georgie.

Mae forced a calm tone. "And you want to tell me…" She hoped one of them would fill in the blank before she screamed.

"Well, Charles and I took the dogs for our morning stroll along the beach—such a rough current, but still lovely—and we saw a man walking along the jetty. I said to Charles—"

"She said the tide's high to be walking out that way," finished Charles.

Georgie awarded her husband a scowl. "Yes, and the man must have realized it, too, because he turned back. He stopped when he saw us. By then we were maybe… how far would you say, Charles?"

Charles had caught his breath, and when he answered, he sounded his normal self again. "Oh, I'd say half a football field? Less than that, maybe. Close enough to tell it was a man, pick out the color of his hair and clothes, but—"

Georgie interrupted. "But nothing. We both thought it, Charles." To Mae, she said, "I'm embarrassed now to say it, but we both thought it was William for a moment. Just for a moment. We laughed at our foolishness and chalked it up to the anniversary date being so near."

Charles nodded. "Very common, and not just with us seniors."

"Not just seniors," agreed Mae. "It happened to me and Feather Anne today. I was telling Georgie we saw a man across the pond earlier who reminded us—no, more than reminded—of William so much. He even dressed the same way. And his hair. I almost…" She laughed in a self-deprecatory way and tucked her hair behind her ear. "Well, let's just say I almost made a fool of myself."

Charles hugged her and kissed her temple. "You could never look foolish, my dear."

"Thank you, Charles. And you, too, Georgie. Georgie? What is it?"

The platinum-haired woman wore a thoughtful, troubled expression. "You said the man was dressed like William and his hair was the same, too. Just like the man we saw."

"I suppose they could be the same. But who is he, then?" Charles looked from one woman to the other.

Mae forced a laugh. "Well, if it's the ghost of William Grant, he'd better do something more useful than lurking about." To the air, she said, "The goat pen could use a cleaning, for starters."

When she looked back at the Brightsiders, her face fell, and in a stricken voice, she asked, "Was that terrible of me?"

The duo hurried to reassure her, and she believed they meant their testaments, that joking around showed a healthy attitude and perspective in their eyes. She thought so, too. It was a tightrope she walked; balancing her and her children's sorrow with gratitude and joy. Sometimes she wobbled. Other times—especially in the first weeks and months—she fell. But she got up again and kept moving forward. Today, she'd wobbled. First when she saw the man who looked like William, then again when Bruce joined them.

"Hey," said a familiar voice behind Mae.

She turned and looked up into Bruce's ocean blue eyes. Mae tried to make her face a neutral canvas, but against her will, a smile spread. "Hey, yourself."

He gave her sleeve a shy tug; a boyish gesture that was so Bruce-like that her heart caught in her throat. God, she'd missed him. She'd missed him because he'd baled on her. *Abandoned* her. Just like that, the smile faltered and fell. Mae crossed her arms over her chest and thrust her chin.

"So, you came," she said.

Underneath those words were all the unsaid accusations. *You left me alone in my darkest days. I needed you, and you weren't there. You hurt me.* Yet still another voice, another part of her brain rebutted the accusations. *It's not his job to carry you. You've already asked too much of him for too long. You needed to learn how to stand on your own again. He loves you.*

She had little doubt that his internal battle equaled her own. It showed in his eyes, so easy to read. He managed one word. "Yes."

Charles, watching the pair with knowing eyes, said, "We'll see you two at the café," and took his wife's arm. They strolled away like the dignified royalty they were, and left Bruce and Mae with their awkward, tense silence.

"Are you coming to the luncheon?" Mae held her breath.

"I—"

"Of *course*, he is," said Feather Anne, who'd sprung up behind them. She looped one arm through Bruce's and the other through Mae's, and gave them each a wide, toothy smile meant to look innocent and cheery. "Shall we hit the road, kids?"

Bruce jabbed a thumb in Feather Anne's direction and said, "Give the girl fifteen minutes of fame, and now she calls *us* kids?"

"Well, she is a big star now, so to her we're positively infantile." Mae affected a haughty British accent.

Feather Anne rolled her eyes and said, "Weirdos. But seriously, let's roll. I think those girls recognize me." Mae and Bruce turned in the direction she'd cut her eyes to. She hissed, "Don't make eye contact."

A devilish grin appeared on Bruce's face. A second later, Mae wore a matching one. In a booming voice, he said, "Feather Anne, it's so great to have you home."

Mae—just as loud—said, "Yes, our Greatest American Singer, home at last."

It was all the group of six girls—in the eleven to thirteen age range—needed to hear. Their suspicions confirmed, they rushed up to Feather Anne with cell phones, pens, and papers.

"I am literally, like, your biggest fan, Feather Anne," gushed one girl around a mouthful of braces.

Another elbowed her way forward. "I want to be a singer just like you."

A third blurted, "Where's Nick? Is he coming back to Chance, too?"

One of the other girls sneered, "He's already in Chance, dummy."

Feather Anne froze mid-autograph and looked at the girl. It lasted long enough for the girl to shift in discomfort under Feather Anne's scrutiny. Mae watched her sister's eyes flick to the nearest cell phone trained on her and flashed a smile. She ignored the questions like a pro.

"Thanks for the love, everybody, but I've got to get going. I'll see you around town, I'm sure."

Feeling like a bouncer or a security guard, Mae blocked their view as best as possible while Feather Anne strode to the car. Bruce caught on, wrapped an arm around Mae's waist and shuttled them forward. Once in the driver's seat, Mae rolled down her window to speak to Bruce.

She laughed. "Well, that was an experience."

From the passenger side, Feather Anne deadpanned. "Yeah, welcome to my life."

Mae ignored her and said, "So, we'll see you at the luncheon?" This time she tried to convey all the hope and welcome she could.

"Somebody's gotta play bodyguard here. Might as well be me," said Bruce. His way of saying yes, he'd be there.

Mae drove out of the parking lot musing over how light she felt, given that she'd expected the opposite. Maybe William had been there; not in the form of a man across the pond, but in sending her dearest friend back to her. Or maybe it was wishful thinking, and things just happened the way they happened.

One glance in Feather Anne's direction alerted her that not everyone felt as light-hearted as she. If only she could get her to talk about it.

8 Brandon

He'd managed to avoid the memorial luncheon. Now it was twenty-four hours before Feather Anne's welcome home party—which he was not attending, no matter what his sister said—Brandon Bourdreau stood in the middle of a party supply store. His sister loomed a few steps away, hands on hips, and towering over a nervous salesperson.

"And this is why I only ever use my wholesalers, and not you… you chain stores."

In her right hand, she held a roll of ribbon in a color she called crimson. In her left hand, she waved another roll that seemed damn close to the first, but according to Brianna, it looked nothing like the one in her right hand.

"Ma'am, we have no control over what the-the—
"

"Distributors. The word you are looking for is *distributors*. Who checks your inventory, a color-blind person?"

She prattled on about how two rolls from the same brand, with the same name and item number should blah, blah, blah. Brandon tuned her out and checked his Snapchat. There were a few funny snaps from his buddy Kade, and one from a girl named Kya. It was the last one that jolted him.

It was a shot of Feather Anne. The caption above it read, "OMG, I just met THE Feather Anne. Pinch me if I'm dreaming," followed by too many exclamation points to count. He took a screenshot of the snap before it disappeared without thinking.

Bullshit. You were thinking.

He just wanted to study it for a second, that's all. Brandon stared at her face, then the background. Center Park. It was taken the day before. She looked good. Better than good. But he knew that already because her face was everywhere. Feather Anne singing on television. Feather Anne being interviewed… being photographed, being recorded… being every-fucking-where but with him.

Brianna said his name, and he snapped. "*What?*" He steadied himself. "Sorry. What's up?"

She narrowed her eyes at him. "I said, we're done here. Do you want to grab a bite to eat?"

He wanted to go for a run. But he could also do with some grub. "Yeah, sure."

In Brianna's SUV, they said little. Mostly because his sister barked commands into her Bluetooth to her assistant. He didn't mind, not one bit. Less opportunity for conversation meant less grilling about going to the party. Bad enough he'd gotten roped into helping her today.

The second Brianna ended her call, Brandon said, "And why exactly did you need me to come with you for this?"

"Because," began Brianna, her tone caustic, "I thought I would have a gigantic box to carry. But those baboons in there screwed everything up. So, you're stuck getting a free meal out of it. Poor you." She waved a dismissive hand at him.

"Where are we going, anyhow?"

He looked up from his phone with interest and suspicion. Brianna had turned onto Old Main Street, and while there were several restaurants to choose from, he had a sudden mistrust of where she might go. When she ignored the question and turned the radio up, he knew.

"Bri, no. Don't even think about it. I'm not going in. Jesus. Is she there? Is that why you're bringing me to the café? I told you—"

"Oh, shut up. Are you a boy or a man?"

"That has nothing to—"

"You're being a coward, Brandon. Is that who you are? I'll tell you the answer. No. No brother of mine will be a chicken-shit. Not on my watch."

"All right, all right. Calm down," said Brandon. He sunk down in the seat and crossed his arms.

But his sister, now revved up, wasn't ready to calm down. "Just because cowards raised us doesn't mean we're destined to be them, too. No. Fucking. Way. So, you are going in there whether or not Feather Anne is in there, and you will man up and confront this—this elephant between you once and for all. If she's there, I mean."

It was a dangerous time to say it, but Brandon couldn't help himself and countered with, "You know, Bri, modern psychology is warning against over-masculinity. They say it's toxic and that today's women need more of a—"

"Shut *up*." It came out a whisper-hiss.

He shut up… for about thirty seconds. "Speaking of good old mom and pop, what's the latest with Gordon and Martha and their respective new lives?"

Brianna's face tightened even more. "Martha and her lady friends are on a senior singles cruise. Gordon is fuck knows where doing fuck knows what, with—"

"Fuck knows who," finished Brandon. Where most people said *God knows*, Brianna substituted with *fuck knows* instead. She rarely used the Lord's name in vain… or at all. Not out of respect, but disdain. "If you hate them so much, why do you keep tabs on them still?"

He wasn't trying to be a dick; his curiosity was genuine. *He* never checked up on them. Not on social media—they were both on Facebook, and both had blocked the other—not by phone, and not by visiting. But Brianna, who had more reason than him to erase their existence from memory, kept tabs.

She parked and faced him. "Because it's my job to make sure neither one of them ever do anything to disturb our peace again. Especially Gordon. Knowing where he is means I know where he's not."

"Here." Brandon understood.

They climbed out and walked to the café. Brandon, on impulse, swung his arm over his sister's shoulders. She was older by quite a few years, but he had at least six inches on her, and she let him tuck her under his arm. He hadn't done that in some time and had forgotten what a comfort their bond was.

When he'd lost the scholarship, he'd expected Brianna to lose her shit, but she kept her cool; even gave him some uncharacteristic sympathy. Then, when he sat them down and confessed it had been a relief to lose it and that he didn't want to go to college—at least not yet—he waited for her to explode. Instead, she and Ricky made him an offer that pleased them all. A steady job at the shop and free room and board until he saved up enough money to either move out or pay rent to them.

Brandon figured out that car sales—Brianna's first pick for him—was not for him and auto body work, Ricky's recommendation, suited him. He'd already been helping his brother-in-law on and off for years, so it seemed a no-brainer to take the hands-on training and learn a usable trade… *and* have no student debt burden after to boot. He'd made out well, in his estimation. Plus, he was happy. Mostly.

What he couldn't quite get his head straight about was how it all looked from the outside. Feather Anne Byrd's former boyfriend—onetime jock with a bright collegiate future turned local grease monkey. Or so the tabloid headline read over a grainy picture of him in his overalls, leaning over a mustang engine. That was at the height of the Feather Anne—*and Nick, don't forget him*—frenzy.

That had sent him down a rabbit hole. One he'd just started coming out of until word came back Feather Anne had returned. He couldn't tell his sister or Ricky—especially not Ricky—the actual reason he avoided her. It embarrassed him. Shamed him. And he felt like a loser, or at least like *she'd* think him a loser. How could he say something like that to Bri or Ricky, who'd built their entire life on that career choice? The answer was: he couldn't.

Regardless, Brianna was right. Time to suck it up and deal. Only it turned out Feather Anne wasn't at the café and his relief outweighed his burst of courage. Mae greeted him warmly—as if they didn't see one another regularly around town—and sat them in a corner table by the windows. Their food—Brianna's Salade Nicoise, Brandon's Everything but The Kitchen Sink burger—came out, and he dug in.

"Must you eat like a savage? Use your napkin, for fuck's sake."

Brandon smiled at her with a mouthful of burger and a mixture of ketchup, mayonnaise, and mustard running down his chin. Before she could say anything more, a shadow fell over them.

"I see you're still eating like a caveman," said Feather Anne.

He snatched the napkin dangling from Brianna's hand, ignored her smug, *see, that's what you get* expression, and wiped his face. He half stood, then sat, then stood up, knocking the underside of the table as he did.

Fucking hell.

He tried to come up with his own, *I see you're still...* but had nothing. "Hey, Feather Anne," he said.

"Missed a spot." She pointed a finger in the vague direction of his chin.

He felt around, then saw the teasing look in her eyes. There was no spot. She was fucking with him, just like she always did. For some stupid reason, this made a lump lodge in his throat. He had to blink fast to clear the sting in his eyes. She saw it, though. Of course she did.

"Well, I am stuffed," said Brianna. She'd taken two bites. "I've a few things to discuss with Mae, so if you two will excuse me." She stood and offered her seat to Feather Anne.

"Oh, I—" Feather Anne gave Brandon a panicked, *is it okay* look, and he pointed his chin to the chair.

"There," said Brianna.

The self-satisfied smile Brandon saw on her face spoke volumes. If she hadn't orchestrated the meet-up, she at least approved of it. Feather Anne slid into the vacated chair and pushed aside the barely touched salad. Brandon sat, too. She untucked her long hair from behind her ear and let it fan out to hide her face from the tables next to them. The move of a girl grown accustomed to stares.

His first thought was, *oh please. You're in Chance, not Hollywood.* But then he glanced around. Maybe every eye wasn't on them—*her*—but it was damn close enough. Brandon wiped his mouth once more, threw his napkin down, and stood. She looked up at him, startled.

"Come on. Let's get out of here."

He reached his hand out to her. Feather Anne stared at it for a long second, then took it. Brandon pulled her to her feet and led her out the side door at the back of the café at a half-walk, half run pace. Neither looked to see if anyone followed them out.

"Bikes are still in back. You remember how to ride one?" Brandon called over his shoulder.

"Yeah… it's like riding a bike. You never forget," she replied.

He smirked. Same old wiseass. Maybe she hadn't changed so much. The bikes leaned against the building, unlocked, and they each hopped on one. They pedaled up Elm Street as if being chased by paparazzi and continued that way until Brandon directed them onto Heron's Way. When they reached Beach Access Road, they stopped side by side, panting for breath.

He glanced at her and turned away just as fast. It hurt his heart to look at her too long. The glance was enough to see her chestnut hair tangled and wild from the wind and her cheeks flushed pink. And those damn eyes of hers. Those damn eyes.

"Brandon, I—"

"Come on. To the jetty, okay?" He looked straight ahead.

In a quiet voice, she said, "Okay."

They wedged the front tires of the bikes in the rusty bike rack and walked toward the beach, then the jetty without talking, touching, or looking at one another. She took the lead at the boulders, and he followed her over the flat stones set like puzzle pieces all the way to the end. The ocean looked calm.

First time all week it had. Brandon wished he could steady his racing heart the same way. Feather Anne stared at his profile; he could feel her eyes on him.

"Why won't you look at me, Brandon?"

He didn't answer, not at first. His jaw worked and his temples pulsed, but his throat tightened up so hard it hurt. She touched his wrist, then held it. He let her. She slid her hand down into his and held it. He let her. But he didn't curl his fingers around hers. They twitched, but they didn't curl.

"Brandon."

It wasn't a question, but a command. Her will always was stronger than his. He looked at her. Still, the words refused to come. Feather Anne stepped closer, then she stood in front of him. With her free hand, she touched his face. Against his will, he leaned into her hand and tipped his forehead to hers. Deep tremors shook his body, yet he didn't cry. He wouldn't let himself do that. His hands—no longer like dead weights—found their way to her face. His fingers tangled in her hair, and his palms pressed against her damp cheeks. She was crying. The girl who never cried was crying… for him. No, for *them*.

It opened the floodgates. Brandon told her everything he'd been thinking and feeling since she'd left. He didn't hold back. If they were to have a chance—if that was anywhere in the cards—they had to have total, brutal honesty between them. Even if hearing what *she* had to say tore his heart out.

They'd sat by then, side by side on their favorite rock. The same rock they'd opened their hearts to each other years ago, when none of this seemed imaginable. Feather Anne sat mute while he spoke; he could tell it burned her up to keep her mouth shut a few times, but she did it.

"So, that's everything, Feather Anne. The good, bad, and the ugly. The embarrassing, too. It's all laid out. Now I need you to do the same. Even if it hurts." It would hurt; this much he knew. Hearing about her and Nick Amendola… part of him didn't think he could take it, but he had to.

Feather Anne licked her lips and frowned at him. "Brandon, Nick and I…"

9 Feather Anne

She hesitated when he recoiled. Then she pushed on. Brandon needed to hear this. She needed him to hear this.

"Nick and I were never together."

Feather Anne watched Brandon for his reaction. She could tell her words hadn't sunk in; he still wore the pained expression of a man awaiting a death sentencing. She wanted to laugh but bit her cheek instead. Teasing him right now would be cruel. She would sit and wait for the slow smile to creep across his face. But when it didn't come, Feather Anne touched his arm.

"Brandon, did you hear me? I said—"

"Yeah. I heard you, Feather Anne. I thought you were going to be honest with me? Huh? You expect me to believe after seeing all the pictures, and videos, and—and the interviews, Feather Anne. The *interviews* with the two of you cozied up together—"

"Brandon." Feather Anne slapped her hands on her thighs. "I am telling you the truth, jackass. It was all for publicity. I was against it from the start, but I signed the contract. They called the shots. I swear to you. Nick and I never even kissed." *They came close. Tell him. Honesty, even if it hurts.* "We almost did. But something… held me back."

"Oh, yeah? What was that?"

He tried to sound indifferent, but Feather Anne knew better. "You dummy. It's always been you. Yeah, I got… swayed for a minute. But it was only because—"

"I acted like a total dick," finished Brandon.

"Yeah, that," said Feather Anne.

At long last, they laughed. All their glass shards poking at each other fell into the ocean. They were Brandon and Feather Anne again. They talked about stupid stuff for a while and let the big stuff rest. When that wore down, Brandon asked what sat between them.

"So, what now, Feather Anne? What happens next?"

She took a breath so deep it hurt her lungs and told him the honest to God's truth. "I don't freaking know." She forced the breath out until her spine curved, and her chest caved.

Brandon rubbed her back, a gesture so Brandon-like it made her eyes sting. "I guess it all comes down to what do you want?"

She barked an ironic laugh. "What I want? How about… all of it? None of it?"

Brandon laughed through his nose; a brief burst. "Yeah, sounds about right."

"They want me to sign a solo contract. Exclusive. Lots of money on the line, big plans. Even bigger promises."

"Sounds like that would be a good thing. Why don't you seem excited? Isn't that what you wanted?"

Feather Anne shook her head. She looked out across the sea and kept a little sailboat in her sights as she spoke. "I thought so. In the beginning, I mean. But this hasn't been what I imagined, you know? All these… fake people and empty compliments. They took my music and…"

"Made you Britney Spears?"

Feather Anne elbowed him. "She's a nice lady. I met her at… shit, I don't even remember where. But she was sweet. She said, *never let them own you, honey.* Stuck with me. I mean, she should know. Look what that life did to her, right?"

Brandon shrugged and offered a bright side. "Afforded her the best care and recovery in a mansion, then a Vegas show. All's well that…" he saw Feather Anne's dirty look. "Yeah, no. I see what you're saying. Look, I'm not trying to convince you to do this. Not by a long shot. Just, you know, be sure whatever you choose. You don't want to have regrets."

He was right. That's how she knew he was on her side, no matter what, even if it went against what he wanted. How had she forgotten that? Above and before everything else, Brandon Bourdreau was the truest friend she'd ever known.

"I love you. You know that?" She blurted it, but she meant it.

He didn't act surprised though. All he said was, "I love you, too, Feather Anne. Always have, always will."

By unspoken agreement, they stood and brushed off the sand from their pants. Like nimble Billy goats, they hopped and sprang across the jetty back to the shore. Brandon helped her down, not because she needed it but for an excuse to have his hands on her again. He didn't have to tell her this. She knew.

"So, you coming to this thing tomorrow, or what?" Feather Anne planted her fists on her hips and squinted at him.

He kicked at a shell and grinned at her. "Yeah. If you want me to, that is."

"Duh," said Feather Anne. She gave him a shoulder bump hard enough to make him stumble, then ran off toward the bikes.

She beat him there, but not by much. The slower ride back to the café gave her time to think. And to steal glances at Brandon. He looked different. Longer hair. A glimpse of a tattoo on his inner forearm that hadn't been there before. Stubbled cheeks and chin where he used to be clean shaven. None of it bad—this fresh look—just… different.

The only thing that *did* bother her was the trace of wariness still in his eyes. He didn't entirely believe her about Nick, and it pissed her off. But she also understood it. The producers had run full steam with the whole Feather Anne and Nick Amendola thing. *Are they, or aren't they? Will they, or won't they? Should they, or shouldn't they?*

In the beginning, Feather Anne had minded little. It all seemed too surreal to matter. And silly. Like, who the heck is watching or caring about this? Turned out, millions of people—and not just hormonal teens—cared a little too much for her liking.

As for Nick, he enjoyed it. Not at first—he grumbled about it even more than her—but then… she didn't know what happened. He enjoyed the attention. No, the adoration. Before her eyes, he became a persona and not a person. All the plans they'd had for making music together when the show and their contracts ended vanished like smoke on a breeze. He baled on her and left her in the dust without so much as a backward glance. Something Brandon would never in a million years do.

"Yo, you good?"

They'd reached the café and Brandon had climbed off his bike. Feather Anne realized she'd been staring at him.

"What? Yeah, good. All good. Hey, what's the tattoo of?" She gestured to his arm; half covered by his pushed-up sleeve.

Brandon approached her, a shy smile tugging the corners of his mouth, and pushed the sleeve up further to reveal his whole forearm. Still holding the handlebars of the bike, Feather Anne watched as he twisted the arm to reveal an intricately detailed feather. She let the bike fall over and took his arm in her hands and bent over it. Strands of her hair danced over his wrist and he tucked them back behind her ear with his free hand.

Her head stayed down, but she looked up at him with just her eyes. "Does that… it says Anne in the middle, doesn't it?"

The pattern inside the feather appeared just that at first glance—a series of lines and swirls—but on further inspection, and if you stared long enough, the curves of an A, then two N's and an E became clear. Now a slow grin spread across her face. He'd done this while they were apart and not speaking.

"I'd like to say I was drunk when I got it, but I was stone-cold sober, Feather Anne."

She wanted to kiss him then and almost did. But the screen door of the café kitchen opened, and Mae stepped out with a loud, "Oh."

Feather Anne released Brandon's arm and stepped back, shoving her hands in her back pockets. "Hey, we—I…"

"Don't let me interrupt you two. Just taking out some trash and... okay, bye."

Mae pivoted and fumbled with the door a minute before flinging it open and tripping inside. Brandon and Feather Anne exchanged wide eyed stares before the laughter burst out. When it died off, another one of those awkward moments stretched out. Feather Anne opened her mouth to speak, but movement on the opposite side of the street drew her eye. When she saw no one, her brow creased.

"What's wrong?" Brandon followed her gaze.

"Nothing," said Feather Anne, but she took a few steps toward the road. "I thought I saw... eh, it was probably that asshole reporter John St. James sent to interview me. I've been dodging him."

Another step brought her to the curb where the intersection of Elm and Old Main Street became visible. Brandon followed close behind, a hand on her hip. "There," he said. He pointed to a man standing at the corner of Lucky Loo's. The building cast him in shadows, but Feather Anne felt certain he looked back at them. *It's the man from the park.*

"William?" It came out a whisper.

10 Mae

From inside, Mae and Brianna watched the pair from the office window until they moved out of sight. William would have called their behavior adolescent, but Mae didn't care, and she could guarantee Brianna Baker didn't, either. A giggle welled in her chest, and she stifled it. One look at Brianna's face told her the ice queen had a similar urge.

"I knew it. I knew if we could just get them in the same room," said Brianna. She stabbed the air with a lacquered fingernail. "You see?"

Mae considered reminding her the idea had been hers, but bit back the words and replaced them with, "It seems to have worked. Do you think he'll come to the party now?"

"He better. All right, well, looks like our job is done here. Well met, as William would say," said Brianna. A stricken expression came over her. "I hope that's okay to say."

"Better than okay," said Mae. She looked out the window again. "Where'd they go? Around front, maybe?"

Brianna shrugged as she checked her phone before slipping it back into her oversized purse. She'd already moved on from the Brandon/Feather Anne situation. *Problem solved, next please.* That was her attitude. Mae admired it. And felt a bit tilt-a-whirled, too. The woman changed gears as fast as Mae chopped onions.

"Unconcerned. We have bigger issues. I've just gotten reliable intel that Nick Amendola is in town. What are we going to do about that?"

The sudden realization that she, Mae Huxley-Grant, was now in cahoots with Brianna the Ice Queen Baker disconcerted her. When did this happen? How? She tried to think, but Brianna took no breathers and dragged her along—figuratively—with her.

"I'll tell you what we will do," continued Brianna, tapping her chin and gazing off in a Cruella Deville-like manner. "We will keep him away from our girl." With a sharp turn of her head, her blue eyes pierced Mae's gray ones. "*You* will keep him away."

"Me?" Mae pressed her fingertips against her chest. She suspected she looked every bit the Disney character Feather Anne teased about. Which one? Perhaps Snow White when the witch—disguised as an old woman—offered her the poison apple?

"Well, who better," snipped Brianna. "He's Bruce's son. And that—what's her name again—anyhow, you're friends with the parents. Keep *them* close, and you'll be able to keep taps on the boy-man."

"I-but Mia is visiting her mom in Arizona. She won't be back until—"

"Fine, Bruce, then. Oh, please, don't give me that look, Mae."

"What look?"

"The doe-eyed one. The Disney princess one, as Feather Anne calls it. Bruce's blatant adoration at the altar of Mae is well-established. And in case no one else has the balls to say it to you, the feeling is obviously mutual."

Mae took a step back and stammered, "Well, I-I, of-of course, I adore Bruce. He's been my dearest friend since—"

"Stop. I can't *even* with you right now. If you're not ready to admit you love him, so be it. But you, more than most, know that life is short and love like that is rare. You should grab it and hold on to it for dear life if you get the chance. Well, I'm off. Tell Brandon to get a ride home."

She left Mae standing, mouth agape, swallowing a mouthful of her perfume. That tilt-a-whirl feeling was nauseating now. Dazed, she stepped over to the full-length mirror hung beside the doorway of the office. Mae smoothed her already smooth hair and pressed down her apron. She fished around in the deep pocket for her lipstick and reapplied, careful to avoid her own gaze, afraid of what she'd see there. *Coward.* She let her eyes drift up from her mouth, nose, then her eyes.

"You still love and miss your husband," she told her reflection.

It answered back. "But you love *him*, too."

The screen door creaked behind her, and she spun around, expecting to see her sister.

"Feather—"

There was no one there.

11 Jared

Jared Simon unzipped his travel-sized toiletry bag and removed a box monogrammed with the name Wilde & Harte. Inside the box sat an absurdly expensive razor; an extravagance that set him back nearly two-hundred US dollars, but one he harbored no regrets over. If he were to embody the man, he had to do it fully. Besides, he expected to see that money back tenfold if he played his cards right.

He despised shaving, but without the beard the resemblance was undeniable. So, he ran the faucet until the water turned almost scalding, then rinsed and lathered his face, neck, and nape. Gripping the steel handle, Jared had to acknowledge the heft and craftmanship of the thing. But was it worth two-hundred bucks? Damned if he knew. But it was the razor *he'd* used, and that alone made Jared want it bad enough dip into his meager savings account.

The lighting in the motel bathroom was crap—the yellow light flickered in an erratic pattern—and the walls were so thin he heard the couple in the next room fighting, then making up. Jared dragged the blade down his cheek and shifted his dark eyes to the photo he'd taped by the mirror.

"Bet you never stayed in a shit hole like this, did ya? Not even when you were *on assignment*, huh?"

That was petty, he supposed. It wasn't *his* fault Jared grew up in a series of foster homes until he aged out of the system. Some of those people were all right. Most weren't, but some were. He liked to believe his big brother—half-brother, sure—never even knew Jared existed. To believe otherwise—that his brother knew and didn't care—was an unacceptable concept.

"*Did* you know, big brother? Hmm? Did you know our father had an extramarital affair that resulted in me?"

Just like the photograph taped to the wall, the actual person it captured could never answer that question for Jared.

"I found you a year too late. I'm not giving up just yet, though. If you knew I existed, you'd have told that pretty wife of yours. And maybe that pretty thing will want to share some of that money she got, too. Or maybe not. But I betcha I could persuade her."

He saw in his head, clear as day. Grieving widow meets look-a-like long-lost brother of her deceased husband, gets overcome with emotion—*why, it's like getting him back again, isn't it*—and invites him to stay with her. He's family. They get friendly. Hell, maybe she even falls in love with him. He'd be all right with that, sure he would. Just like the movies. Not that those always turned out right. It didn't matter much either way; he was getting *something* for his troubles. He deserved it.

"It is owed to me, damn it."

Jared rapped the razor hard against the sink edge, then winced. If he broke the fucking thing… nah, it was fine. For two hundred, it better be. He rinsed and dried it, set it back in the box and zipped it inside the toiletry bag. Out of long habit, he slicked back his damp hair. Then he remembered. *Uh-uh. That's not how big brother wore it.* With his fingertips, he created an off-center part and smoothed it down. Backing out of the narrow bathroom— keeping the mirror in view—Jared studied his reflection from a distance.

There. A near-perfect Doppelganger of the late, great William Grant. One sure to buckle the knees of Mrs. Grant and get him through the door of that sprawling ranch of hers. And once the kids saw him? Well, that'd be icing on the cake for Jared. They'd beg their mommy to let him stay. No doubt about it.

12 Bruce

The "family and friends" gathering for Feather Anne's official welcome home ended up being more like a three-ring circus, with Feather Anne as the reluctant key attraction. It didn't help the kid to have a reporter and that mannequin called Claire trailing behind her everywhere she went, either. Bruce watched it all from his perch at the bar with a mixture of awed frustration.

"Crazy, huh?" Miles Hannaford sidled up next to Bruce and thrust his chin in Feather Anne's direction. She had a mini mob arced around her.

"Yeah, can say that again. Who *are* half these people?"

Miles hitched up a shoulder and let it fall. "No clue, brohan. I guess people let it slip that there was a party for the kid, and *boom*, in come the groupies."

Rosabelle joined them. "Yep, this is her life now. At least for as long as she stays in the spotlight."

"Speaking of spotlight, what's up with your boy? Heard he's in town, too." Miles ordered another round of drinks for him and Bruce and a seltzer for Rosabelle.

It was Bruce's turn to shrug. "Eh, you know. Layin' low."

Truth was, he and Nick had a minor blow out back at the house. Nick wanted to come to the party; Bruce thought it a terrible idea.

"All I'm saying is, I think you two have some unfinished business that needs to be addressed privately, and not at her welcome home party," Bruce had declared.

Nick shot back, "Must be nice."

Bruce had raised his eyebrows at his son and asked, "Do you want a welcome home party, too, Nick? Is that what this is about?"

Nick plopped down onto the couch and swung his feet on top of the coffee table. He lifted his guitar—it never seemed to be far away—and settled it on his lap. After he'd strummed a few notes—and kept Bruce waiting—he grinned and said, "Hell, no. I've got writing to do. No time for nonsense."

"So, what's the problem then?" By now, Bruce's irritation had blossomed into full-blown aggravation.

It was like Nick had reverted to that sullen, angsty teen from seven years ago. Except now he was a sullen, angsty man who looked like he bought the Chris Stapleton starter kit. He'd gone Nashville, all right. It wasn't a bad look—kid knew how to pull it off—but it sure differed from the boy band heartthrob look he'd had going during the Greatest American Singer season.

"No problem, Pops. Just thought it'd be fun to stop by and say hey. That's all. But if I'm not wanted, then…"

"Jesus Christ. Nobody said you're not wanted. It's just not the time or place to make a grand entrance. Have you talked to her at all?"

"Who?" Nick blinked at Bruce with an innocence he'd bet his life was bullshit.

Bruce gritted his teeth. "Feather. Anne. Is. Who."

"Oh, right. Yeah, no. Listen, I tried. She's not taking my calls, so what's a guy to do?"

"Uh-huh," said Bruce. He eyed his son. He acted *too* nonchalant. "She wouldn't have a good reason to ignore your calls, now would she?"

Not looking up, Nick asked, "Why? What'd she say?"

"Well, nothing. And *that's* the problem. You must have really done it good, son."

For the first time, Nick's ultra-chill facade cracked. "Me? Fuck that. She's the one who screwed it all up. Not me. We had a shot to—you know what, never mind. Go celebrate little Miss Martyr. I'm cool staying here."

Bruce had hesitated, but Nick made a big show of ignoring him and by then, he'd had enough. At some point, he'd get both sides of the story and straighten it all out. In the meantime, he had a party to get to. *And Mae would be there.*

Miles elbowed him, jolting him back to the present. "Is that who I think it is?"

Bruce followed the line of his gaze with a sick sense of dread that Nick had ignored his wishes and shown up. Instead, the sight at the end of the line was none other than Ophelia Torres. *Effie*. Sister of Marisol Villeneuve, onetime fling of Bruce Grady, and jet-setting girlfriend of millionaire developer, Jason Marsdale.

Bruce hissed, "What is she doing here?"

Rosabelle heard him. She tilted her head close to Bruce's and said, "By the looks of it, she's here to find *you*."

Bruce saw Effie respond to her sister- and brother-in-law without looking at them; her interest lie somewhere else. With a devilish glint in her eyes, Effie scanned the room until they landed on Bruce. Mae's best friend was right.

"And there's our cue to disappear," said Rosabelle to her husband.

Miles seemed about to protest, then thought better of it upon seeing his wife's no-nonsense stare.

"You guys, stay—"

"Hello, Bruce." Effie stood close enough for him to inhale her perfume; something tropical. Or maybe it was just her.

Bruce took a reflexive step back, a move which Effie raised an eyebrow at.

"Effie. What are you doing here?" Bruce blurted it.

She offered him a seductive pout. "Are you not glad to see me?"

"I-yeah, no. I mean, sure. I just wasn't—I didn't know you'd be here. In Chance. Tonight."

Her pout became a sly smirk. "You seem nervous, *Moosie*. Do I make you nervous?"

Bruce's eyes darted around the room, then back to Ophelia. "What? No, I—"

"Oh, I understand," said the dark-haired Cuban temptress. "You are afraid *Mae* will see us together, hmm?"

"No," said Bruce, his voice high and about as unmanly as anyone could get. In a deeper voice, he said, "Not at all. Mae and I are just friends. So, uh, how have you been? What brings you here? Back to Chance, I mean. Well, obviously, you're here because your family is here. How are your parents?"

Effie folded her arms and waited for his stream of babble to cease. When it did, she answered each question like he were a toddler. "I have been well, thank you. Jason is in Barcelona. And I want to spend time with family. My parents are also well and will, in fact, be on a plane to Connecticut tomorrow. Is there anything else you would like to ask me?"

Bruce had to laugh. Mostly at himself, but also at her amused, playful expression... also at his expense. "I think that about covers it. Except, how long you here for?" No longer flustered, Bruce asked this in a more casual tone.

"Indefinitely. Buy me a drink." She gestured to the bar.

"It's an open bar, so..."

"So, order me a drink, Mr. Big." She waggled her eyebrows at him.

Bruce's face heated as he recalled the last time she'd called him Mr. Big. It was after they'd had sex on the beach. She'd been one hell of a summer fling. He needed to stop thinking about that. He cleared his throat. "You still drink gin and tonic?"

"Excellent memory," replied Effie.

He ordered her drink and another beer for himself and asked, "So, I guess that means Jason's not joining you tonight, or..." he let it hang. He swore. Bruce didn't want to seem like he was flirting. As gorgeous as Ophelia Torres was—and sexy as hell—Bruce wasn't interested in rekindling anything with her.

"We broke up," said Effie matter-of-factly.

"I'm sorry to hear that," said Bruce. And he was.

It had come as a shock when she'd taken off with Marsdale, but their thing had been nothing more than casual. It neither hurt nor upset him to get the news. Besides, that was years ago. They'd both moved on. Her to a wealthy boyfriend; him to a string of short-lived relationships and a current status of borderline celibacy. Without the borderline.

Effie downed her drink, plunked it on the counter, and said, "Don't be. Now, maybe you and I—"

"Bruce, there you are," exclaimed Mae, coming up beside them. "Oh! Ophelia, hi. It's so nice to see you. Marisol told me you were coming."

Effie gave Mae a hug like something out of a catty women's show. He couldn't come up with the name of one, but that's what the hug reminded Bruce of, anyhow. "Mae, it's so nice to see you, too. I was so sorry to hear of your husband's passing. How *are* you?"

Mae looked down and tucked her hair. Bruce cringed for her; he knew how she disliked the attention William's death cast on her. The *poor Mae* faces and sickly sweet tones. She stammered a response—one Bruce knew would be awkward—so he jumped in and changed the subject.

"Hey, how about another round of drinks, hmm? Mae? What are you drinking?"

"Oh, I—red wine would be great. Thanks."

The look she awarded him said thank you for more than the drink. As for the look on Effie's face… that said something else.

"So, Mae," began Effie as she squeezed her way in between her and Bruce. "How is your little coffee shop doing? It must be so hard to be a small business owner."

Bruce took a long swallow of beer and searched for someone to rescue him. Instead—smelling blood in the water—Brianna slithered up beside him and whispered, "That looks positively unfriendly." Her eyebrow twitched, and she did not try to hide her Maleficent-like glee. On the other side of Bruce, Mae squared off.

"The *café* is doing well, thank you. And how about you? Are you still Jason Marsdale's… receptionist? If not, I could always use another waitress. I'm sure one of the high school girls would be happy to re-train you."

Bruce felt a bead of sweat trickle down his temple. "Do something." He hissed to Brianna.

"Oh, hell, no." Brianna crossed her arms and leaned in closer.

Effie cackled. "Oh, that is too kind of you. But, no. My skill set is way above your little coffee shop, and you couldn't afford me anyhow."

Mae set down her glass. "It's a café and from what I recall, your so-called skill set involves lying flat on—"

"Okay, ladies. This has been great catching up, but—" Bruce made eye contact with Pedro who, with one glance, understood the situation and strode over.

"Ophelia, I have some friends who want to meet you," cut in Pedro. He took his sister-in-law's arm and led her away.

The moment the conflict resolved, Brianna drifted away, leaving Bruce and Mae alone at the bar. He lifted her glass and handed it to her. Two spots of pink flushed her cheeks and her eyes blazed. She drank it in one sip, then ordered another.

"So that was—"

Mae cut him off. "The nerve of that woman. *How is your little coffee shop*?" Mae mimicked Effie, Spanish accent and all. "What's her problem, anyhow?"

Bruce tried not to laugh. "Um, I don't think it's politically correct to do accents."

"Oh, shut up," said Mae. She cracked a smile. "Seriously, though. What's her issue with *me*? Does she think… oh." Her face suffused with color. "She thinks I—that we… well, that's—"

"Yeah, I know. It's—she's… wrong. Obviously. You don't—I mean, we're not…"

"This is excruciating to watch." Feather Anne had come up behind them.

Bruce looked at Mae, and Mae looked at Feather Anne. By unspoken agreement, Bruce and Mae spun and walked off in different directions. Feather Anne followed him.

"Slow down, you big ape," said Feather Anne.

Bruce didn't want to talk. He wanted to leave; go somewhere quiet to think. Too many thoughts and possibilities tangoed in his head. He pretended to not hear Feather Anne and reached for the handles of the double doors. They opened before he touched them. Feather Anne's hand grabbed his arm. It dropped away when they saw who stood in the open frame.

"Nick. What are you—"

"Hey, Pop. Feather Anne." He gave a shrug to Bruce and a smile to Feather Anne. "Decided I didn't want to miss the party."

Bruce seethed. Leaving now became a non-option. His own troubles aside, this had the making for a catastrophe. He became acutely aware of the heads turning and gasps from the crowd.

Cell phones were being held up and the reporter who'd been trailing Feather Anne all night elbowed her way to the front of the forming half-circle; her cell phone raised. Bruce looked back at Feather Anne, expecting to see fury. But Feather Anne Byrd had spent enough time in the limelight and under the scrutiny of the public eye that time had made a professional of her. Instead of unmasked rage, her expression smoothed into something glacial and unreadable... if you didn't know her.

Like Mae, Feather Anne's eyes told her every emotion. Bruce saw the myriad. Contempt, disbelief, hurt. Nick must've been able to read her, too. He ducked his head in a way that could only convey both apology and pleading. Neither spoke. Someone from the back of the crowd shouted, "Play us a song!"

Feather Anne faced them, turning her back to Nick and Bruce. "Would if we could, guys. Sorry, no instruments."

An audible murmur of disappointment rippled across the group, but then Nick's voice rang out over it. "Actually, I have my guitar outside if someone wants to—"

"I'll get it," squeaked a girl who must have been a relative of one of the invited guests. Bruce didn't recognize her from town. She ran out the door at breakneck speed.

Nick breezed past Bruce, hooked a proprietary arm around Feather Anne's shoulders—she stiffened—and announced, "It's great to be back home, surrounded by family and friends, and by Feather Anne's side, doing what we love to do. Make music together. Right, Feather Anne?"

Feather Anne addressed the guests. "Always good to be home. In the spirit of family and friendships, Nick and I have to ask that you don't share our performance on social media." Nick opened his mouth, but Feather Anne gave him no chance. "Right, Nick?" She awarded him her sweetest smile.

"Y-yeah, right. Thanks for, uh, understanding."

Mae had made her way over to Bruce's side. "What do you think of all *that*?"

Bruce kept his gaze on the pair. "Don't know yet. But it doesn't look good to me."

Brandon Bourdreau joined them. "Yeah, me either."

Bruce pinched the bridge of his nose and closed his eyes. The night may not have quite been a disaster, but it felt damn close to becoming one the longer it went on. And since it was his kid who added the icing to the cake, he'd have to stick it out to the end.

13 Mae

Mae collapsed a folding chair, passed it to Bruce, and moved on to the next one. Across the room, Chris and Gina did the same. They were the last ones in the hall, somehow relegated to clean up duty with Brianna—the one who'd planned the entire thing—nowhere in sight.

Every so often, she stole a glance at Bruce. Each time, she discovered he was looking at her. They grinned and looked away. When she'd slid a fifth chair onto his outstretched arm, she laughed and said, "Okay, macho man. That's got to be getting heavy. Why don't you go stack them with the rest?"

Bruce shook his head. "Nah. I'm strong like bull. Two more."

Mae's eyebrow flicked but all she said was, "All right, then. Here you go."

He winked at her and carried the awkward stack to the far end of the room. She watched him walk away, unaware of the smile on her face until she caught her mother staring at her with a curious expression. Mae busied herself with the next set of chairs and hoped Gina would stay on her side of the room. No such luck, though.

"So, looks like Bruce is back in the picture, huh?"

Mae offered a noncommittal, "Hmm? Oh, I suppose… yes."

"Must be nice to have your…" Gina paused, "friend back."

"Mhm. It is," said Mae. She glanced at Gina, then back down at the task at hand.

"Yeah, I couldn't help but notice you seem happier these past few days. Don't suppose old Moose has anything to—"

"No but thank you for asking. How are you and Chris? Any closer to setting a date?"

Mae knew that would derail Gina's attempt at nosiness. For as reluctant as Mae was to think about—let alone discuss—her feelings for Bruce, Gina was a thousand times more reluctant to plan her wedding.

"No," said Gina.

"I mean, he asked you, what, a year ago? Don't you think it's time to, you know, tie the knot? Become the old ball and chain? Say I do and—"

"All right, all right. You made your point. All I'm saying is happy looks good on you. Looks good on both my girls. It'd be nice if you could try it at the same damn time, though."

Bruce returned, rubbing his hands together. "What are you two ladies discussing?" He looked from one to the other.

"I was just telling Mae—"

Mae jumped in. "She was just telling me about her wedding plans. Weren't you, Mother? Oh, look, I think your fiancé needs your help."

They all looked at Chris, who'd tangled himself in the balloon bouquet strings. Gina scowled at Mae before calling out. "Stay still will ya? I'm coming." Under her breath, she muttered, "Idiot." To Mae and Bruce—and with a sly smile—she said, "Well, I'll just leave you two alone so you can… talk."

When she'd gone out of earshot, Bruce jabbed a thumb in her direction. "What's her deal?"

Mae rolled her eyes. "You know Gina. Who knows, maybe she's back on the sauce." She regretted saying it.

Bruce winced. "Ouch. How is that going, if you don't mind my asking? Uh, Chris confided in me about a month ago."

Mae looked over at Gina and shrugged one shoulder. "It was a slip, not quite a slide, thanks to Chris. The whole Feather Anne thing—her not talking to Gina—I think it just…" She didn't finish; Bruce understood like he always did.

"Speaking of Feather Anne, does she know about Gina's… slip?"

"No. God, no." Mae shuddered. "That would've been—ugh, I don't even want to think about it. We all agreed it was best for Feather Anne to focus on her career and let us handle Gina."

"And now?" Bruce stared at Mae.

"And now everything is fine. It's good. Under control." *I hope*.

"You hope," said Bruce.

Mae had forgotten how easily he read her thoughts. She couldn't hold back the smile that stretched across her face any more than the next words from her mouth. "It's good to have you back, Bruce."

"It's good to be back, Mae."

They grinned and held one another's gaze until a series of balloon pops assaulted their ears and made them jump. Across the way, Chris called out. "Sorry."

He still had tangles of ribbon around his arms, waist, and legs. Gina held what might have been a thumbtack up to the one remaining balloon. She looked at her future husband with nothing short of contempt, popped the balloon, and left him standing in his chaos.

"Well, I'm calling it a night. Either of you can drop him off on your ways home. Or let him walk. Whatever."

"I'll bring him," said Bruce. "I've got to stop by Brookhaven anyhow."

"Hey, that reminds me. Weirdest thing… ah, you know what? Never mind. It's stupid." Gina turned away.

"No, wait," said Mae. "What is it?" A knot twisted in her stomach. She had a feeling she already knew, but she needed Gina to say it.

Chris—dragging the strings and popped balloons—joined them. "Oh, you telling her about seeing—"

Gina glared at Chris. "I wasn't telling her nothin'. Geez."

Mae swallowed. "Were you, by any chance, going to tell me about seeing a man who looks a lot like William?"

Gina's eyes widened. "Yeah, but—"

"Feather Anne and I saw him, too. At the memorial."

"You did? But you said nothing." She crossed her arms and darted glances around the room. "What, is it like a-a ghost or something?"

Mae wanted to laugh and tease Gina. She really did. But she couldn't because part of her wondered the same thing, silly or not.

Bruce said, "Hang on a second. What are you all saying here? That you think you're seeing William's... spirit around Chance? Come on, now. Where'd *you* see this guy, Gina?"

Gina didn't hesitate. "Saw him across the street from Brookhaven. Chris and me, we'd been visiting Chris's buddy Timmy for a while but came out of there around one thirty."

"Nah, it was more around two," said Chris.

Mae asked, "You saw him, too, Chris?"

"*Psh*, yeah I did. Clear as day. W-well, not that clear, I mean. He was across the street, like Gi said, and neither of us had our glasses on, so—"

"So, you can't be sure what, or *who* you saw," finished Bruce. "You guys hear yourselves?" He took Mae by the shoulders, his grip gentle. "I know what you want to believe, and I get *why*. But—"

"No," said Mae, stepping out of his grasp. "That's not it—not what I want. I don't want William's... ghost hovering around. The idea is heartbreaking. Too many people have had the same vision, or sighting, or whatever you call it. It's *real*, Bruce."

It sounded crazy, yes. In was in Bruce's eyes. But what else could it be?

Bruce folded his arms and studied Mae. After a moment, he asked, "So, who else had one of these… sightings? And where?"

Mae ticked them off. "The Brightsiders. *Both* of them, mind you. Now Gina and Chris. Me. Feather Anne. Twice, too. The time at the memorial, then again with Brandon outside the café."

She paused, and Bruce used the pause to ask another question. "And did anyone try to—I don't know—approach or talk to the… person?"

"He keeps disappearing before anyone can," said Mae.

"How about you guys?" Bruce addressed Gina and Chris.

"Same. Plus, we felt kinda stupid. I mean, it wasn't William," said Chris.

"Well," said Gina. "He was a dead ringer. Pardon the term."

Bruce quipped, "Dead ringer you could hardly see without your glasses on."

The three traded barbs but Mae stayed silent. Something out the far window held her gaze. A man cast in partial shadow under the streetlamp. She couldn't be sure—there was no way, given the distance and darkness—but, God, it looked like William. Her chest grew tight and her throat constricted. She opened her mouth, but nothing came out.

"Mae, tell her I—Mae? What's wrong?" Bruce's tone sharpened and it drew her eyes away from the window.

"I—he… *look.*"

They all turned to see… nothing. In the brief second she looked away, the man—*William*—disappeared once again. Mae moved toward the door, but Bruce halted her. "Stay here. Please. Whoever it is out there— it's *not* William—is playing some kind of game here. I'll deal with him.

"Bruce, do you really think—"

Gina never finished her question; Bruce had already slammed open the doors and stepped out into the night to chase the mystery man. Part of Mae felt relieved he'd done so; part of her wanted to run after him. She should be the one confronting… whoever this was.

Not William.

"Should I go with him?" Chris looked from Gina to Mae.

"No," said Gina.

Mae said, "Yes."

The trio argued, but it proved pointless. Bruce returned, alone and with his face set in stone. Mae froze, eyes locked on him.

Chris asked the question stuck in Mae's throat. "Well, did you find him?"

Bruce shook his head and fixed his gaze on Mae. "No. No trace of him."

"So, maybe it *is* a—"

"No," said Bruce. "It's some asshole, dicking around with us. With *you*, Mae. I'll find him. Don't worry."

"Bruce? Maybe we should call Joel?" Mae wasn't sure if it was an overreaction, but if there *was* someone lurking around, they should involve the police.

"Ahead of you. I called him on the way out. He dispatched a patrol car to look around. They'll be doing more passes in your neighborhood, too. Whoever this guy is, he won't get away with this."

Mae saw the flaw in the plan. "Yes, but what has he done?" She looked at each of them. "Nothing. Not really. Maybe we're being—"

"We're being cautious, Mae. You—*we*—live in a bubble here in Chance. It's easy to forget there's a world of whack jobs out there. Voyeurs, scumbags who prey on people with money, fanatics. You name it, they're out there. And you aren't low profile."

"Me? I don't—" Mae scoffed but Gina cut her off.

"You're the sister of a pop star and widow of a famous author. And your café is a tourist attraction. Bruce is right. You're a flashing neon sign for flag-flying freaks."

"Say that ten times fast," snorted Chris. No one laughed.

Mae protested. "Stop, now. This isn't the movies or-or a television show. Do you seriously think someone is out there—what—pretending to be the ghost of William? To what end?"

Bruce rubbed his jaw. "I don't know, Mae. Not yet. But until I do, I'm not letting my guard down and neither should you."

Gina chimed in. "Old Moose here is right, kid. In fact, I know I'd feel a whole lot better if I knew he was staying with you until this all resolved itself."

Mae stared open-mouthed at her mother, who appeared expressionless on the surface. But Mae knew Gina well, and saw straight through the innocent façade. "Isn't that a bit—"

"Your Mom is right, Mae. We'd all feel safer is Bruce was there with you, Feather Anne, and the twins."

Bruce stayed silent, watching Mae for her decision. She sighed. "For the kid's and Feather Anne's sake, yes. Fine. If you wouldn't mind, that is."

"I—" began Bruce.

"He doesn't mind at all," finished Gina.

Bruce said, "Looks like it's decided. I'll, uh, swing by my place and grab a few things. I should only be a half hour."

"We'll stay with them until you get there," said Chris.

"Guys, you're being ridiculous." Mae gaped at each one, expecting at least Gina to back her up. They wore coordinating grim expressions. She threw her hands up and let them drop to her sides in defeat. "I give up. Let's go, then."

Instead of Bruce driving Chris home, Gina going to her house, and Mae heading home to Feather Anne and the twins, she now had them all trailing her home like the Secret Service. Bruce made another last-minute decision to have Nick bring him an overnight bag. Gina and Chris were coming over *just because.* That's what they'd said, but not meant.

Mae gave the wake-up command to her phone, then said, "Call Feather Anne." When her sister answered, Mae cautioned, "So, don't freak out, but—"

"Okay, never start a phone call with *don't freak out,*" interrupted Feather Anne. "What's wrong? What happened? Where are you?"

"See, now that's why I said don't freak out. Everything is fine. I'm on my way home… and Bruce is staying overnight."

After a pause, Feather Anne said, "Well this is an interesting development." There was laughter in her voice.

"No, wiseass. Not—not like that. Geez. There was a-a minor incident and just for peace of mind— his and Gina's, not mine—he's going to, I don't know, hang out."

"What—wait a sec," said Feather Anne. She must have covered the phone because her voice muffled as she spoke to someone. "Sorry. I was just telling Brandon what you said."

"Oh. Brandon's still there, is he?" *Shit. Nick is coming to the house with Bruce's overnight bag.* "Is he, um, staying long or…"

"Uh, yeah. We were going to watch a movie. Mae, what is going on? What is this incident? Does it have to do with the William look-a-like?"

"Did *you* see him again?" Mae's tone came out sharp. She exhaled. "Sorry, our mother and Chris and Bruce have got me on edge now. Nothing happened, exactly. I-I saw him again."

"Holy shit. You did? When? Where?"

"He was outside the country club, across the street," said Mae.

"And…" Feather Anne drew out the word.

"And nothing. I turned away to tell Bruce and Gina to look, and when we did, he was gone. Bruce went out to find him but couldn't."

"Yeah, because it's a ghost," said Feather Anne. There was no humor or teasing in her voice.

"Feather Anne, you don't believe—"

"Well, why not?" Feather Anne's defiant streak from her younger years poked through her newfound Zen. "Why couldn't it be?"

Mae rubbed away the crease in her forehead. "Sweetie, you don't believe William's.... it's not...

listen. I'll be home in five. We'll talk more when I get there. Twins are asleep, I hope?"

"Yep, since about an hour ago. They woke up when Brandon and I got home but fell back asleep quick enough. See you in a few."

"Wait, I forgot to tell you..." The line clicked. *I forgot to tell you Nick is on his way over.*

She knew she should call back and forewarn her sister, especially after the tense scene at the party. The only thing that had kept it civil was the crowd and cameras watching their every move. A face-off without all that? Trouble. Then again, whatever drama those two had going on needed to resolve somehow.

"And what about your own drama?" Mae met her own eyes in the rearview mirror and scowled.

Was this a sign from William that it was too soon to... to what? Move on, as they say? Whoever the hell *they* were. And she had been *moving on* with life. Unbidden, William's last letter came to mind. Or rather, the last line.

"*... know that love—a second chance at love— waits patiently for you. Don't resist for too long, sweetheart. Time is short, as we know all too well.*"

He'd meant *Bruce* waited patiently for her. Of this, she had no doubt. William never blinked at Mae and Bruce's uncommon friendship. In fact, he encouraged it. As if he knew one day...

Mae turned into the driveway. She parked but didn't get out right away. Her gaze fell to her hand still on the steering wheel. Her wedding ring sparkled in the light above the garage.

"Oh, William. What am I doing? *What* do I do? I don't know if these... sightings are a sign that it's too soon or that you're giving me your blessing, or..." She sighed and closed her eyes. "Can you maybe give me a clear sign?"

A knock on her driver side window caused her to jump. Mae sprang away from the door and may have screamed, too. The blood rushing to her ears deafened all sound. It took a few beats for her to realize it was Bruce's apologetic face staring at her through the glass. She climbed out swearing.

"God damn it, Bruce. You scared the hell out of me."

"Sorry, sorry. You, uh, all right?" Bruce squinted at her.

"Yeah. I was just... I'm fine. Let's go inside. Feather Anne doesn't know Nick is coming yet."

"Uh-oh. I'll keep him outside." Bruce held the door for Mae, then followed her inside. Gina and Chris followed.

Feather Anne and Brandon sat cozied together on the couch, watching A Star Is Born, but she paused it as soon as they all walked in.

"So, what's going on? Feels like you're not telling me something here."

Mae gripped her sister's shoulders and looked her in the eye. "You know as much as we do, I swear. Bruce doesn't quite see the same... mysticism in this as you do, I'm afraid."

"Okay, fine. But what do *you* think, Mae?"

"I've been asking myself the same question, Feather Anne."

"And?" Feather Anne crossed her arms and stared hard at Mae.

"And... I don't have an answer yet. I don't know *what* to think." Mae's tension headache returned. She rubbed her temples.

"Feather Anne, give her a break, okay?" Brandon came up beside Feather Anne. He softened the admonishment. "You guys have had a long night; you're both exhausted. I will head home and let you sleep."

Feather Anne dropped her head on his shoulder. "Fine, I guess. I'll walk you to the door."

Gina spoke up. "Looks like everything is under control here. Chris and I are leaving, too. G'night everyone."

The moment their car pulled away, Mae remembered. *Nick.* Bruce must've thought it at the same time. They both called, "Feather Anne," but they were too late. She'd already swung the door open. Standing in the doorway was Nick, hand poised to knock.

"Uh, hey. I'm, uh, dropping stuff off for my dad."

Feather Anne spun around to glare at Bruce and Mae. "Thanks for the heads up, guys."

"I was going to..." Mae sighed.

Bruce squeezed her shoulder and went to the door. Mae held her breath, half expecting the boys to take swings at each other. Or for Feather Anne to throw a punch at Nick. Either seemed possible. But Brandon surprised them all.

"Hey, Nick." Brandon nodded at him. It was neither friendly nor unfriendly. It sounded neutral. "I'm heading out. Maybe it's time for you two to talk and—"

"No, thanks," said Feather Anne. She kissed Brandon. "Pick me up tomorrow? Around eleven?"

"Yeah, sure. Goodnight."

He smiled at Feather Anne in a way the made *Mae's* heart melt. He loved her kid sister as much as he ever had, but now with a maturity and confidence of a man. Mae couldn't help but hope the two would have a future together. Then she turned her attention to Nick still in the doorway, and her heart clenched for him.

He'd stepped aside to let Brandon pass, and now stood with Bruce's bag in one hand and the other shoved into his jeans pocket. The odd man out. He kept his expression disinterested, but he couldn't hide his eyes. Hurt, plain as day, for anyone observant enough to notice. God, she wished Mia hadn't gone to Arizona to visit her mother. If this boy-man ever needed a mother's affection, it was now.

"Thanks for dropping off my stuff, bud. I'll, uh, see you tomorrow?"

"Yeah, sure, Pop," said Nick. He glanced quick at Feather Anne, then nodded to Mae. "Good to see you again, Mae. Goodnight."

Before she knew what she was doing, she called out, "Wait. Nick, you came all this way… come inside for a cup of tea with us."

Bruce and Feather Anne stared at her like she'd asked Atilla the Hun in for tea. Her return glances were defiant before she beckoned Nick inside.

"I'm going to bed," declared Feather Anne.

"Nope," said Mae. "You're joining me in the kitchen. All three of you." She spun on her heel; confident they'd follow. She filled the tea kettle and pulled four teacups from the cabinet. Without looking at them, she said, "Sit."

Three chairs scraped across the floor. Feather Anne sighed. Bruce cleared his throat. Nick stayed silent. Mae lit the tealight in the warmer, and when the kettle whistled, she poured the boiling water over the tea leaves in the floral teapot that once belonged to her grandmother. The trio at the island said nothing. To break the silence, Mae put Keely Smith on the record player, low enough to not wake the twins, but loud enough to sooth at least *her* jagged nerves.

She poured tea for each of them, avoiding eye contact with Feather Anne—who she knew would glare at her—and Bruce as well—who'd be giving her an, *are you crazy* look—and smiled encouragingly at Nick. However, he missed her show of support because he was too busy staring at Feather Anne.

"So," she began. Mae had no idea what to say next. She mouthed, "Say something," to Bruce.

He straightened, clanked his teacup onto the saucer and stammered. "Y-you guys uh, want to—"

Feather Anne had fire in her eyes and venom in her voice. "Go on, Nick. Tell them. Might as well. Tell them what a rotten snake you are, or I will."

14 Brandon

Brandon tossed his keys on the foyer table and kicked off his sneakers, already anticipating the hot shower awaiting him upstairs. His shoulder ached, and the heat helped. He'd gone only two stairs when Brianna called his name from her office. He debated whether to pretend not to hear her.

"Don't act like you can't hear me, brother dear. Get in here. I need to ask you something,"

He hung his head, then backtracked. Brianna was talking to someone. Who did she have over this time of night? The answer: no one.

"Who were you just talking to?" He looked around the room and saw only Brianna and her laptop.

Several voices called out, "Hi, Brandon," and "Hey, handsome," and a voice unmistakably Elise's said, "Show us your face, kid."

He answered his own question. "Ah, you're video chatting. Hey, ladies." He turned to leave.

"No, don't go. Come, say hi to the girls. We're using Zoom." Brianna waved her wine glass dangerously close to the keyboard.

"Oh, Jesus. Don't spill." He tromped over and bent down to get eye level. "Hello, ladies. Good to see you, now goodnight."

He tried to leave again.

"Oh, Bran, don't go yet. I told you, I need your help. Look. I can only get three of them on my screen. How do I get the others?"

"Bri, I don't use Zoom. I don't know." He supposed he could figure it out, but...

"Oh, come on. You can figure it out. You're a genius with this stuff."

He was nowhere near being a genius. But his injury *had* given him a lot of time to mess around with audio-digital programs. Turned out, he was kind of a natural. Even though having Bri's friends watch him made him awkward, he saw right away how to fix her problem.

Ignoring the catcalls from Elise, Brittany, Katie, and even Charlotte, Brandon clicked a couple icons and said, "Just open this, then click that, and ta-da, you're all visible."

"Yay for my baby brother," said Brianna. She clapped her ring against her wine glass. "Stay for a minute. Tell us what's going on with you and Feather Anne. Come on. Don't be shy."

From the laptop, Charlotte said, "Oh, let him be, Brianna. Run, Brandon, while you still can."

Elise said, "As if you don't already know, Brianna."

Brittany said, "I already know, too."

Katie said, "Am I the only one who doesn't know anything? Oh my gosh. Are you kids back together?"

Brandon rubbed the back of his neck and hooked his thumb through his belt loop. "I-we, uh, it looks… that… way? I'm, um, not sure what the plan is, you know? We're taking it day by day, I guess."

The women on screen went silent. Brianna stared at him; her eyes narrowed. "I'm going to say goodnight now, girls. Anyone meeting for coffee tomorrow at Mae's should be there by eight-thirty." She closed the laptop and stood. "You, me, kitchen."

He was in no mood for a Brianna grilling, but he'd opened his big mouth, making it his own fault. She motioned for him to sit at the kitchen table and grabbed two cake plates from the drying rack by the sink. After cutting him a generous wedge of chocolate fudge cake and herself a narrow sliver, she sat across from him.

"Well?"

His fork hovered. "Well, what?" He knew what she was asking, but he figured he'd make her work for it a little.

"Well, what is going on with you and Feather Anne? Duh."

He smirked. "I told you—and your posse—day by day."

"Have you two talked about the future? Is she staying in Chance? Signing the contract? Are you a couple?"

"Whoa, easy, there. Yeah, we've talked about it. She's... undecided."

Brianna slapped her knees, then raised her hands in the air. "So, tell her you love her and you want her to stay, dummy."

Brandon laughed. "She knows I love her, Bri. And that's why I will not tell her to stay. She's got to decide on her own, without my influence. Whatever she does, I support her."

"Hmm." Brianna tapped the fork tines against her plate and eyed him. "Very mature of you. And what is the Nick situation? He made his mark at Feather Anne's party. He's lucky I didn't throw him out on his ear."

Brandon shrugged. "I'm not worried about Nick Amendola. I'll never like the guy, but I trust Feather Anne. There's nothing between them."

"Brandon, they—"

"Nope. Her beef with him isn't some… jilted girl thing. It's between them. If she wants to talk about it, she will."

"Wait, you know what all the drama is about? And you're not going to tell me? Your own sister?" Brianna looked both incredulous and offended.

"Can't tell you what I don't know, sis." He shoveled the cake into his mouth in three giant bites. He spoke with his mouth full, knowing how much she hated it. "Love you. Night sis."

Brandon snicked the carton of milk from the fridge and dashed upstairs, smirking the whole way. He knew what Feather Anne's problem with Nick was, but it was for her to share or not share. He'd already made the mistake of weighing in, now he planned on butting out. In the meantime, he had the glimmer of a plan of a different—yet related— matter.

Carton of milk drained, Brandon sat down at his desk, opened his laptop, and reached for his phone. Time to get in touch with his old buddy Kade. On the second ring, he answered.

"Hey, bud. Long time no talk, man. What up?"

Brandon's smile grew. He hadn't talked to his old high school friend in months, but it was like no time passed at all. "Nothing much, man. Hey, your dad still own that music store?"

"Sure does. Whatcha need? I'm working there part time, so I can hook you up."

"Excellent. You there tomorrow? I'll come by. It'll be easier to explain in person."

"We open at nine. Come after that, bro."

"Sweet. Thanks."

"I hear your girl is back in town. What's up with that?"

"Eh, you know. We'll see."

"This little trip to the music store have anything to do with her?"

Brandon chuckled. "You could say that."

"No, shit, huh? Cool. Bring her by, man. It'll be good for business, you know? Tell you what. You scratch my back, I'll scratch yours. Feel me?"

"That sounds kinda gay, man."

"Shut up. You know what I mean," said Kade.

"Yeah, yeah. I'll see what I can do," said Brandon.

He hung up and tossed the phone onto his bed. Phase one, done. Bringing Feather Anne with him to the store might ruin his plan, but it could still work out. It all might be a colossal waste of time, too. But it was worth the risk. *She* was worth the risk. Next, all he needed was to clean out his savings account. *No biggie*. He kept telling himself that. The last phase involved Mae, but Brandon felt confident she'd like the idea.

Correction: last phase would be Feather Anne getting onboard.

Maybe if he had someone else onboard who knew what she was going through, he could sway her? His gut clenched at the person his mind led him to. Yet, there was no one else.

15 Nick

"You haven't told them yet?" Nick had assumed they all knew by now.

Mae and Bruce looked from Feather Anne to Nick but said nothing. They were waiting on him. He held Feather Anne's gaze until she looked away. Small victory for Nick.

"No," said Feather Anne after a pause.

"Why not?" He pressed. "If I'm the shit you think I am, why not tell them yourself? Maybe it's because I'm not the bad guy here? Huh? John St. James is, Feather Anne. Deep down, you know that."

He was getting through to her; he saw it in her body language. Maybe she never loved him the way he loved her, and he supposed she never would. But he could at least get her friendship back. He could hope for that.

"Uh, listen," said Bruce, glancing at Mae for her agreement, "we'd love it if one of you would clue us in here. How about it, Nick?"

"Fine. But Feather Anne, you need to hear me out this time." It would not be the version John St. James had sold Feather Anne, but his. The *truth*. Everything he would have told her if that asshole hadn't blocked him at every chance.

"St. James offered us—*us*, Feather Anne—a contract outside the show. That's what he told me, at least. *Everything you kids have been asking to do and more*, was what he said. He told me you were on board." He sat forward, his arms on the island, and hands clasped. "I was an idiot, Feather Anne. I admit it. I signed the contract without even reading it. I trusted—no, that's a lie. Truth, Feather Anne? I wanted us away from that stupid, soul-sucking show tour and I thought that was our ticket out."

"Yeah, well, you made no secret of that," agreed Feather Anne. She still wouldn't look at him, though.

"No, I didn't. You know what a smooth talker he is, Feather Anne. I—"

"So, you're telling me John St. James tricked you into signing a contract to get you off the tour?

Why, Nick? Why would he do that when he told me we—*you and me*, Nick—got them their highest rating out of all seven seasons put together? Why would he try to separate us?" She pressed her back against her seat and folded her arms.

Nick's hands curled into fists. "I don't know, Feather Anne. But if I had to guess? He knew you were the one with the genuine talent, the bigger future. I was just the guy in the way."

She forgot her anger, if only for a moment, and said, "Bullshit. You've got more talent than anyone I know." She remembered her anger again. "You're still an asshole."

"But you believe me?"

"John St. James is a snake. We never trusted him."

He repeated, "So... you believe me?" Nick smiled but held it in check. He wasn't out of the woods with her yet.

Bruce and Mae hadn't uttered a word. They just watched the pair like a tennis match.

Feather Anne skirted the question again. "You're an idiot for not reading the contract."

"Yes, I am." Nick agreed easily enough.

"And you're a bigger idiot for not telling me this sooner."

Nick had to defend himself, even if it risked his chances at reconciliation. "Now, hang on, there. I tried. Repeatedly, Feather Anne. You wouldn't take my calls. They wouldn't let me anywhere near you. That contract I signed? There was a shit-ton of legal language in there that came down to my having to pay back close to a million dollars if I breached any of the terms. And one of them was no talking about the show with the press. My hands were tied. I swear."

"Nick, that sounds like—" Mae interjected.

He shook his head. "I had a buddy of mine look. It's airtight, *and* I signed it. I'm stuck for three years."

The last of Feather Anne's icy contempt melted right before his eyes. "John told me you came into his office and demanded he let you off the tour. That you threatened to leak to the tabloids that the whole Nick and Feather Anne romance was a lie." She shook her head and sniffed. "He said he just wanted to protect me from your spitefulness. He, uh, he spun it pretty good."

"He manipulated both of you," said Bruce. "He's the asshole here."

Nick didn't disagree, but what about Feather Anne? As far as he'd been able to tell, John St. James had his hooks deep into her brain. "Feather Anne? What's he promising *you*?"

She glanced at Mae, and Bruce, then held Nick's gaze. "To make me a big star." She waved jazz hands at the *big star* part. "He's been pressuring me to sign a five-year deal."

Bruce exploded. "That's bullshit. This guy is a slimeball. You don't—and this goes for both of you—sign a contract without a lawyer. And you shouldn't sign one with him, period."

"Yeah, well, too late for me, Pops." The nasty taste in Nick's mouth was from the bitter pill of reality.

"Don't be so sure, son. We're getting a lawyer to look at that contract, pronto. As for you, Feather Anne. I can't tell you what to do, but I would suggest you do nothing without a professional by your side. He's taken advantage of you enough."

Feather Anne wriggled in her chair and pressed her palms to her eyes. When she dropped them back on the island, she fixed them with wide eyes. "I don't know what to do. If I don't sign, I lose this chance, and it might be my only one. If I sign, I blow my chances of controlling my music and I'll be their puppet. At least for a while. Then, maybe after I've paid my dues, I can—"

"Five years is a long time to make music you hate, Feather Anne," said Mae.

Nick's phone buzzed. He looked at the time. Eleven-eleven PM. "Make a wish," his mother would've said. The text message came from an unknown number.

Meet me tomorrow morning at eight outside the café. It's important.

A second message followed.

It's Brandon. Don't tell Feather Anne.

Nick's gaze flicked across the island at Feather Anne and back to his phone. What the hell does Brandon Bourdreau want? To flex his muscles and mark his territory? He could blow him off; let him stress about whether Nick and his girl were rekindling the imaginary fires again. But his curiosity always got the better of him. He typed a brief reply.

Sure. See ya then.

He slipped the phone in his back pocket as he stood and stretched. The others stood. "It's late. I'm sure you're all beat. We can talk more tomorrow... if you want to, that is." He directed the last part at Feather Anne.

"Yeah, sure." Feather Anne awarded him with her first smile in months. "I'll walk you out."

At the door, he stopped and faced her. "What do you say, short stuff? We cool again?"

She punched his arm. Hard. "Yeah, I suppose. You're still and idiot though."

"True. I am. And I'm sorry how everything went down. Listen, there's no question St. James is a sleazy bastard, but I have to be honest. I'm making the music I wanted to make. Yeah, it's under his label, but I've got a lot of say in the record. Maybe, I don't know, this can all work out and we can still make music together, like we planned in the beginning."

Feather Anne shrugged. It wasn't a shrug of indifference, but of uncertainty. "I guess I've a lot of thinking to do, huh?"

"Contracts are negotiable. You don't have to make the same mistakes I made, and you can still get what you want," offered Nick.

"Yeah, but what if I don't *know* what I want?" She punched his arm again, this time not as hard.

He punched back. "Well, then, I guess you have some thinking to do."

She blew her hair out of her eyes and held the door open. "Yep, I do."

Nick stepped onto the lamplit porch. He turned back once more. "I, uh, I've missed you."

"It's good to have you back, Nick."

Nick gave a slight smile and jogged down the stairs. He turned back to wave when he reached the truck, but Feather Anne had already gone inside, and the porch light was off.

What'd you expect, dumb ass? That she'd follow you out and give you a big, fat kiss?

He drove away in his old truck with the all too familiar jumble of emotions that had been his constant companion since he'd met Feather Anne. Hope and disappointment, *ping pong, ping pong*. If they could just go back to the first months of the show. They'd gotten close, really close. They had this complete experience—the show, the tour, the fans, and the music—binding them together, and yet it still wasn't enough to prove to her they belonged together.

"Damn, it, Feather Anne." He pounded the steering wheel with his fist.

Somehow, this caused the visor to drop, and a flurry of papers fell into his lap. He looked down for a second to grab them. When he picked his head up again, his heart jolted.

"Shit." He yelled and swerved, but not before seeing the startled face of a man.

Nick's heart felt like it might bust out of his chest and his entire body felt liquid, He pulled over to the side of the road and tried to calm down. "Fucking hell, man." He opened the door and hopped out. The man was nowhere in sight.

Nick turned around, his hand on the top of his head. "Hey," he called. He was alone on the empty street, unless he counted an orange striped cat crossing the lane a few houses down. "What the fuck." He muttered and climbed back in the cab.

He drove home at a crawl, his nerves jangled. Soon enough, though, his thoughts drifted away from the jackass in the road and back to Feather Anne. He replayed everything; especially the part where she forgave him. Then he remembered Brandon's mysterious text. He seemed chill leaving Mae's house; nothing like before. The jealous streak was gone, which either meant he had no feelings for Feather Anne anymore—Nick wished—or he was that confident in their relationship. That was the more likely scenario.

"And that means Ole Nick hasn't got a chance in hell."

16 Marisol

The Villeneuve house, as large as it was, had too many people in it. This, according to Pedro, at well after midnight. He'd returned to his and Marisol's bedroom with a hand towel clutched around his waist. It gaped open, exposing a generous show of muscular thigh and buttock.

"Why are you smiling, Mari? This is funny to you?" Pedro scowled and tried to adjust the scant towel. It slipped from his grasp and gave his wife a full frontal of her husband's goods.

Marisol's eyes drifted down, and her eyebrows up. "Not funny, mi amor, but perhaps fun."

Pedro's indignation vanished, and a slow smile spread across his face. He locked the bedroom door and turned down the lights. After the Villeneuve's made love—quietly—and Marisol had curled against her husband's side, he reignited his earlier lament.

"I know your tricks, Mari. But I haven't forgotten. We have too many people here, I feel claustrophobic. Worse, they're eating us out of house and home using all our towels, and they are so *loud*, cariño. I can't hear myself think."

"Pedro, my family has been here less than twenty-four hours." She pinched him.

"Ouch. Yes, and how long are they staying? I hear no talk of leaving. You know your sister almost got into a catfight with Mae?"

This was news to Marisol. She sat up. "With *Mae*? But why—" Dawning lit her face. "Oh, because of Bruce. Ay dios mio."

"Exactamente. You need to talk to her, Mari, before she makes a colossal mess of everything."

Marisol bristled. "She has a broken heart, Pedro. You should be more understanding and supportive."

"I'm trying. And for a woman with a broken heart, she seemed fine." Marisol pulled away, but Pedro hugged her against him. "Sorry, sorry."

Marisol softened. "She really is upset about Jason. Flirting with Bruce is her way of making herself feel better. It meant nothing. But I'll talk to her tomorrow."

"And… you'll also ask what her long-term plans are?"

Marisol sighed. "Yes, I will. Now, what great offense have Mami and Papi made?"

"None, unless you count your father using the last of my shaving cream, or your mother giving the children ice cream before dinner, or—"

"Okay, okay. Suffer for one more week. They'll miss their friends in Florida and will be ready to go back, too."

They lay quiet for several minutes, and even though she suspected Pedro had fallen asleep, Marisol mused aloud. "I wonder if Bruce and Mae will finally get together now."

Pedro startled beside her. After a pause, he replied. "It is none of our business, Mari."

She propped herself on her elbow and squinted at him in the dark. "Pedro Miguel Villeneuve, are you to tell me you are not at *all* curious?" He spoke, but she interrupted. "You lie, if you say so. This is more exciting than a Telenovela, and I've caught you watching them."

"That's different, Mari. This is real life. Real people that we know and love. I would hate to see either of them get hurt."

"Get hurt? Why would anyone get hurt?" Marisol was being obtuse. She understood how either or both could get hurt. She spoke again, as if Pedro had explained. "Okay, but they love each other. They always have. I believe that Mae realized it during all that time Bruce stayed away."

"It was a wise move," allowed Pedro.

Marisol considered her husband anew. "Did *you* have something to do with that, Mr. Don't Get Involved?"

She felt rather than saw him shrug in the dark. "I may have suggested they could benefit from having some space."

Marisol considered this. On one hand, she disagreed. Mae's heartache had doubled after William's death when Bruce all but disappeared. But then, his absence helped Mae find her own footing *and* have time to miss his presence. A risky move that paid off, judging by the pair's recent reconciliation.

Mae's tiff with her sister sounded like a display of jealousy to Marisol. Perhaps her husband was right, after all. Instead of commending him for his sage advice, another recollection—one triggered by her thoughts of William—came to mind.

"I just remembered something." She hesitated. "You'll think I'm loca."

"Nothing new, mi esposa." He chuckled.

Marisol ignored his teasing. "Yesterday, when I left the office, I saw..." She hedged, not knowing how to say it.

Pedro shifted in the bed to face her. "Who did you see?"

Goosebumps rippled along her skin. *Who did you see*, not *what did you see*? Marisol's gut told her that Pedro saw, too. She said, "We'd just left the office. We both stopped at the light on the corner of Old Main and Birch—"

"The one that takes forever. I was going left, you, right," said Pedro.

"Yes. I looked around and noticed someone on the library stairs. I-I don't know why he caught my attention."

"I saw him, too," said Pedro.

"He looked like…" She wanted him to say it.

After a silence, Pedro said, "William. The man looked like William."

"Well," said Marisol, "at least now I know I didn't imagine him."

Pedro rested his head back on the pillow and patted hers. "He was at a distance, Mari. He *resembled* William. It happens often after someone dies. There's probably a name for it." He yawned.

Marisol settled back backside him. "When I was a girl, I thought I saw my abuela everywhere. At the grocery, in the store, on the street. Every time, I would get so excited. *She's come back*, I thought. Of course, it was never her." She yawned, too. "I suppose that's all it was."

Pedro caressed his wife's bare arm and kissed her nose. He closed his eyes, and within minutes, his breathing slowed and deepened. Marisol envied her husband's ability to capture sleep with such ease. For her, it proved more elusive. The image of the man on the library stairs floated before her eyes. Bruce and Mae followed. Her sister. Her parents. Scenes of confrontations played out in her mind. Worry for her parent's health and safety on their travels. Trepidation about her sister's future. Anxiety for her children.

This was nothing new to Marisol. She'd spent many a night this way; lying awake in the dark, imagining all the things that could go wrong. It was bad enough when things seemed fine—Mari found things to worry about anyhow—but when things were *not* right in her or her loved one's worlds, it became so much worse.

Pedro had often teased her—calling her *mamá gallina,* or mother hen—and though it annoyed her, she supposed he was right. Her nature made her a nurturer, a worrier, and a protector. Right now, her sister needed protection from herself. Mae needed protection from… hopefully not her sister. Bruce needed his heart protected. She had no idea how to help any of them, but she'd find a way. She had to.

Pedro rustled beside her. Without lifting his head or opening his eyes, he muttered, "Go to sleep, *mamá gallina,* tomorrow is another day to cluck over your brood."

He turned over but took her hand with him, pulling her arm around him so she had little choice but to snuggle against his back. His body radiated warmth and smelled of his men's soap, so she allowed herself to be lulled by the rise and fall of his steady respirations. She tucked her arm under his and splayed her hand over his chest. Part of his muttering repeated in her brain as she invited sleep.

Tomorrow is another day…

17 Jared

For the first time, Jared questioned his plan. Not the morality of it, no. The *duration* caused him to pause. Had he carried this on too long? With too many people? How would they—Mae, most importantly — receive him now?

He hadn't needed to see her up close to know her reaction at seeing him through the window at the hall wasn't one of happiness. It was… fear? Jared ceded to himself that he might have misjudged. His fantasy had not yet aligned with reality. Neither Mae nor the girl—Feather Anne—had run to him. They'd both frozen, wearing matching expressions of an emotion he didn't understand. *Was* it fear?

It wasn't fear that made the giant—*Bruce* was his name—charge out the doors in search of William's ghost. This gave him a chuckle. That he'd almost been caught sobered him. He took a swig of the cheap gin he'd nicked off the package store shelf and dabbed at the cut on his forehead. Getting almost hit by a truck hadn't been part of his plans, either.

"Fucking rose bushes."

The scrapes and gouges in his arms, legs, and torso felt like tiny fires all over his body. He'd been stuck—literally—lying there until the jackass kid from the truck finally drove off again. Then he had to run two blocks over, bleeding and in pain, to his car at the beach parking lot. He'd have to lie low for a few days. Let doubt settle back in.

"Then onto phase two."

18 Feather Anne

Feather Anne looked at her phone screen. Six missed calls. Seven unanswered texts. All from John St. James. Tomorrow was his supposed deadline. He'd made it clear he expected Feather Anne would sign the contract; no other option made a blip on his radar. Every conversation had the words, *when you sign the contract.*

"John, I'm not sure about the language in it. I'm going to have a lawyer look at it," she'd said in their last phone call.

"Sure, sure. Whatever you want. I've got a guy you can use. Listen, when you sign the contract, we'll sit down and talk about what your vision is for the album. We'll do whatever you want, kid."

"Isn't that what you told Nick?" She held her breath. Here was the moment. John would either fess up or — "Nick? Nick Amendola? Kid, why we even talking about him? This is about you, and your future. Don't let his bitching and moaning distract you. When you sign the contract, you'll see. This will be *major*. Gotta go."

Feather Anne had stared at her phone in disbelief. He'd blown off the entire thing. No denial, no explanation. Barely an acknowledgement. And he expected her to do the same because he waved a crazy amount of money in her face.

"Knock, knock." Mae stood in her bedroom doorway. "Feel like coming into the café? I could use a hand in the kitchen."

Feather Anne hopped off her bed, shoved her phone in her pocket, and said, "Yeah, sure. Why not? Nothing else to do since Brandon and Nick became besties."

Mae scrunched her face. "Yeah, I'm still not understanding all that. Explain again on the way?"

"I'll try. Damned if I get it myself, though. Let's ride our bikes in. It's nice out."

Mae agreed, and they took their time, chatting as they peddled. The air was summer-warm, even though fall had officially begun, and they both breathed it in, wearing matching smiles.

They started with idle talk. Feather Anne asked, "Open mic should be fun tonight." She added, "Now that everyone is acting normal around me again."

Mae laughed. "Well, there seems to be a lot more people than usual. Not that I'm complaining, mind you. I know Charles is hoping you'll sing with him again."

"Can't say no to Mr. B.," said Feather Anne.

"Nope, his YouTube followers would be mighty upset with you," said Mae.

Thanks to Feather Anne and the Greatest American Singer show, Charles Brightsider had amassed quite the following once the show aired a segment of them playing and singing together. Since then, the nearly ninety-year-old man had fans of all ages following and sharing his videos. Mrs. B. was less than thrilled, but still good-natured about her husband's newfound fame.

Feather Anne ventured a comment on another subject. "So, Bruce has been around quite a bit lately."

Mae kept her eyes forward and feigned a casual tone. "Yes, well… with the sightings, or whatever we're calling it, he's just being helpful."

"Uh-huh," said Feather Anne. "And, um, when was the last… sighting?" She tried not to smirk.

Mae shot her a glance, then peddled a little faster. Feather Anne caught up and matched her stride. Mae answered. "Almost a week."

"Mhm. And yet, Bruce is over every. Single. Day." Feather Anne openly grinned now.

Her sister shot back—a slight smile on her lips—with a retort. "Yeah, unlike your on-again boyfriend and music boyfriend."

"Touché," said Feather Anne.

"So, what the heck *is* up with those two?"

They'd reached the café, parked their bikes against the side of the building, and took off their helmets. Feather Anne twisted her hair into a messy bun and spoke around the elastic between her teeth. "I don't know. One minute, Brandon wants to take me somewhere, the next, he cancels out because *something came up*." She secured the bun and made air quotes. As she followed Mae inside, she continued. "Come to find out that something was a meet-up with Nick. *Here,* of all places. Like, did they not think it would come back to me? Idiots. Anyhow, they've both been avoiding me like the plague and saying things like, *all in good time*. And *patience is a virtue*."

Mae flicked on the lights and turned on the stereo system. "Well, clearly they are up to something."

Feather Anne gave her a sardonic look. "Ya think? But what? That's the question. What the hell could Brandon Bourdreau and Nick Amendola have in common?"

Mae returned the look and said, "Um, *you*? Duh." She threw an apron at Feather Anne and they began prepping for the breakfast crowd.

They worked companionably for a while, singing and bopping along to the music like old times. Chris and Gina delivered bread, pies, and pastries for the case out front and they had coffee together.

"Shit, I've missed this," said Feather Anne.

The others exchanged looks, but it was Chris who spoke. "Nothing says you must sign that contract, Feather Anne."

Gina piped in. "From everything Mae's said, you *shouldn't* sign the damn thing. Tell that floppy-haired, shady bastard to fu—"

"We all agreed we'd let Feather Anne make her own choice, without our influence, remember?" Mae scolded their mother and Chris. To Feather Anne, she said, "We support you no matter what you decide."

Feather Anne said, "So, you *do* think it's a mistake to sign with John St. James?"

Mae held up a hand to stop her. "I'm not saying that. I only suggest—strongly, I might add—that you not let him bully you into signing before a lawyer combs through it. There's a reason he's pushing you so hard, and it can't be good. Just ask Nick."

"I would if I could find him." Feather Anne snorted.

Chris perked up. "I saw him and Brandon at—" Gina stomped his foot. "Ow. Wh—"

"We saw them getting coffee the other day," finished Gina.

Feather Anne narrowed her eyes at her mother. "What do you know, Mother?"

"Would you look at the time? Come on, Chris. We got to go. More deliveries and such. See ya."

"Hey," called Feather Anne after them. Chris stammered an apology just before Gina yanked him through the door. "Well, that was super subtle. You know something I should know, Mae?" She turned her attention to her sister, who'd begun to knead dough aggressively for the quiches.

"Hmm? What? No, I—"

"Forget it. You're all shitty liars. Fine, whatever. I'll find out soon enough, I suppose."

If there was one thing Feather Anne knew about Chance, it was that no one could keep a secret for very long. Except for Georgie Brightsider, that was. She'd kept hers for a hell of a long time. But that had turned out all right, so maybe this all would, too. She hoped.

19 Brianna

"You two? Together? My garage?" Brianna looked from one boy to the other.

Boy-men. That's what they were. Her brother and his new best friend, Nick Amendola, sat across from her at the kitchen table and stared at her, wearing identical, *c'mon, mom, can we.* expressions.

"Yeah, us, yes, ma'am. We'd pay rent, or lease for the use of the space," ventured Nick.

Brandon added, "And it's far enough back from the house that we shouldn't disturb you guys."

"Or the neighbors, ma'am," said Nick.

Brianna snapped. "Ma'am me one more time, Amendola, and I will hurt you."

"Yes, ma—Mrs. Baker."

"Oh, Jesus Christ. *Brianna*. Just call me Brianna." She rapped her fingernails on the table, again looking at both. "You've bought all the equipment already, haven't you?"

Nick looked at Brandon. Brandon offered his sister a sheepish grin. "Maybe? Okay, yes. But—"

"And—I'll go out on a limb, here—you have not discussed your brilliant idea with Feather Anne yet?"

"Ah, well, no," admitted Brandon.

Nick said, "We wanted to surprise her."

"Mhm. I see. And what about your recording contract I've heard so much about?" She pierced Nick with her stare. Instead of squirming, he smiled.

"My dad got a contract lawyer to look it over. I don't understand the specifics, to be honest, but there's, like, some shit in there that makes it so I can get out of it without penalty."

Brianna leaned forward and folded her arms on the table. "Let me see if I understand. You are walking away from a recording contract with one of the biggest names in the industry—yes, boys, I've done my homework, too—where you'd stood to make millions of dollars, all for… a garage band?" She made no attempt to hide her incredulity. It *was* inconceivable.

Nick rushed to explain. "Not a garage band, ma'am—Mrs.—Brianna. A recording studio. A legit, real recording studio where Feather Anne and I can make our own music, the way *we* want it."

"I see," said Brianna. She turned her attention back to her baby brother, who was her only actual concern. "And how do you fit into this, Brandon? Last I knew, you didn't play an instrument or sing."

"True, I don't. But I've been learning—on my own—about the digital side of things. Mixing, audio, recording… the technical stuff. I've still got a bunch to learn, but—"

"Dude, you're a natural at it." Nick clapped him on the shoulder.

Brianna sat back. "Well, I guess hell has frozen over. I suppose you two have some work to do, then."

Their faces lit up. Brandon said, "So it's a yes?"

Brianna stood. "It's a conditional yes."

"Great," said Brandon.

"Cool," said Nick.

Brianna rolled her eyes. "And this is why you idiots get into trouble. Don't you want to know the conditions?"

The pair of dummies looked at each other. Brandon shrugged, Nick laughed and said, "Nah, whatever you say is cool, Bri." Her eyebrow quirked at him. He corrected himself. "Uh, Brianna."

"Fine. I'll draw up a lease. Once you let Feather Anne in on your plan, we'll talk again. Now get out of my kitchen."

At the door, Brandon paused. "Bri, you sure Ricky will be okay with this?"

She waved him off. "As long as you let him bang on the drums once in a while, he'll be fine."

"Ricky plays the drums? No shit?"

"The way he bangs on the steering wheel all the time, he should."

Brandon chuckled. "He *is* always banging on stuff at the shop. Hell, maybe he can play. Hey, Bri? Thank you. For real."

"Yeah. Yeah. Fuck off now, please."

She waited until the door closed behind him before she smiled. If Feather Anne bought into their scheme, this home studio thing had potential. For what, she wasn't sure. All she had was a feeling, and when Brianna Baker got a feeling about something, she was rarely wrong.

Wheels and gears churned in her head. She grabbed her laptop from the office and brought it to the kitchen. These boys weren't businessman; they'd need help. They'd need to make plans. Their best chances hinged on Feather Anne's involvement, although Nick's name held plenty of appeal on its own. The two names together, on the heels of their current popularity, had the potential to make their little recording studio a mecca for local artists. As the word spread, they could attract artists from everywhere.

Brianna left the kitchen table and stepped onto the back porch to view the detached garage. Ricky had used it as a home auto body shop for years, fixing up old cars and fucking around out there. He wouldn't mind her—them—taking it over. And if he did, he'd get over it once he saw a drum kit. He'd talked about learning for years. Here was his chance. That's what she'd tell him, at least. Later. First, she needed the space cleared. Who could she get on short notice, though?

She grabbed her phone and began scrolling through her contacts. The fifth name jumped out at her. Bruce Grady. Didn't he have a complete team of construction workers at his disposal? Brianna tapped the call icon.

"Bruce? Brianna Baker. I need your help." No time for small talk.

"Brianna? Hey, what, uh, what's up? Everything okay?"

"Fine, why?" She snapped.

"Be… cause you never call me? And you just asked for help, so—"

"Right. Whatever. Listen, I need four of your best guys for a… project." It behooved her to add, "It's for your son and Feather Anne, and Brandon, too."

There was a pause. Then, "Okay, I'm intrigued. I'll need more details before I commit, though."

Brianna clenched her fist and gritted her teeth. "Fine. Come over in an hour and I'll explain. And bring your guys. I want this started immediately."

"Yes, ma'am," said Bruce.

Before he could add any other annoying comment, Brianna disconnected the call and went back to her laptop. Knowing Brandon's finances and both boy's stupidity, she guessed they'd bought less than top quality equipment for the studio. They probably hadn't even thought about proper soundproofing, furnishing, or… *any*thing. Thank God they had her in their corner, even if they didn't know it yet.

20 Mae

Life had resumed as normal in the Huxley-Grant home. Mostly. Brandon's sudden and bizarre sneaking about with Nick Amendola seemed to be at an end and according to Feather Anne, and the explanation would be forthcoming that evening. The other, even more disturbing mystery of the William look-alike—*or ghost*—seemed to have vanished with little more than frayed nerves left behind. She mentioned as much to Bruce as they unlocked the café doors.

"Seriously, Bruce. You don't have to keep doing this. He's gone, whoever he was."

"We don't know that for sure, Mae," said Bruce. "Stay here."

He checked the café from office, to kitchen, to dining room, storage, and bathrooms for an intruder. It had become the morning routine. One Mae found endearing… and also annoying by the third day. She'd reminded him, more than once, that the café was locked *and* she had an alarm system. Bruce remained unimpressed and insisted on doing his own investigation.

He returned, nodded at her, and said, "All clear."

She tried and failed at not smirking. "Thanks, Detective Grady."

"Ha, ha. Hilarious." He poked her ribcage.

She swatted at him with her apron, but his reflexes were quick, and he captured it mid flick and tugged. The move caught Mae off guard, and she fell against him. What followed happened so fast, and yet in slow motion, too. Bruce's arms were around her, their bodies pressed together. His cologne—one so familiar and comforting—filled her nose. She gazed up at him; he, down at her. Was she breathing? Her heart thundered, so yes. How had she forgotten how blue his eyes were?

Don't think, just…

Her arms, which had been pinned between them, slid up his chest to his shoulders. The muscles underneath his t-shirt twitched at her touch. He pulled her closer and lowered his head to hers. Mae tilted hers. Their lips brushed. A long-forgotten fire sparked low in her pelvis. She moved her hands to his face and ran her thumbs across his stubbled jawline. He kept one arm around her waist and slipped his free hand into her hair. He teased her mouth with his.

She wanted him. But not there. It had to be somewhere special; somewhere *right*. "Bruce, I…"

He released her. "Shit. I'm sorry, Mae. I shouldn't have—"

"No, I—"

The chimes over the front door rang, signifying a customer. A voice called out, "Hello, anybody here?"

Mae sprinted to the doorway. "I'll be right with you." She turned to tell Bruce she'd call him later, but he was gone. Their moment together now felt like a dream. Maybe, after all this time, his feelings for her had changed, and she'd just humiliated herself by reading the moment wrong. Heat flooded her cheeks.

"Hey, Mae. How's—hey, you okay? Your face is all red," said Melina, hanging up her purse and sweater.

"Hmm? Yes, oh. I-I'm fine. It's, um, warm in here, no?"

Melina looked at her funny. "No, actually, it's pretty comfortable."

"Huh, guess it's just me. You mind taking care of the customer out front? I've got…" She looked toward the back door, "something to take care of."

"Sure, no problem," said Melina, watching her with interest.

Mae grabbed her keys and walk-ran to the door. "Thanks. Call me if you—"

"All set, Mae. No worries. Oh, and Bruce was still in his truck when I came in. Just so you know."

She looked back at her long-time employee to see her grinning. Mae's face flamed. Instead of responding, she dashed out the door. Bruce's truck was gone.

Damn it.

This couldn't wait. Either Bruce felt he'd made a mistake, or that she had. Mae knew it wasn't so on her end, but what about his? Would it be crazy of her to drive around town looking for him? Yes. Yet she didn't want to call. This wasn't a phone call conversation; it was a face to face one. Settled and determined, Mae got in her car and drove to the most obvious place first, his house.

She drove past at a crawl, but his truck was nowhere in sight. Next, the Brookhaven. No Bruce there, either. He could be any number of places by now. She saw the Brightsiders walking their dogs and stopped.

"Hey, there!" She smiled and waved.

"Well, hello, dear," said Mrs. B.

Mr. B. said, "Great open mic we had," and blew an imaginary saxophone.

"Yes, it was," agreed Mae. "Say, you haven't seen Bruce around, have you?"

"Aside from your place, you mean?" Mr. B. gave her a salacious wink.

Mrs. B. swatted him. "Oh, Charles. Behave. Don't listen to him. No, we haven't seen your Bruce this morning."

Mae deflated. "Thanks anyway. See you for lunch later?"

"Wouldn't miss it," said both.

Mae drove away and left them to their stroll. Where the hell did Bruce go?

Your Bruce.

The reference hadn't escaped her. Did the entire town assume they were together? If so, what did they think about it? Were they pleased or appalled? *Some* had to think she'd moved on too soon after William. It *was* only a little over a year. Those closest to them seemed more than accepting; they were downright pushy. This included Feather Anne, who'd loved William fiercely. She wished someone would just tell her what to do. But the only person she knew who'd give it to her straight and not pull punches was on a Mediterranean cruise and wouldn't be back in the States for another week.

"Damn it, Auntie Tree. Just when I need your advice, you—" Her cell phone rang. Mae hit the speaker button and said, "Hello?"

"Hey, kiddo. My Spidey-senses were tingling. Everything kosher with my beautiful niece?"

Mae cry laughed. "How the hell do you do that?" She looked at the time. "And it must be the middle of the night there."

Katrina chuckled. "Told ya, it's my Spidey sense. It's early dawn, technically. Jimmy is snoring away, so I've been out on the balcony relaxing. All of a sudden, I thought, *Mae needs me*. So, here I am. What's going on?"

Mae filled her in on everything up to the kiss in a rapid-fire monologue. At the end, her aunt whistled. "Well, that is a hella bunch of goings-on right there. And the William ghost-guy has just up and vanished, huh?"

"Seems that way," said Mae.

"My opinion? That ain't the ghost of your husband, toots. I think Bruce is right. And speaking of that big hunk of a man, you know how much I love that boy. So, my thoughts on that are a given. But it doesn't matter what I think, and it definitely doesn't matter what anyone else thinks. It's about what you think, Mae. If you think you love that boy—*love* love him—then tell him so. If you're *not* sure, tell him that. Either way, all you can do is be honest."

In fairness, her aunt told her nothing she hadn't already considered. Yet, somehow, hearing it from her brought a fresher sense of clarity. "I *do* love him,

Tree." Saying it out loud felt terrifying and freeing at the same time.

I love him. Oh my God. I love Bruce. Now What? What does that mean for our friendship? What—

"Hey, sunshine?" There was laughter in her aunt's voice.

In Mae's… shell shock. "Yeah, Tree?"

"Don't overthink it, huh?"

Mae grinned. "Okay, Tree. I'll try not to. Love you, be safe."

"You, too, kiddo. I mean it. I don't think that creeper is gone yet." No laughter remained in her tone.

Mae forced herself to sound serious, too. "Okay, Tree. I promise, I'll be careful."

They said their goodbyes and Mae realized with a start that she'd turned onto Brianna's street instead of her own. She gave a double take as she passed the Baker's house. Bruce's truck, as well as Nick's and two more she didn't recognize, filled the driveway. She noted several people at the far end, in front of Brianna's open garage.

The Bakers were doing some sort of remodeling; something Mae felt only mildly curious about. That she'd now have to wait to talk to Bruce weighed more on her mind. Resigned, she drove back to the café.

You escaped me for now, Grady. But we will talk this out. Tonight.

She took out her phone and texted him.

Dinner, café. Just us. 7 PM.

Her finger hovered over the send button. Then she added one last thing.

xo

She held her breath, hit send, and exhaled. Now she just needed to get a sitter for the twins. She called Gina. "Hey, any chance you and Chris could watch the twins for a few hours tonight?"

"We never turn down an Evvie and TK fix. What time?"

"Six okay for you?" That should give her just enough time to shower, change, and get back to the café.

"You got it. So what's up? You got a hot date or something?" Gina laughed. Mae didn't. "Holy shit," said Gina. "You *do* have a hot date. Bruce?"

"It's not a—yes, it's Bruce—but it's not a date... exactly. I mean, I guess it is? But—"

"We'll be at your place at five-fifteen," said Gina.

Mae almost protested, but then agreed. "That would give me more time to get ready. Thank you."

Sitter secured; Mae drove back to the café. Staying busy would help keep her mind off the evening ahead. And her nervousness. God, she was nervous. Why was she so nervous? It's *Bruce*. The man she'd known forever, even intimately once upon a time. He'd been her best friend and confidante, her rock. A man she'd always adored, trusted, and respected. Someone who'd seen her at her worst, who was there for the birth of her children, and who'd helped parent Feather Anne. He was the man who'd been waiting for her, without hope or expectation.

An additional worry crept in. What if she couldn't measure up to what he believed her to be? What if, when he got to know her in this novel way, he decided he'd wasted his time? If Bruce had her on a pedestal—and she wasn't saying he did—how could she live up to his illusions? She'd never so much as burped in front of him. Then again, she'd never done that in front of William, either.

What else? Morning hair. Morning *breath*. The twins. What would they think? Maybe they'll be traumatized by the change. Maybe they'll hate Bruce; a show of defending their father's memory.

Oh my God. I can't do this.

Mae parked in her usual spot behind the café, turned off the ignition, and cried. It didn't last long, nor was it hysterical. She reined it in, blew her nose, and flipped the visor down to fix her makeup in the mirror.

"Calm down, Mae. You're getting way too far ahead of yourself."

She switched back to rational thoughts, repeating the ones she'd already laid out and adding fresh ones. Friends to lovers; a natural transition. Perfect, really. None of the awkward getting-to-know you phase. Straight into comfortable companionship.

But you need sparks and fire. What if there's no fire?

She recalled their kiss. There was fire, all right. No worries in that area. Although, it made her blush. She'd kept Bruce in the friend lane so long—ignoring his good looks, his masculinity—that to allow herself now to have these carnal thoughts seemed... wrong. No, wait. Not wrong. Naughty.

Mae fanned herself and went inside. The familiar sounds of the busy café—grills sizzling, music playing, customers and staff conversing—brought her back to her senses. She had a business to run; no time for silly romantic fantasies about her... whatever Bruce was to her.

Guess I'll find out tonight though.

21 Bruce

"So, you want *all* this stuff cleared out? Everything?" Bruce scratched the back of his neck and gave Brianna a doubtful look. "Ricky know about this?"

Brianna fixed her ice cube eyes on him. "Yes, Bruce. He does, thank you. I need this done quickly. Are your men able to do this, or what?"

Bruce heaved a sigh. "Yeah, we can do it. Today's the only day we got, though. So—"

"Perfect. That's what I want. Today, done. Start to finish. I'll let you get to it."

Bruce opened his mouth to reply, but she'd spun fast on her pointy little heel and left him staring after her. He wondered if he should call Ricky, just to make sure. But then he didn't want to hear any grief from Brianna when she found out he'd gone behind her back.

"What d'you think, boss?" Stan, his newest guy, shot a glance at Brianna's backside.

"Do what the lady wants, Stan. Let's start over there and work our way back."

Screw it. It's between Ricky and Brianna if there's a problem.

For Bruce, this kind of mindless grunt work was just what he needed. He let his mind travel back to that morning with Mae. That kiss. He wasn't crazy; Mae *had* kissed him back. She didn't push him away. Where would it have led if that customer hadn't come in?

Whoa, don't go there, buddy. A hard-on at work is not cool.

When she had drawn away, he ran off like a chicken, afraid she'd say the kiss had been a mistake. For him, it was *everything*. Their drunken one-night-stand all those years ago couldn't come close to comparing. This sober, sexy as hell kiss...

"Yo, boss? You, uh, need a hand?"

Fricking Stan again, staring at him with a look of amused interest. Bruce looked down at the tire rims in both his hands. "What? No, I'm good."

"It's just... you been standing there for—"

"All good, Stan. Grab those tires and stack them over there." Bruce hollered down the driveway.

"Billy, go get the dump truck." He set down a rim and tossed him his keys. To everyone else, he yelled, "Stack everything over here. And do it neatly, assholes."

The next few hours werc full on manual labor, and he spent all of it with images of Mae in the back of his mind. By the time he got back in his truck again, he'd accepted the fact he'd have to talk to her, even if what she had to say wasn't what he wanted to hear.

He looked around the truck cab for his phone and realized he'd left it at home. The clock on the dash told him he'd have no time to get it, either. That meant the phone call would have to wait, as would her rejection. Bruce tried to remind himself it wouldn't be the first time she'd turned him down, anyhow. It didn't make him feel any better, though.

A tap on his window led to another distraction that was no less uncomfortable for Bruce. "Hey, Effie. What are you doing here?"

Ophelia flipped her dark tresses over her shoulder and licked her lips. "I was taking a walk, and I saw your truck. What are you doing?"

"Doing? Now? Uh, nothing. I mean, I have stuff to do." Why did she always make him feel like a twelve-year-old kid looking at his first nudie mag? Bruce coughed into his hand and pulled his shit together. "I've got some repairs to handle at Brookhaven. I'm heading there now."

Effie pouted. "I am so bored, Bruce. Take me with you."

Bruce failed to compute. "Take you... with me? Where? To Brookhaven?"

Effie didn't answer, but walked around the front of the truck—*sauntered* around the front of the truck—and climbed into the passenger seat. "Come on. Let's go. I can help you with your repairs. Then you can take me out to dinner."

"I—you—you're not exactly dressed for manual labor," said Bruce. "Aren't you afraid you'll break a nail." He grinned.

She looked at her nails, considering. "Hmm. Well, I can watch you work. But you can still take me out to dinner after." She smiled and batted her eyes.

He couldn't explain it if he tried, but right then, his blinders fell off and he saw Effie—the real Ophelia Torres—for maybe the first time. Yes, she was beautiful and sexy as hell. But it was all an act, a show she put on. Underneath the hair and makeup and tight clothes was a girl trying too hard to be loved.

Beautiful girls, ones like Ophelia Torres, were way more insecure than people might believe. How could they not be, when their entire existence revolved around people—okay, men—focusing only on their appearance? Bruce felt a wave of sympathy and affection for the woman who was, in many ways, still a girl. The affection extended no further than friendly, though, and he needed for her to know it.

"Okay, I'll take you out to dinner on one condition."

"Name it," said Effie.

"We go as friends."

She stared at him for a long moment. "You're still in love with Mae." A statement, not a question.

Bruce, for maybe the first time, owned it. "Yes."

Effie tilted her head and asked, "And she loves you, yes?"

Here, Bruce hedged. "I—she—ah, hell. I don't know, Effie. Maybe?"

The flirtatious, sexy woman's demeanor changed. Her shoulders relaxed, and her expression softened. "All right, big man, let's get your little job done and go figure this out over dinner. I will help you figure it all out. Okay?"

Bruce started the truck and grinned. "It's a plan. But how about you tell me what happened between you and Jason Marsdale in the meantime?"

"Fair enough. You drive, I talk."

Bruce did as ordered, and Effie told him all about the argument—one that started over a dress she wore, then escalated—that led to her jumping on the first flight home. Bruce listened without interrupting and failed to stop home for his phone; something he didn't realize until they reached the Brookhaven. He considered borrowing Effie's phone to call Mae, but then reconsidered.

The job at Brookhaven took longer than expected, and Bruce apologized to Effie. "If you want to take the truck and go, I understand, Effie."

She waved a dismissive hand in his direction from her spot on the condo's balcony. "This is fine, really. I have a beautiful view, and my new friend to spill my guts to."

Bruce nailed the last section of crown molding in place and grinned over at her. "You might not call me friend when I tell you my thoughts on your situation."

She narrowed her eyes at him. "You think *I'm* wrong, do you?"

Bruce considered. "Not *wrong*. It sounds like you're seeing this one-sided. You both are. You think he's trying to control you. He thinks he's being protective."

"Protective?" She snorted. "I do not need protection, thank you very much."

He tried again. "No, I mean, like, protective of your... honor. Effie, you are a knockout. You've got... all that," he gestured to her figure, "and men—"

"Are pathetic animals that can't control themselves?"

"Something like that. Listen, I'm not saying it's okay or right by any means; I believe in behaving like a gentleman."

"I know you do." Effie's defensiveness eased. "But I shouldn't have to change the way I dress because men look at me and he's got insecurity issues."

He packed up his tools with painstaking care. What he wanted to ask next might piss her off, but it needed to be asked. "Effie, why do you dress… the way you do?"

She glared at him, then looked out over the ocean. "Because I can." Her chin jutted.

"Of course, you can. And no one has the right to tell you otherwise. But who are you dressing *for*, Effie? What I mean is, if it's for you—because the clothing feels good and comfortable—then great. But if it's for… attention? You don't need to do that. You'd be stunning in a brown sack, with no makeup, and your hair a mess."

She resisted a smile, but a smirk snuck through, anyway. "Thank you." She came back inside. "Are we ready to go? I'm starving and ready to put *you* under the spotlight." She poked his chest.

"Yes, I'm ready. For both food and scrutiny. Where to?"

"The Marsdale. We'll have lobsters and filet mignon and the best wine in the house. On Jason's tab, of course."

Bruce raised his eyebrows but made no comment. Who was he to turn down lobsters and filet mignon? He looked at the time. Five-thirty. Dinner should only be an hour or so, he'd have plenty of time to call Mae. He dropped his gear in the truck's bed and opened the passenger door for Effie. Any other time, she'd have done some slinky, sexy maneuver, but this time, she hopped up into the cab with no fanfare. Bruce smiled.

"What?" Effie caught his smile.

"Nothing, Effie. It's nice having you as a friend, that's all."

Four and a half hours, a full stomach, and a mild buzz later, Bruce and Effie pushed back from the table. They were laughing over something she said when her face froze in apparent shock. Her eyes fixed over Bruce's shoulder. He turned to see what had evoked such a reaction and saw none other than Jason Marsdale storming toward them.

Bruce stood—he'd be damned if another man stood over him while he sat—and held up a warning hand. "Easy does it, man."

Jason glared at him, then looked at Effie. "This is what you do? Come running back to… *him*?"

Effie stood, too. "What do you care? Mr. Big Shot. Go back to your island and your office and leave me be." She crossed her arms over her chest and pivoted away.

Bruce felt like he was in a bad soap opera. "Listen, you two obviously need to talk, so I'm just going to—"

"What do I *care*? I flew commercial to get here, Ophelia. That's how much I care. You're the one who doesn't care, obviously, since you're here with *him*." Jason shot daggers at Bruce.

Bruce tried again. "Bro, Effie and I are just friends. How about I just leave—"

"At least he doesn't try to change me," spat Effie.

Jason threw his hands in the air. "All I suggested was that you wear a shall over your dress because it was a chilly night."

She spun back toward Jason and jabbed a finger at him. "You wanted me to cover up because you didn't want anyone to look at me. Admit it."

Jason looked at the ceiling, then back at Effie. "People look at you all the time. You're gorgeous. I'm proud to have such a beautiful woman on my arm."

"So, now I am just—just arm candy to you?" She turned her wrath on Bruce next. "Ha. You see? You are wrong, Mr. Know It All. He doesn't want me to cover up."

Bruce stammered. "N-no. Wait. That's not what—you're getting it—"

Jason moved beside Effie and turned on Bruce as well. "Why are you telling my fiancée to cover herself up?"

"I'm not, I—wait, fiancée?"

She'd left that part out. Based on her expression, he forgot to mention it to her, too. She stared at him, and he at her. Bruce felt more and more like a wobbly third wheel. The handful of diners still in the restaurant all stared at them. A few women gasped as Jason reached into his pocket and kneeled before Effie.

The rest played out in a standard, cliché way. At least Bruce assumed it had; he'd quietly excused himself from the now oblivious couple and made his escape. Effie would say yes, of this he felt certain, and the pair would live a dynamic, often explosive life together. She would return to Chance to see her family and occasionally catch up with her friend Bruce and they would laugh over old times. But where would Bruce be in his life? Would he be with Mae? Alone? Or with someone he couldn't yet imagine? He knew who he wanted it to be with. Now he had to find out if she wanted it, too.

22 Nick

Nick and Brandon stood on Mae's front porch, planning their argument. "Okay, so I'll start by telling her I got out of my contract," said Nick.

"Right, yeah. And I'll bring up... who?"

"Billie Eilish, man," said Nick.

"Yeah, her. She's the one with the home studio that just made, like, a number one selling album?"

"Exactly. Then, I say, *hey, why don't I do that*? And then you say—" Nick prompted Brandon.

"I say... I say..."

From the window above them came Feather Anne's voice. "You say, *gee, Feather Anne, you and Nick should just start your own recording studio.*

Then Nick is supposed to say, w*ow, what a brilliant idea, and hey, Brandon, you can be the engineer and sound guy.*"

Nick and Brandon exchanged *oh, shits*. Seconds later, Feather Anne opened the front door and joined them on the porch. She didn't look pissed, but she didn't look happy, either. Maybe, if Nick could explain the plan, she'd be down with it. He started to talk.

"Hear us out, Feather Anne. We—"

"Sit. Both of you," said Feather Anne, motioning to the Adirondack chairs. They sat. She paced as she spoke. "First, your stealth skills suck. I heard your whole Heckle and Jeckle plan from my bedroom window."

Nick whispered to Brandon. "Who's Heckle and Jeckle?"

Brandon shook his head.

Feather Anne continued. "Second. Did you really think you could pull all this off without me finding out? Yeah, that's right. I know all about your recording studio idea."

"Who—" Nick asked.

"Who do you think?" Brandon snorted. "Brianna is my bet."

"No, smartass," said Feather Anne. She held up her phone, which showed a photograph of Brandon and Nick walking out of Kade's father's music store.

"Nothing Nick or I do is private these days. Get used to it."

Nick moved to stand again. He hated being at the disadvantage. Feather Anne glared at him and he sat again.

"So, using my superpowers of deduction, I'm guessing you two knuckleheads have already set up this home studio. The question is, where? And with whose money? Oh, and what makes you so sure I'd give up a multi-million-dollar contract to hang my hopes on your rinky-dink operation? And don't say Billie Eilish."

Here was Nick's opening. This time he stood. He looked her dead in the eyes and said, "You'd be miserable being John St. James trained monkey, and you know it. Stick with us, Feather Anne. Make the music you—*we*—wanted to make all along. I'm not saying we'll be Billie Eilish big, but we'll have the same satisfaction of being in control of our music. Oh, and I put up my earnings from the show."

Feather Anne's eyes widened. "All of it?"

Nick shrugged. "A good part of it. Brandon put in money, too."

She looked at Brandon. "This is what you want to do? With him?" She thumbed in Nick's direction.

Brandon stood, too. "Yep. I know it sounds crazy, Feather Anne. And I support you know matter what you choose. But this... this feels right, babe."

Nick's teeth and fists clenched. *Babe*. He willed his hands open, his jaw to relax. *Get used to it.* He would not be that guy—the sad sack loser who never gets the girl. Unbidden, the image of his father popped into his head and he felt guilty. Bruce Grady was no sad sack, nor was he a loser. He was just the guy who didn't get the girl. Like father, like son. He pushed the thoughts aside.

"What do you say, Feather Anne?" Nick held his breath.

Feather Anne stared from one to the other for what felt like an eternity. She kept her expression unreadable, but a glance at Brandon's smiling face told Nick they had a shot. Unless it was a hopeful smile and not one of happiness. She folded her arms.

"I'm in... *only* if I'm a full partner. This is *our* recording studio, not yours. We split the expenses. No fucking boy's club bullshit. Got it?"

Nick pumped his fist in the air. Brandon clapped his hands twice and high-fived Nick. "Yes," cheered Nick.

"See, that right there. No exclusive high-fricking-fives. Palm me, assholes." Feather Anne held her hand up and raised an eyebrow at them.

Nick high-fived her and Brandon followed. Then he swooped Feather Anne into a bear hug. Nick's smile faltered. He shoved his hands in his pockets and looked away. Before he could wrap himself up in too much self-pity, the two tackled him into a group hug. No less awkward for him, but it was all right. Maybe even better than all right.

Feather Anne stepped back. "Um, so where the hell is this recording studio?"

Brandon looked like a kid at the circus. "Babe, that's the best part. It's close to home, cheap, and when we're done, it'll be fully loaded and functioning."

"*Where*, Brandon?"

He hedged, now looking less sure of their plan. "My garage. Well, Bri and Ricky's garage."

Feather Anne gave another one of her scary looks. "Your... garage. You mean where Ricky fixes up old junk cars and smells like oil and beer?" She dropped onto the porch swing and threw her head back. "What have I gotten myself into?"

Nick interjected. "Come see what it looks like tomorrow. I swear, you're going to feel a lot better about this when you see it." He had his own trepidations about that part—namely, Brianna's sudden interest and involvement—but he'd keep his mouth shut since she helped them out big time. "By then it should look closer to being ready and we can show you."

She narrowed her eyes at him, then at Brandon. "Why not today? Now?"

"W-well, it's not perfect yet. We want you to see it all done, so—"

"So I don't freak out?" Feather Anne challenged them with a look. "No. Take me there now." Brandon pleaded, but she cut him off. "I'm not the princess going to her new castle, dummies. We're *partners*. And as a partner, I want a say in how this is set up. Let's go."

She led the way to Brandon's truck, and both guys followed like puppies after her. When they'd left the Bakers, the driveway had been loaded end to end with outgoing stuff *and* ingoing. It resembled a junkyard, not a recording studio. Not the best first impression if they wanted her to feel like giving up a multi-million-dollar contract was a good idea. Still, she had a point. If they were in this together, they had to each have a say.

Holy shit. We're in this together. What the hell are we doing?

23 Miles

Miles jotted down numbers with his free hand while he held his cell phone against his ear with his shoulder. The office buzzed with activity; just the way he liked it. Busy equaled money, and money—despite what some might say—equaled happiness. Or at least, the means to buy the things that brought happiness. Based on the numbers he jotted, the Hannafords were in for happy times indeed.

"All looks good, Barb. Yep. Great. Talk to you later. Bye." He released the phone, letting it fall into his lap. He shouted out for Nora, and when his office door opened, he said, "Tell Papa what a good Dad—" the words died on his tongue.

It wasn't Nora at his office door, but Brianna Baker. The ice queen hadn't stepped foot in

Hannaford Realty in over seven years. A memory and time he cared not to revisit. She looked as icy as ever.

"Hello... Papa," said Brianna. A smile thin as a razor blade cracked her face.

"Brianna. What are—what can I do for you?"

She made no small talk and got straight to her reason for darkening his door. "I need you to draw up a lease agreement. I could do it myself but I need the real deal, with all the legal jargon."

"Ah, sure." He stood and walked over to a filing cabinet. "You, uh, could've emailed—"

"I was in the neighborhood." She glanced around the office. "You've redecorated since the last time I was here."

Miles coughed. "Mhm, yeah. I-we did it a few years ago." He checked the folder, closed it, then slid it across the desk to her. "This should have everything you need."

She thumbed through the papers, then stood. "Thanks. How much do I owe you?"

Miles blinked. "Owe me? Oh, no, nothing. All good. It's just some papers. So, you're, uh, leasing... a property?"

And who did you buy the property from? I'm the only real estate broker in town.

"Oh, calm down, Miles. God, you should see your face right now. I didn't buy a property. Brandon, Feather Anne, and Nick are using the garage for a studio. I'm just making them responsible and accountable."

"Oh," said Miles. He tried to sound indifferent. "That's cool. So, they're going to be our long-term local celebrities, then? That's good for the town."

The sliver smile returned. "You mean good for business. Nothing like a celebrity presence to attract new homeowners."

Miles drew himself up to his full height. She was wrong, and he couldn't wait to tell her so. "Actually, it could be a deterrent. People love spotting celebrities, but they don't necessarily want to live near them."

Brianna waved a hand and yawned. "Whatever. Thanks, again. Say hello to Rosaline." She sashayed out.

"It's Rosabelle, and you know it," called Miles after her.

She lifted her hand and waggled her fingers in a wave without bothering to turn around. The air temperature returned to normal, as did Miles blood pressure. The ice queen cometh and the ice queen goeth. He felt surprisingly unscarred. Stunned, but not scarred.

"Nora? Come in here, please." He needed to brainstorm ways to make this little development benefit him. Nora entered with a notepad and a smirk. "Have a seat. I just received some interesting information about—"

"Those three kids renting the Baker's garage for a record studio. I know. It's all over town," said Nora.

Miles gritted his teeth. "And yet I'm last to know."

"Sorry," said Nora with a shrug. "You were busy, so—"

"Never mind. It's fine. I'm thinking we need to get to these kids before they sign Brianna's little contract."

Nora scoffed. "They're kids, Miles. What are you going to rent them, a storage unit?"

Miles pointed his pen at his favorite silver-haired real estate shark. "You're forgetting something, Nora. They're kids *with money*. They can afford better than Ricky Baker's greasy garage. They just need someone to point that out to them.

A fresh light brightened Nora's brown eyes. "I think I might have just the property for them, it so happens."

Miles winked. "I knew you would, darlin'." He sent her off again, content all wheels would turn without squeaks or wobbles while being guided by the steady hands of Nora Halpern.

That night, over dinner, Miles told Rosabelle about the day's events. She fixed him with one of one of those looks she gave the girls when they misbehaved in a public place. "What?" He pulled his head back and offered an innocent grin.

"Miles." She stretched his name out. "These are friends. The *children* of friends. You will *not* take advantage of them, I hope."

"Babe," said Miles. "Come on, I would never. I'll make sure they get an impressive deal... and that we profit from that great deal. Win-win, see?"

"Okay. So, when Mae comes over tomorrow night for our book club meeting, I won't have any reason at all to feel nervous, or uncomfortable, or guilty, or—"

"Not at all. I promise. And come on, even you can admit it's kind of fun to yank Brianna's chain."

Rosabelle smacked the table. "Ah-ha. There it is. This isn't about making a sale. It's about zinging Brianna. Aren't we past all that by now?"

Fiona and Poppy began smacking the table like their mother and laughing at each whack. Miles distracted them with a Donald Duck imitation. Then he resumed the conversation. "We are—I am—but she just plunked the opportunity right in my lap, babe. And besides, I've got Nora on it. I can plead ignorance."

"Really, Miles? *Your* office, *your* agent. I'm sure she'd be able to see right through that." She sighed and began clearing dishes. "I just don't want any trouble, Miles. We have enough on our plates without adding a Brianna Baker vendetta."

Miles jumped up and took the dishes from his wife. "You go relax. I'll take care of this and the kiddos. And I promise, no trouble is coming our way."

She gave Miles another look, this time it was her, *don't make promises, Miles* look. He kind of regretted the choice in words, but they were out and now he'd have to make good on them. A rare wave of doubt knotted his stomach. Maybe antagonizing Brianna Baker wasn't such a hot idea. But, damn, was it fun.

24 Brandon

Feather Anne stayed silent on the ride over to see the garage. He tried to read her mood, but she had her walls up. Was she pissed? Scared? Excited? For Brandon, this was the first time since... he couldn't *remember* when he'd last felt this energized and alive. He'd been treading water these past months and only now realized how far he'd sunk.

"Okay, so, remember, it's a work in progress. We're clearing out the entire thing, even the loft. It's gonna take a hot minute. You just have to try and, like, visualize it. Okay?" Nick rambled the whole ride. "I thought we could, you know, use the loft area to write and stuff. Get a fridge up there and—"

"Nick?" Feather Anne turned those unreadable eyes on him.

"Yeah?"

"Please stop talking." She looked back out the window.

Brandon grinned. He turned his head to hide his mirth. He and Nick were cool, sure. But he couldn't help if he liked it when she cut him down. And then, somehow, he felt guilty for feeling that way.

When he'd sent that text the other night, he hadn't expected discovering Nick Amendola might not be the major asshole he'd always thought him to be. Brandon didn't expect to *like* the guy. In fact, all of Brandon's perceptions and expectations changed that morning outside Mae's Café, when the former enemies sat down over coffee and talked.

"Gotta tell ya, man. For a second, I thought maybe you wanted to duke it out or something," said Nick. He added a laugh—not to mock, but as self-derision—and studied Brandon. "Then I remembered how chill you were at Feather Anne's when I showed up." He looked away for a long moment. When he turned back to Brandon, he'd looked him dead in the eye. "I tried, man. Tried like hell to get her to want me and forget you. Never happened. Never will. I realize that now."

Brandon hadn't anticipated such frankness. He imagined smugness, indifference, and maybe even contempt. Nick threw him off with his openness and he stammered for a reply. "I, uh... we've got an extensive history, me and Feather Anne. I've loved her since... forever. Watching her go off with you? Man, that was the shittiest feeling ever. I hated you, bro. Envied you, too. Still do, in a way. You two share something I can't be a part of—this music connection—and I'm just the outsider looking in."

Nick flapped a hand at him. "Nah, man. I mean, yeah, the music thing? It's a bond, for sure. And, fuck, I've missed making music with her. But it's not... well, anyhow." He cleared his throat.

Nick told Brandon the complete story, all the way up to his talk with Mae, Bruce, and Feather Anne the night before. It shed a whole new light on the Feather Anne and Nick drama, and Brandon found himself feeling sorry for Nick. It also made him realize he needed to save Feather Anne from making the same mistakes Nick had made.

Brandon's original thought-out and rehearsed plan drifted away like the steam from his coffee cup and a new one came out his mouth before his brain processed it. "We should start a recording studio, together. For you and Feather Anne, I mean. I've got the perfect location and it won't break the bank. You guys will make your own music, your way."

"What about that contract she's about to sign? And the one I'm already under? My dad is looking into getting me out of it, but who knows, man?"

"How soon will you know?" Brandon's plans now hinged on this.

Nick looked up at the sky, exhaled, and dropped his head back down. "Not sure. Bruce had a fire lit under him this morning. Got the contract over to a guy he remodeled a home for. Guess the dude owes him a favor, or something. Today, maybe?"

Nick pushed back from the table, sat forward, and rested his elbows on his knees. Then he steepled his fingers under his chin and stared hard at Brandon. "I really want to do this... this recording studio. *If* I can get out of my contract, I want in. But I gotta ask, man. What's *your* role in this? No offense, but I can't have another John St. James trying to run my life. And neither can she."

Brandon bristled at the comparison but forced himself to calm down. The guy had been manipulated and taken advantage of; he had a right to be wary. "I hear you. It's not like that at all. Actually, I'm hoping to be a useful part of this thing and not just the creepy boyfriend who hangs around all the time." Nick chuckled. Brandon ducked his head and picked at his jeans a moment before he went on. "I, uh, I've been dicking around with sound engineering and, like, all kinds of audio stuff. More than dicking around, to be honest, and I think I'm getting good at it. So, my thought is, I could be your sound guy and you two can focus on the making the music."

Fuck, I feel like a freshman trying to impress a senior.

Instead of laughing at him, as Brandon half-expected, Nick said, "No, shit, huh? That's fucking awesome. I mess around a bit with the mixers and shit, but I prefer just making the music and writing the songs, you know? It'd be a fucking lifesaver having someone else handle that shit." He shook a finger at Brandon and squinted at him. A grin spread across his face. "You know what? Fuck it. Let's do this." He stretched out a hand for Brandon to shake. After, he said, So, how do we sell this to Feather Anne?"

"Well," said Brandon, "I thought I'd bring her over to the music shop and show her all the stuff I'm buying, and—"

"Nah, don't do that. Let's me and you go, get all the stuff, set it up, and then tell her. She's gotta see it all laid out, you know?"

Brandon hedged. "I don't know, man. You think—"

"Yeah, yeah. Come on. It'll work. Text her you had a change of plans and you'll catch up with her later. Me and you are gonna go to that music store. So, where's this studio we're making?"

That was when they'd gone over to talk to Brianna and lay out their proposition. She'd been more receptive than Brandon expected, but then he also knew she'd harassed Ricky to clean out the garage for years, and now she had an excuse to do it. After that, they'd bought everything they needed from the music store and loaded it into Nick and Brandon's trucks.

Their last and scariest stop had been Feather Anne's. Just before arriving, Nick had gotten the call from the lawyer that contract could be broken without penalty thanks to some crap John St. James added in after they'd signed. It seemed like everything had lined up just right for them. All they needed was Feather Anne to say yes. And, to his amazement and relief, she did. So far.

That could all change the minute she saw the work ahead of them to make the garage usable. Even for him—the guy who'd masterminded the whole thing—it was hard to visualize. A hint of panic crept underneath his excitement. She could still back out. Then, it would be just him and... Nick Amendola. His new best friend? No. His new business partner. In a business neither knew enough about.

Shit. Shit. Shit.

He was so engrossed in his inner spiral down the rabbit hole, he didn't at first hear Nick say, "Yo, bro. What's going on?"

Brandon blinked and looked out the window at what Nick pointed at. They were two houses away from the Baker's house, but the dump truck and two pick-ups in the driveway couldn't be missed. "What the..." Brandon hunched forward for a better view.

Feather Anne snorted. "Brianna. *That's* what's going on."

They parked across the street from the house. He and Feather Anne jumped out, but Brandon fell back against the seat and moaned. He covered his faced. "No, Brianna, no. No, no, no."

Feather Anne tapped the glass and her muffled voice said, "Come on, Bran. Let's see what she's done, at least."

Brandon climbed out as if he had lead shoes on. Feather Anne hooked her arm through one of his, and Nick clapped him on the back. "It'll be fine... I think," said Nick.

The dump truck revved and pulled away revealing Brianna in the center of the driveway, hand on hip and gesturing to a pair of workers. She spotted them and waved.

"Bri, what are you doing?" Brandon looked around; his mouth hung open.

The garage stood empty of every automotive remnant, including Ricky's latest junkyard car and all the equipment that Nick had in the back of his truck, was now in it. Brianna blasted them with her ultra-bright smile.

She swept an arm out toward the garage. "Helping."

"You mean taking over," muttered Brandon. His heart sank. This was so... so *Brianna* of her.

Nick nudged him and spoke out of the side of his mouth. "Dude, this is awesome."

"Sure, on the surface it is," said Brandon, adopting a similar speech.

Feather Anne followed suit, talking out the side of her mouth. "Well, if she's in, it must have a potential to be big."

Brandon couldn't decide whether to be insulted or relieved. Brianna's involvement insured Feather Anne's; that was the good part. Without that involvement, Feather Anne thought they might fail. That kind of stung.

"The three of you suck at whispering. Relax, I'm not *taking over,* you fucking crybaby. I am merely fast-tracking your setup so you can get started. You're welcome, by the way." She closed the gap between them, her heels click-clacking on the driveway. Her smile grew when she looked at Feather Anne. "So, you're taking your chances with these two, huh?"

"Looks like it," said Feather Anne. She added, "God help me."

"Never mind *him,* you've got me," said Brianna. "Come on, I'll show you what's been done so far." The trio followed until she halted. "You two can go unload Brandon's truck while us girls go inside."

Great, she's already ordering us around.

Nick looked at Brandon. Brandon shrugged and said, "Let's go. No arguing with her."

So, while Brianna gave Feather Anne the grand tour of their new studio, he and Nick humped amps, chairs, a drum kit—piece by piece—and mixer equipment into the space. When they set down the last of the truck's contents, they looked around for the women.

"Up here, toolboxes." Feather Anne leaned over the loft railing and grinned down at them.

"That's *Mr.* Toolbox to you," said Brandon.

Feather Anne threw a dusty tennis ball at him, which he caught. They tromped up the wooden staircase and joined Feather Anne and Brianna, who lounged on a well-worn brown leather sofa. Behind her hung a mural of music instruments. Feather Anne sat in a coordinating chair, her legs draped over the arm and a plush scarlet pillow clutched to her chest. A small refrigerator took residence in one corner and a coffee bar stood in another. She had swept—or more likely had someone sweep—the plank floor clean and a Persian rug sat under a scarred, rectangular coffee table.

Brandon, once again, stood with his mouth agape. Nick verbalized his thoughts. "Holy shit, man. This is fucking awesome."

"Fuck yeah, it is," said Brianna without a hint of modesty.

"Bri, how the hell did you get all this done it such a short time? We met with you this morning."

Feather Anne answered. "Um, because she's Brianna, bitch."

The two women cracked up at this, leaving Brandon and Nick baffled. Insider joke, obviously. Despite Brandon's trepidation at having his sister involved, two things became clear. One, Feather Anne seemed happy about it. And two, his sister was kind of a badass businesswoman. Whatever she didn't know about the industry, she'd make up for by finding the people who *did* know their shit.

"So, what do you kids say? Partners?" Brianna looked at each one, saving Brandon for last.

Brandon stammered. "I, uh, we—can we have a few minutes to discuss you—this, I mean?"

Brianna stood, walked over to a small, kitchenette-type table he hadn't even noticed before, and opened the blue folder lying on it. She extracted a small stack of papers and placed them on top of the folder. "Suit yourselves. I drew up a lease agreement and partnership papers. I've some errands to run, so we'll chat when I return."

After they were sure she'd gone, Nick blurted, "Damn, she's scary."

Feather Anne said, "They don't call her the Ice Queen for nothing. I think it'd be good to have her on our side. I vote yes."

"Cool by me," said Nick. "I vote yes, too."

They looked at Brandon. "This is why you two get into trouble. Has anyone looked at the contracts yet? Don't answer, I know you haven't."

He picked them up, sat in the middle of the couch, and patted the cushions on either side. Nick and Feather Anne sat down like scolded children. He read the first contract—the lease agreement—aloud.

When he finished, Feather Anne said, "Seems straightforward, no?"

Nick raised his hands, palms up. "The rent isn't bad, either. Six hundred split between three people? That's like—" he looked skyward.

"Jesus. Two hundred a piece. Did you not take elementary school math?" Feather Anne rolled her eyes.

"I knew the answer. You just said it first."

Nick grabbed a decorative thing from the bowl on the coffee table and whipped it behind Brandon at Feather Anne. She blocked it and it hit Brandon in the temple. Feather Anne snatched another decorative object from the bowl and chucked it at Nick, proving why she never excelled as a softball pitcher.

"Can you two toddlers cut the shit for five minutes, please?" Brandon took on the role of daycare manager. He suspected it would be a permanent job, too.

Chastised, both mumbled an apology and pretended at paying attention. Brandon continued where he left off. "So, if we're all in agreement that we accept the terms of the lease, then—"

"You didn't vote," said Nick.

"Well, I'm saying now that I agree with—"

"Nick's right. You gotta vote, Brandon," said Feather Anne.

Brandon rubbed his temples and replied through clenched teeth. "All right. I. Vote. Yes. Happy now?" He turned to Nick, who nodded. He turned to Feather Anne, who also nodded. "On to the partnership agreement."

He read through this one twice, then a third time because it turned out both Feather Anne and Nick had been playing on their phones the whole time. When he finished, he re-explained it to them as if they were children and not grown adults who'd just toured the world and should have an ounce of common sense and basic concept of how things work.

"Are you, like, mad at us, bro?" Nick asked.

Brandon replied, "No. I'm not mad at you."

"You kind of sound mad. You're using your stern voice," said Feather Anne.

Brandon forced his tone to sound nicer. "I am using my regular voice. See? Do you—and you understand that, by signing these papers, Brianna has a say in how we do things?" The man-child and woman-girl nodded again. "And you are cool with that?" They nodded again. "All right, then. I guess we sign. Ready?"

Brandon grabbed a pen and signed his name on both contracts. He slid the papers to Nick, who also signed. He slid the papers across to Feather Anne. She took a deep breath, held it, and signed. When she finished, she let the breath out and looked at Nick and Brandon.

"Let's not fuck this all up, okay?"

Brandon stuck his hand out, palm down. "To not fucking this up."

Feather Anne rested hers on top of his. She echoed him. "To not fucking this up."

Nick placed his hand over hers. "To not fucking this up."

Brandon, used to team huddles, said, "One, two, three, *break*," and they all raised the stacked hands in the air.

Nick looked around. "Uh, now what?"

"Now," said Brandon, "we get this place set up right. I'll start working on the sound equipment layout. Nick, you and Feather Anne get everything you need from your places. Guitars, laptops, mics, notepads... everything and anything you can think of. Let's make this space ours."

Feather Anne had gone quiet and bit her nail. "Actually, the first thing I have to do, is tell John. St. James that I'm not signing his contract."

"Oh," said Brandon.

"Shit," said Nick. "You should do it with us here. For, like, moral support."

Brandon added, "Yeah, and so he doesn't try to bully or trick you into signing."

Feather Anne seemed relieved. She took out her phone, and switched spots with Brandon so that she sat in the middle. With the phone on speaker on the table, she hit the call button. John St. James' assistant answered, and after giving her name, she asked to speak with him.

The man sounded giddy upon realizing who was calling. "He's been waiting impatiently to hear from you. I'll put you right through, you just hang tight two tics and a shake."

"What the hell does that mean?" Nick muttered.

Feather Anne shushed him and resumed biting her nail. Her leg bounced. Brandon resisted the urge to clamp down on her knee to stop the movement; it would get him swatted. Instead, he waited beside her. The line clicked, making all three jump.

"Hey, how's my girl? You ready to make some killer music, or what?" John St. James wasted no time getting to the point.

"H-hey, John. How's it going?" Feather Anne stalled.

"Going just fine... once you're on the St. James team. Why don't I send a car for you, getcha back in the city that never sleeps, and we'll get this show on the road. Or in this case, the studio I've had designed just for you."

When Feather Anne didn't respond, he tried again, this time sounding nervous. "I, uh, heard you had a run-in with Nick while you've been home. That must've been... nice. Too bad I had to let him go. He just didn't have what you do, kid."

Feather Anne had to clamp her hand over Nick's mouth to keep him from going off on the guy. As she wrestled him, she said, "Oh, is that how it went down? Funny, Nick's story is a little bit different."

Nick broke free. "Yeah, dickhead. A *lot* different."

Without missing a beat, John St. James said, "Nick, buddy. Come on, now. No need for hard feelings. All's well that ends well. I mean, I still have a multi-million-dollar studio, production company, and all the industry contacts a man could dream of, and you have... what is it *you* have, Nick?"

Nick's jaw clenched and unclenched. Feather Anne leaned forward and said, "He's got me, John. I'm not signing your contract. I'm out."

There was a lengthy pause. Then, "You sure you want to do this, kid? You understand what you're walking away from? Hitching your wagon to Nick Amendola's will only get you in a bad way. No offense, son."

"Fuck you," said Nick.

"Feather Anne, once this offer is off the table, there's no getting it back. You'll be walking away not just from millions of dollars, but opportunities, too. And if Amendola is using Billie fricking Eilish as your We Can Do It poster child, you should know she's an anomaly, not the norm."

"Thanks, John. I'll take my chances."

"Jesus, kid. Think of the money. You—"

"That's just it, John. It was never about the money for me. You kept trying to make it so, but it's just not," said Feather Anne.

John St. James snorted. "Yeah, okay, kid. Keep telling yourself that. Well, I wish you the best of luck. Both of you. You're going to need it."

John St. James ended the call without adding a goodbye. Feather Anne fell back against the cushions, her eyes wide and unfocused. She'd untucked her compass medallion from her shirt and slid it back and forth on the leather cord. Nick looked at Brandon, and Brandon looked at Feather Anne.

"Babe? You, uh, okay?" Brandon spoke in a gentle tone.

She turned toward the sound of his voice but continued to stare into space. "I have no fucking idea."

Nick chuckled. "Fair enough. I say we have a drink. Lucky Loo's?"

Brandon tilted his head at Nick. "Bro, Feather Anne's still underage."

Nick blinked several times at them. Then he started laughing. He laughed so hard, he doubled over. It was enough to shake Feather Anne out of her fugue. She grinned at him, then at Brandon, who grinned back. Soon, they were as hysterical as Nick.

The trio's manic laughter died off. Nick was the first to notice Brianna standing at the head of the stairs, watching them with one perfect eyebrow quirked and her hands behind her back. He nudged the others and pointed his chin toward Brandon's sister.

When she had all eyes on her, she asked, "So, is a celebration in order?"

Brandon gathered up the contracts and waved them at her. "Yes, landlord slash partner, it is."

"Excellent," said Brianna. She held out a bottle of champagne and four glasses. "Then let's celebrate."

By the time their celebrating wrapped up, it was after nine. Feather Anne jumped up and said, "Shit, I haven't checked with Mae all day. She will freak when we tell her the news. Brandon, can you take me home?"

Brandon stood too fast and felt the room sway. "Uh, I'm afraid not. I'm buzzed. Nick, how're you?"

Nick had sprawled out on the couch and snored. Brianna laughed and said, "I'll call you an Uber. I'm afraid we're all sauced."

"No, don't be silly. It's not far. I'm sober, so I can just walk."

"I'll walk you, babe." Brandon grabbed his jacket and almost toppled over the chair.

She chuckled. "Stay here, jackass. I'm fine to walk by myself. See you guys tomorrow for our first recording session."

She left them in the loft despite their—granted, weak—protests. It was Chance. Nothing to worry about. Something wriggled in the back of Brandon's mind, though. Wasn't there something to worry about in Chance? Someone? He puzzled a minute longer, then gave up and downed the last of second champagne bottle. He fell into the chair across from Brianna and watched her leave through slitted eyes. He was asleep before she reached the bottom stair.

25 Jared

The cuts and scrapes healed up well enough. The minor bruising over his left eye and temple took longer to fade and thus delayed his plans longer. He was a lion pacing the cage, marking the time until he could meet her face to face. *Mae*. She'd been much more attractive than what he'd envisioned. The more he watched her and looked at her pictures, the more his feelings grew. Jared might even *love* her.

Now, *that* would be something. He could pull off the pretense of love to get what he wanted, sure. But to win her love *and* reciprocate those feelings? A most welcome surprise... and helpful in making the time pass more pleasantly. A pity, too. Once he'd gotten what he deserved, he'd be on his way again.

No moss grows on this rolling stone. Especially when the stone might still have arrest warrants in three states.

He allowed himself to imagine Mae falling so in love with him she begged him to take her with him. They could go to Colombia or Brazil and live a life of decadence and leisure. When the money ran out, they'd work as a team. The greatest cons in the world.

A knock on his motel door startled him out of his fantasy. Jared saw the time—eight-twenty PM—and peeped out through a sliver of the blackout window curtain. A man with a severe comb-over and beer gut stood with his head tilted toward the door, listening for sounds within. His nametag designated him as *Jim, Manager*. Jared stayed silent, waiting for him to leave.

After a few seconds, *Jim, Manager* left, but not before slipping a sheet of paper under the door. Jared snatched it up and read the print letting him know his card was declined and he'd have to provide another form of payment or vacate immediately. He couldn't postpone his plan any longer. It was time for Mae to meet her long-lost brother-in-law.

26 Mae

By seven-thirty Mae had to admit to herself that Bruce wasn't coming. The near-constant text checks told her he hadn't replied to her message, either. It was unlike the normally attentive Bruce, but then, this wasn't normal times. They'd kissed that morning. She thought it had been the start of a new phase in their relationship, but obviously he felt otherwise and just didn't know how to break it to her.

She blew out the candles and cleared the settings. Singing along with Billie Holiday to cheer herself up, Mae carried the empty plates to the café's kitchen. The Cornish hens and roasted vegetables would come home with her; Feather Anne and the twins would happily tear into it for lunch the next day.

"At least it won't go to waste," said Mae to no one.

She turned off the stereo and lights, locked the front and side doors, and went back through the hall to the kitchen. Her hand hovered over the knob, but the soft light emanating from her office caused her to pause. Mae couldn't remember leaving the desk lamp on, but there it was. She considered leaving it, but her practical nature made her turn away from the exit and go left, to the ajar office door. Like the light, she could've sworn she'd shut it earlier.

A nervous knot twisted in her stomach, but she laughed it off.

This isn't a scary movie, silly.

Not that she ever watched them. Still, she knew how they went and couldn't help mentally narrating her steps.

Woman sees light under door, ignores trepidations, dramatic music plays, she opens the door, and...

Nothing. No ax murderer, no monster. The ridiculousness of allowing herself to get worked up made her laugh as she released the breath she'd been holding. It was a shaky laugh at that. "Stop acting stupid." Mae turned off the light and closed the office door, listening for the click. Her keys jangled on the keyring dangling from her finger as she turned back toward the kitchen door.

"Hello, Mae," said a familiar figure in the doorframe.

Mae swayed. Black starbursts bloomed around her peripheral and spread. Her mouth opened and closed, but no sound came out. Then everything went black, and the blackness swallowed Mae whole.

27 Bruce

Bruce hung his keys on the rack by the front door and called out. "Yo, Nick. You home?" No answer. He located his phone on the kitchen table, right where he'd left it. Eleven missed calls and double the missed text messages. But the one that stood out was Mae's.

Dinner, café. Just us. 7 PM.

xo

"Shit." He looked at the time. Eight-forty. He swore again, louder. He hit the call icon below her name.

On the fourth ring, it went to voicemail. Bruce hung up before the *leave a message* tone. He needed to see her in person. He unhooked his keys, hopped in the truck again, and headed straight to Mae's house. On the way, he spied Feather Anne walking. He pulled up alongside her.

"Hey, you want a ride?"

"Sure, thanks."

Feather Anne filled him in on her latest news. "Holy shit, kid. That's outstanding. All of it. Shocking, but awesome. You sure this is what you want, now?"

Feather Anne awarded him with a serene smile. "It's the first thing I been sure about in a year." She jerked her chin at him. "What's your deal? With my sister, I mean."

"Well, kid, I'm not sure. But I'll find out now, I guess." He parked in front of the house. They walked up the driveway together and Feather Anne led them inside.

Gina lifted her head from her book, looked from Feather Anne to Bruce, then behind them. She frowned. "Where's Mae?"

"She's not here?" Bruce felt a prickle of concern. He looked at his watch again.

"No, I thought she was having dinner with you," said Gina. She stood and dropped her book and blanket on the couch.

"I missed her message. Just saw it fifteen minutes ago. I called her, but no answer," said Bruce.

Gina reached for her phone and said, "Let me try her."

Feather Anne looked at them and scoffed. "Guys, over-reacting much? She's probably still at the café with the music up loud."

"The café," echoed Bruce. "Right. I'll check there. You two stay here in case she comes home."

"Bruce? Should we call Joel?" Gina's tone was grim.

"Not yet. Sit tight. I'll call you when I get there."

Now Feather Anne looked worried. "The ghost-guy. That's what you're worried about, isn't it?"

Bruce looked at Gina, who said to Feather Anne, "Why don't you give Rosabelle a call and see if she's talked to her?"

Bruce left them inside and ran to his truck. Thank God the café was only minutes away; if his heart pounded any harder, he'd give himself a heart attack. He winced at the too close to home reference and thanked God again that he hadn't said something so stupid to Feather Anne.

The gravel crunched under his tires as he pulled into the back lot of the café. To his relief, Mae's car was there, and light streamed from both the kitchen and office windows. No other cars sat in the lot. But it didn't mean no one else was in there with her. He jumped out and slid the heavy wooden baseball bat from under the seat.

He turned the knob, expecting to find it locked, but it rotated easily. Inside, he held his breath and listened. Voices came from the office; one male, one female. Mae and… who? He crept up to the partially closed door and listened again for signs of distress. Instead, the melodic sound of Mae's laughter floated out through the crack. He pushed the door open.

Mae sat on the edge of her desk, holding an icepack to her temple, and looking down. Her head jerked up, and the smile on her lips froze. He took this in as he also registered the view of a man's back sitting in the chair in front of her.

The man stood and faced Bruce. The bat slipped from his hand and clunked to the floor. Bruce's brain refused to process the name that came out of his own mouth.

"William?"

28 Feather Anne

Feather Anne stared at her phone screen for several seconds. She hadn't realized her brow furrowed until Gina said, "What's wrong? What did Bruce say?"

"He said Mae has someone she wants us to meet but try not to freak out." Feather Anne looked at Gina. Gina looked at Feather Anne. In matching hushed voices, they said, "The William ghost-guy."

Gina's exact words were, "William's ghost," but it was close enough. She looked at the time—now ten PM—and side-stepped Feather Anne into the kitchen. "I'll put on the kettle, you set some food out on the island."

Mother and daughter were sitting at the far end of the kitchen island—facing the foyer and front door—when Mae walked in. Two men followed her. One was Bruce, and he looked at Feather Anne, a serious but unreadable look on his face. The second man's head was down, and he hung back.

Mae entered the kitchen first, Bruce stood behind her, and the stranger behind him. Her expression differed from Bruce's. She looked from Gina to Feather Anne. The first thing she said was, "Thanks for putting on the tea. I—this will be a shock, so I want you to just stay calm, and listen, okay?"

For more than a split second, Feather Anne held a wild, irrational hope that somehow it *was* William. That maybe he'd been in some kind of witness protection thing and he had to leave them to protect them. But even though Mae seemed happy-ish, it wasn't the happiness of a woman who'd just got her husband back.

"Bruce?" Mae called over her shoulder. "Can you bring… can you two come in now?"

Mae came into the kitchen and stood between Feather Anne and Gina at the island. She rested a hand on each of their shoulders. Feather Anne's stomach tightened, and her chest felt like it had the wings of a thousand birds flapping against it. She hadn't been this nervous since her audition for the Greatest American Singer. She wiped her damp hands on her jeans and met Bruce's gaze again.

The look lasted for only a few seconds, but it was enough for him to relay a non-verbal warning to her. But of what? She turned her attention to the man coming around from behind him. The flapping wings in her chest froze. Beside her, Gina's teacup clattered onto the saucer.

One side of her brain said, "William." The other side said, "Not William." The resemblance could only be called uncanny—a word Feather Anne had never thought, let alone used before—but on further inspection, differences revealed what the shocked side of her brain missed. This was a man who could be William's doppelganger, and that was all.

He styled his hair the same as William, and his clothing might as well come from William's closet. But the more she stared, the more she saw the dissimilarities. The slight bend in the nose. The eye color—William's had been chocolate brown—his were dark, like coal. He also stood a few inches shorter than William had—he and Bruce had stood eye to eye, but this man did not—and his build was stockier.

The comparison reminded Feather Anne of the Fleetwood Mac tribute band she saw one rare night off from the tour. Throughout the show, she, Nick, and the others had stood far enough back to keep the illusion of Stevie Nicks and the others, but when they went up after to meet the band, she lost the impression. Up close, she saw it was only the hair, makeup, and clothing that allowed her mind to accept the fantasy. This felt no different once the initial shock passed.

Mae said, "I'd like you to meet Jared. He is… William's brother."

The man ducked his head with a bashful wave. "It's very nice to meet you."

Feather Anne experienced what she supposed to be the equivalent of Déjà vu. Even the man's voice recalled that of William's. She looked up at Mae, still between her and Gina, and saw the acceptance and joy on her face. Feather Anne wanted to feel it, too, but couldn't. There was something off—besides the obvious—and she couldn't put her finger on it. She looked at Bruce, who stared at Mae, and noticed his jaw clench and unclench.

You're not feelin' it either, are you?

"So, you're William's brother? How come he never mentioned you?" Feather Anne received a hard elbow poke from Mae for that, but she didn't care. It was a reasonable question.

"It's okay, Mae. I don't mind," said Jared. "William never knew about me, Feather Anne. Our… father had an affair, and I was the byproduct of that relationship. I only found out recently that I had a brother. You can imagine my disappointment—and sadness—at learning he'd passed away."

Jared bowed his head again, but his eyes peeked from under his lashes at Mae again. *Dream on, buddy. Not a chance in hell.* Feather Anne looked up at Mae. She expected her to meet her gaze with one of their *get a load of this guy* looks, but she stared back at this Jared dude with a dopey smile on her lips. Feather Anne met Gina's eyes instead. There, she saw hers and Bruce's wariness mirrored. She directed her attention back to the stranger.

"With both William's parents long gone, I guess we can't really confirm any of this, can we?"

"Feather Anne—" Mae blurted.

"What? You can't blame me for being a little... curious. You have money, and you're hot. It's not crazy to think someone might want to take advantage of the situation."

"Oh, my God, Feather Anne. Apologize. Poor Jared has already explained everything once and I believe him," said Mae.

"That's because you're too trusting," said Feather Anne.

She caught Bruce's eye. He tried to hide a smile behind his mug. She checked Gina's reaction, and though she wasn't smiling, she *was* nodding her head. She wasn't wrong here. If Feather Anne had learned anything over the past year, it was to trust her gut. She thought Mae had the same instincts, but based on her mush face, her radar turned off the minute this pale impression of William showed up.

Mae refused to look at Feather Anne. She stared at Bruce and hooked her hair behind her ear. That's when Feather Anne saw the angry bruise at her temple. "Holy shit, Mae. What the hell happened to your head?"

"She fainted and hit her head on the counter," said Bruce. "When *he* showed up." Bruce jerked his chin at Jared. "They were in the office when I showed up."

"I-I carried her in there and found an ice pack. S-she was only out for a second," said Jared.

"You are all being very unkind to our guest. Jared, don't feel bad, please. It was late, I was tired, and you... you can't help that you look so much like your brother." Mae shot warning glares at Bruce and Feather Anne. Since she'd stayed quiet so far, Mae spared Gina.

Gina spoke. "Have a seat, Jared. Tell us about yourself." Her tone sounded neither friendly nor unfriendly. "Where you're from, where you live, what brings you here... all that stuff. Mae, how about you all sit down, too?"

Mae relaxed a little and did as her mother suggested, as did Bruce, then Jared. She poured and passed him a cup of tea and then one for herself. Bruce refilled his mug, took a sip, and said, "Go on, Jared. Fill us all in on where you've been the last... sorry, how old did you say you were?"

Jared met and held Bruce's gaze. "I didn't say, actually. But I am forty-nine." He turned back to the more neutral attention of Gina. "As for your questions, Gina, I'm from outside Boston and I'm... in between residences right now. I was a pharmaceutical rep until two weeks ago. They let me go. I, uh, have some money saved up, so I figured it was as good a time as any to–"

"Lurk around town and freak people out?" Feather Anne challenged him with her eyes. "What's up with that, hm?"

"He explained all that, Feather Anne. He—" began Mae.

Jared interrupted. "It's okay, Mae. I owe an explanation. I'm very sorry about all that, truly. I-I wanted so much to meet all of you, but I-I kept chickening out. I guess I was afraid you wouldn't like me. Call it the old foster kid curse, I guess."

Mae—being the gentle soul she was—pressed her hand to her chest and sympathy poured from her eyes. Feather Anne struggled not to roll hers. Not because the guy supposedly spent time in foster care—she wasn't heartless—but because it sounded and looked rehearsed. The head bowing, the effusive gratitude.

"So, your mother–" began Gina.

Jared cut her off, "Never knew her. Or my father. If you're wondering, no. I never reached out to either."

Bruce said, "But you decided to hunt down the family of the half-brother you never met?"

"Hunt down? That's a strong word choice," replied Jared. He met Bruce's stare. The deferential, almost meek posturing disappeared. "I'd say it was more like... trying to connect with the brother I got robbed of ever knowing."

There you are, creeper. The real you. I knew it was there.

Feather Anne realized that, from Mae's angle, she couldn't see Jared's face. But Feather Anne did. Discussing his parents irked him. Or maybe it was *Bruce* that got under his skin. She'd seen the way jealous male rivals acted enough to recognize the signs. He wouldn't act like that unless... unless he saw Bruce as his competition.

Bruce threw a verbal jab and pressed on. "*Half*-brother. But you didn't want to connect with your parents? Ask them—"

"There's nothing to ask. I was conceived from a one-night stand, unintended and unwanted. I know this for a fact. My mother left a letter she did not want me to contact her. My father..." Jared sneered at the word. "He may or may not have known of my existence. She made no mention of him other than to name him."

Gina asked, "How long ago was that, you said?"

The cool facade melted back into the aw-shucks version of Jared. He stammered, "It-I suppose it was about ten years ago or so."

Feather Anne's ears pricked. "I thought you said you just found out recently that you had a half-brother."

"No, I said—" Jared's composure slipped—it lasted a split second, but she saw it before he plastered on the self-deprecating smile. He restarted. "Yes, I said that I just found out about *him* from the person I'd hired to find my family."

Gina said, "You had someone searching for your family for ten years? That had to be expensive."

Bruce added, "You had your father's name, but it took ten more years to find out he had another son?"

Even Mae appeared quizzical at that. But Jared seemed to have an answer for everything. "It… aggrieved me when I learned my biological mother wanted nothing to do with me. So…" he shrugged. "Burn me once, shame on you. Burn me twice, shame on me."

Feather Anne scowled and said, "Huh?"

Mae said, "He means that once he learned about his mother's wishes, he stopped investigating into his father for fear of the same response."

Bruce looked from Mae to Jared. "Mhm. What changed for you to look again ten years later?"

Jared directed his response to Gina, Mae, and Feather Anne. "I've been a loner all my life. When I aged out of foster care—"

"Aged out?" Feather Anne tilted her head. She'd almost been in foster care herself once upon a time, but never had to experience it, thank God and Mae.

"No family adopted me, so I bounced from one foster family to the next until I turned eighteen. After that, I was on my own."

Despite herself, Feather Anne felt a twinge of sympathy. What a shitty way to grow up. "That must have sucked."

Jared offered a mirthless smile. "Suck, it did. But I'm no worse for the wear. I can honestly say, though, it just made me a more compassionate, caring person, really. I can't bear the thought of anyone ever feeling the way I did growing up." Jared leaned forward and clasped his hands. "That's why I decided to find my brother. I feared maybe he, too, had been a product of one of our father's affairs, only to be forgotten and abandoned. Once the idea took hold of me, I-I had to act." He sat back again and turned his imploring eyes on each of them—except for Bruce.

Bruce, in a dry tone, said, "But then you learned your half-brother had done just fine for himself. Better than fine, actually. Bet that stung a little. I mean, the guy you believe is your father had a whole other family—another son—and they had a pleasant life from what I understand. I could see how that could make a guy feel pretty resentful."

Jared tipped his head in Bruce's direction, but refused to look at him when he said, "*If* this were a movie or a book, sure. But this is *real* life. I'm just a lonely man, looking for a family, and that's all there is to it. Sorry to disappoint you."

"Oh, I'm not disappointed, pal. I'm suspicious. And if you—"

Mae stood so fast her chair almost fell over. "All right, you two. I think that's enough for tonight. We can talk more tomorrow. At the café. We'll all have breakfast together." She nodded her head at each of them. "Gina, we'll wait for you and Chris to finish your bakery orders, so come next door as soon as you can. Now, off with everyone. It's late."

Feather Anne had more questions. There were holes in his story. Had no one else noticed? But none of what Mae said was a request. They stood and muttered their agreement and shuffled to the living room. Gina grabbed her book and jacket off the couch and was the first one to leave. Mae, Bruce, and Jared stood in an awkward circle by the front door. Feather Anne leaned against the kitchen entrance.

"Where you staying? I'll drop you there," said Bruce.

Jared mumbled something about his car.

"Oh, Jared," said Mae, touching his arm. "Are you… staying in your car? We can't have that. You're family. We have a guest bed—"

At the same time as Jared began thanking Mae, Bruce said, "You can stay at *my* place." He glared at Mae.

"That's unnecessary, really," said Jared to Bruce with less warmth than he'd spoken to Mae. He looked back at Mae.

It was clear to Feather Anne—and likely Bruce, too—that Jared hoped Mae would insist he stay with them. When she instead deferred, "Thank you Bruce, maybe that would be for the best. I should prepare the twins." She said to Jared, "The shock of you looking so much like…"

"Their father," finished Jared. "Yes. I understand. I hope—once they've met me—they'll find me a welcome replacement for William."

Mae's smile faltered. "Well, we'll want them to see you as a-an uncle. Not—"

"Of course, of course. I misspoke. I meant a *reminder*, not a replacement. No one could ever *replace* him," said Jared. He directed the last part at Bruce.

Bruce's ocean blue eyes were dead cold as they stared through Jared. "Right. Let's go." He ushered the stranger out the door. When Jared was out of earshot, Bruce turned back to Mae and Feather Anne. "I don't like him, and I definitely don't trust him. You might not want my opinion, but I don't think the twins should meet him."

Mae's tone was cool. "Thank you, Bruce. I'll… consider what you've said. Now, goodnight."

Bruce looked like he wanted to say more. He shot Feather Anne a glance, and she took the hint. "Well, I'm beat. Goodnight, guys."

She left them in the foyer to have whatever argument they were about to have and collapsed on her bed. It was only then that she realized she'd yet to tell Mae *her* big news. In perfect synchronicity with her thoughts, her phone chimed with a text message from Brandon. A moment later, another followed, this one from Nick. Both typed one word:

Well?

Feather Anne grinned and started a group message. She filled them in on the events of the evening, and their responses were as expected given the soap opera-like quality of the news.

Brandon: **No way. That's insane**.

Nick: **I feel like there's a song in there somewhere**.

Feather Anne: **LOL. You would say that. Meet you guys at the loft tomorrow. 10 am**.

Brandon: **Let's call it that**.

Feather Anne and Nick:**???**

Brandon: **The studio. Let's call it The Loft. Or something like that. You two are the writers. Come up with something. Nite.**

Feather Anne and Nick: **I like it.**

She played around with the name in her mind, using it as a distraction to not think about William's weird brother. She'd deal with that tomorrow. Feather Anne grabbed her notebook and wrote: *The Loft*. She tried different variations. *The Loft Studio*. *Studio Loft*. And even just *Loft*. Feather Anne said the word *loft* in her head so many times it sounded strange, like a made up, nonsensical word. So, she dropped the notepad and pen on the floor beside the bed and lie on her side. Her brain switched right over to William's brother. William's supposed brother. *Half*-brother.

Feather Anne reached for her phone once more. This time, she texted Bruce five words.

I don't trust him either.

She didn't wait for his response and instead turned over and closed her eyes. Her mind still raced with conflicting thought. Excitement tangled with anxiety. Doubt twisted through hopefulness. Images of the recording studio—her and Nick making music, Brandon working the sound—interspersed with those of Mae, Bruce, and Jared. Then William's face came to the front of her closed eyelids and she half-consciously reached for the compass around her neck. He was smiling and nodding. It felt like he was sending her a message, telling her that everything would be all right. It was the last image she remembered before sleep claimed her in the wee hours of the morning.

29 Gina

Chris loaded the last tray of French loaves onto the rack and hung his mitts on a peg. "So, you met the guy and you don't like him. Just like that? I mean, shouldn't we at least give him a chance? We ain't everyone's cup of tea either, you know."

"So?" Gina handed him a tray of cinnamon buns. "What's that supposed to mean?"

Chris took the tray and placed it in the oven. "It just means that people once judged *us* on first impressions. *Fat* Chris? Gina the—"

"All right, I get it. This is different, though."

Chris folded his arms. "Oh, yeah? How so?"

She gave him a cold look and said, "Because it's my daughters' hearts involved here, and I think he's playing with them. All of us."

While Chris set the timer for the cinnamon buns, Gina cleaned the flour from the counters. Thinking about that Jared guy had kept her up all night. She hoped he would not be at the café for the family breakfast. Keeping herself neutral the night before had been one hell of a struggle. But she'd figured there'd been enough tension in that kitchen without her adding to it.

Chris yammered away behind Gina, but she only caught half of the last sentence. "… and that's what I think." He looked at her expectantly, then scowled at her. "You didn't hear a word I said, did you?"

"What? Yes, I did. You said…" Gina wracked her brain for what Chris might have been saying. The oven timer saved her. "Oh, gotta get those out and ice them. Mae's waiting for us next door."

Chris gave her that look that said she wasn't fooling him but said nothing. Gina resumed her rant where she'd left off before Chris tried to throw his moral compass at her. "He's got these black, beady eyes that creep me out, too. And the way he simpers around Mae is—"

"Simpers? You been watching the Downtown Abby show again?"

"It's *Downton* Abby, dummy. And you know what I mean. Bruce sees it, Feather Anne sees it. But

Mae is blinded by the resemblance. Which is not so much when you're up close. This Jared guy can't compare even on his best day and wearing William's clothes."

"You done yet?" Chris tossed her jacket at her and took the cinnamon bun tray off the counter. He walked out without glancing back.

Gina stuck her tongue out at his back, then caught their one employee, Luis, staring at her. "What are you looking at?"

"Nothing, boss." Luis raised his hands in a *don't shoot* gesture.

"Whatever. You fine with running the shop while we're gone?"

"Yes, ma'am," said Luis.

"Fine. Be back in a couple hours. Pick up orders are on the board. If any more deliveries come in, call Chris."

"Will do, boss." Luis saluted her and went back to rolling dough.

Gina followed Chris out. Through the café window, she could see Chris handing off the tray to Mae. Bruce and Feather Anne were already sitting, heads bent together in what looked like an intense conversation.

Gina muttered, "Damn it. I want in on that conversation," and hurried across the street.

The second she lowered herself into the chair next to Bruce, Mae called her over. "Gina, could you give me a hand back here?"

Gina swore under her breath and stood again. "Sure thing, Mae." To Bruce and Feather Anne, she hissed, "Wait for me to talk about you-know-who," and quick-walked to the café's kitchen.

Mae stood at the counter, arranging fruit on plates. Easily a one-person job. Gina eyed her daughter. "So, this is nice. All of us together for a family breakfast. We should—"

"You don't like him, either. Jared." Mae dropped a strawberry onto a plate and face Gina, eyes accusing.

"Ah—I… it's not a matter of liking or disliking, exactly." Gina weighed her words. "It's more like not fully trusting him yet. I mean, we just met him last night. And come on, even you have to admit his actions over the past few weeks has been questionable."

Mae cast a caustic look at Gina. "*Even I* have to admit? What's that supposed to mean? You all think I'm being gullible and too trusting?"

"Well, no, I—" Gina wrung her hands. Conflict with her daughters gave her instant anxiety.

"Maybe I can't help but feel compassion for the man. He's William's *brother*. How can we not give him a chance to be a part of this family?"

"*Half*-brother, and you can," said Bruce from the doorway. He came in and stood next to Gina. "But cautiously, with your guard up."

Gina's nerves calmed. Bruce would smooth this over. He had a knack for saying all the right things to Mae.

But instead of calming down, Mae bristled even more. "What, Bruce, you want Joel to do a background check on him? Would that make you feel better?"

Bruce remained neutral. "Yes. That's precisely what I'd like. Sorry, Mae. But protecting you, Feather Anne, and the twins is my priority here. If it hurts this guy's feelings—and if he's innocent, it shouldn't—then so be it."

Mae thawed enough to concede. "It might be a good idea."

Gina had been around these two long enough to sense a tension between them and when to get out of the way. She snagged two of the fruit plates and said, "I'll bring these out. You kids can handle the rest, I'm sure," and made her exit.

She saw that Brandon and Nick had arrived. Both hovered around Feather Anne like puppies. Gina made eye contact with her younger daughter, who motioned for Gina to sit beside her. Before her ass met the seat, Feather Anne started. "*So*? Tell me you don't like this Jared guy. I'll tell you what I think. I think he's shady as fu—" She stopped mid-swear.

Something caught her attention at the entrance of the café. Gina followed her gaze. She nudged Chris on her other side and jerked her head at the door. Silence fell over the room as all eyes stared. Mae, holding four fruit plates and trailed by an unhappy looking Bruce, came out from the kitchen. She saw what had drawn their open-mouthed attention and a smile lit up her face.

"Jared," she exclaimed. "I'm—we're—so glad you decided to join us. Come in, come in. We're just getting started."

Gina looked from Jared to Mae, then to Bruce and back at Jared again. Not one expression matched the other. Bruce scowled. Mae grinned. Jared ducked his head and offered a small smile and a quick wave to everyone. The perfect show of modesty, bashfulness, and hopefulness. Try as she might, Gina couldn't pinpoint what it was that made everything this guy did seem like an act.

As if reading her mind, Feather Anne leaned in and said, "It's the eyes."

Gina said nothing aloud, but to herself, she said, *yes. That's it. Nothing ever reaches his eyes.*

Chris elbowed her. "Holy shit, he looks just like William."

Gina shushed him and stood. "There's, uh, a spot right here for you, Jared. Come on and take a seat."

She placed him between Chris and Nick, where he might be safest from the murderous glare Bruce kept shooting him. Mae mouthed thank you as she set out the plates. There was a long, awkward pause in which the women at the table exchanged tight-lipped stares that meant *say something, will you?*

At last, Mae said, "Feather Anne? Didn't you tell me this morning you had some exciting news you wanted to share with everyone today?"

Feather Anne darted a terse glance at Jared, then around the room. She nodded at Brandon and Nick, who both nodded back at her. Gina's first improbable thought was that Brandon had proposed. However, logic told her Nick would not have been in on that. That meant it had something to do with her music. Feather Anne cleared her throat, and Gina held her breath.

"Right. So, after some not-so-careful consideration, I've decided to not sign the contract with St. James Records, and hitch my wagon to these two dopes." She wagged her thumbs at Nick and Brandon.

Mae beamed, but her brow drew together, and her head tilted. "T-that's… wonderful. I think? I'm so glad you're staying, Feather Anne, but what exactly does that mean?"

Brandon stood. "You're looking at the three founding members of Loft Studio. Feather Anne Byrd, Nick Amendola, and Brandon Bourdreau."

Bruce looked at Nick. "You guys are starting your own—"

"Recording studio," finished Nick. "Feather Anne and me will make the music, and Brandon will handle the sound and all the other crap we don't want to do."

Brandon laughed. "Yeah, that about sums it up. Eventually, we'll invite other musicians in to record, but that'll have to be a little later, when we start making back some money we've spent."

Bruce hedged. "H-how much money have you kids spent; might I ask?"

Gina observed Bruce and Mae exchanging a mutual look of apprehension. Somehow, this pleased Gina. It showed that, whatever their problem had been, they must've resolved it in the kitchen, and they were back in sync. She also noticed Jared watching the exchange with less enthusiasm. His head turned, and he met Gina's gaze. Feather Anne was right. It was the eyes. There was nothing in them. But then he smiled, and it was so like William's, she doubted herself. She forced her attention back to Feather Anne, Nick, and Brandon.

Brandon said, "All of it. Well, all of my savings."

Nick added, "Me and Feather Anne each put in the equal amount, too."

Feather Anne said, "So we'd be equal partners."

Mae and Bruce had a dozen more questions, and the rest of breakfast was spend discussing the kids' plans. Gina didn't much care *what* they did, just so long as it meant Chance was their home base. She looked around the table. This was her family. Arguing, laughing, talking. Caring. Her nose prickled, and her eyes stung. Chris reached for her hand and squeezed. The wonder of it never ceased.

I have a real family; something I didn't even dare dream of growing up.

Gina stole another glance at Jared, who watched everyone in turn. She couldn't know what thoughts were in his head as he looked from one face to the next, but she could imagine what they might be. She was once the outsider looking in, too. Mae's eyes were now on Gina. She met them and nodded.

Fine, I'll give him a chance.

30 Jared

From the moment he walked into the café, he could tell. *They all think they're better than me.* Sure, they acted polite, but none of them meant it. They didn't want him there. Except for Mae. Sweet, trusting, beautiful Mae. She'd be so easy to manipulate if not for the others. He could win over the mother—Gina—but the sister would be more a challenge than he'd predicted. As for Bruce—that pain in the ass—he had to go.

But how? Showing up at the café the night they were supposed to have their little romantic dinner had been an excellent start. Then Bruce threw a wrench in the operations by insisting Jared stay with him. He'd been so close to getting under Mae's roof.

Jared stared at Bruce with barely hidden hatred, then caught himself. These people—some of them, at least—were shrewd and wary of him. He'd overplayed his game of ghost and had to backpedal to win their sympathies. Shooting murderous looks at their beloved martyr, Bruce Grady, would only alienate him further. He needed weak links.

Gina, her husband. Or was he her boyfriend? Didn't matter. They both seemed impressionable enough. The others around the table seemed less persuadable. Who else? The children. But where were they? Why were they not there?

"Where are the twins, Mae?" Jared arranged his face into an expression of mild curiosity. Looking to interested would no doubt raise more suspicion toward him.

The conversation halted. Had he spoke at a bad time? Misjudged the moment? All eyes were on him. The sting of nervous sweat stung his armpit. He forced his face to remain guileless and tried to ignore the daggers Bruce aimed his way.

"Oh," said Mae. "They have school. They join the family breakfast in the summer and on school breaks, though."

Jared noted the she, too, avoided meeting Bruce's eyes. *Good. They must be still fighting.* If he could just drive a wedge between Mae and the others, he'd have a clear run at the money she'd willingly give to him. Sure, he could steal it; clear her bank accounts, take the valuables. But where was the challenge in that? Any petty thief could pull it off. But to make her love him, want him, need him? *That* was skill. That was *talent*. A gift, even. Jared had that gift.

The realization emboldened him. "What a shame. I so look forward to meeting my niece and nephew," said Jared with a warm smile. At least, he hoped it appeared warm.

"*Half*-niece and *half*-nephew," muttered Bruce loud enough for all to hear.

"Yes, but then I suppose being *half* family is better than being nothing at all," said Jared. *You smug, condescending asshole.*

The pro-wrestler sized man stood, and Jared had a panicked moment that he was about to challenge him to fight. Bruce must've seen the fear in his eyes. He smirked and announced he had to get going. "I've got a couple jobs across town to take care of," he said to all. To Mae, he added, "But I'll be reachable should you need anything."

Here was Jared's chance to drop the grenade he'd been waiting to use. As innocently as he could muster, he asked, "Would one of those jobs happen to be the beautiful brunette you had dinner with last night?"

Mae's head jerked up. Bruce's face reddened. Jared couldn't tell whether it was fury or embarrassment. Either way, he got his desired result.

Mae looked close to tears and refused to look at Bruce. Now all eyes were on *him*.

Ha. Consider the tables turned. How do you like it, Captain America? Not quite the superhero after all, are you?

"Mae, it's not what—" Bruce stopped and looked at Jared again. "Hang on a sec. How do you know where I was? Did you follow me, you—"

"That's enough," said Mae. She began clearing plates. "We'll talk later, Bruce. Go do your… jobs. Feather Anne, Brandon, and Nick, I am so proud of you and so excited to see what you will accomplish. Sounds like a perfect reason to throw a party."

The Brandon kid chimed in. "Totally. My sister is already planning something. I can have her call you."

"Great," said Mae. Even Jared could see the smile she wore was forced.

Still reeling from the discovery that lover boy isn't all he seems to be, Mae? Don't worry. Uncle Jared has a shoulder you can cry on.

He had to bite the inside of his cheek to keep from grinning. The urge didn't last long. Watching the way they made a fuss over their goodbyes— hugging, cheek kisses, more hugs, promises to call or see each other later—they acted as if they were jumping into planes and flying to distant parts of the country instead of mere blocks away from one another. Meanwhile, the goodbyes the offered *him* were only perfunctory and polite. Not that he expected or cared.

When the last one left—the mother, reluctantly—Mae turned to Jared and smiled. "I'm sorry. Perhaps that wasn't my best idea, throwing you to the wolves like that."

Jared waved off her apology. "It was fine, really. I understand why they are… wary of me. I'm an outsider, a stranger with nothing more than an uncanny resemblance to the man you loved."

"You are *family*, Jared. They're just a tad over-protective. They'll all come around in time." She gave him a thoughtful look. "The café is closed for the day, so, would you like to come to the house with me? I-I have something I'd like to share with you."

Like your money, maybe?

It wouldn't be that easy, but Jared could hope. More likely, it would involve boring photo albums of beloved Saint William. Apparently, even his rival for Mae's love found his brother above reproach. Nauseating, sappy people, all of them.

"I'd love that, Mae. Thank you," said Jared. "Can I help you clean up?"

It was the last thing Jared felt like doing but it could kill the proverbial two birds with one stone. Further remind Mae of his similarity to William *and* get him more alone time with her.

"Oh, you're too sweet, but I'm all set. Meet you at the house in a half hour."

Stupid. Stupid, stupid, stupid. Never pose what you want as a question. Haven't you learned anything, you worthless moron? I'll help you clean up. That's what William would've said. That's what you should have said, you fucking idiot.

Jared dug his nails into his palms, smiled and agreed. "Sure, see you then." He left through the front door—unlike her family, who'd left through the side door and kitchen—and made himself walk casually to his car. Once he'd driven around the corner, he pounded the steering wheel and let loose the guttural screams that boiled below the calm surface.

Minutes later, Jared wiped the spittle from his chin and slicked down his hair. He flipped down the visor mirror and cleared his throat. A horn burst across the street turned his head. An angry looking shouted something unintelligible. He ignored her.

The tomato-redness of his face faded before his eyes to its natural tan. He was fine. Calm. Collected. Jared turned on the radio—something light and jazzy, like he imagined William listening to—and drove around town until it was time to meet Mae at home. Jared tried the word aloud.

"Home."

31 Rosabelle

Rosabelle held the passenger door in a death grip and hissed at her husband, who had just taken a turn too fast. "Stop driving like an idiot, Miles."

"Sorry, babe. Another contraction?" She gave him a look so venomous; he should've fallen into death throes. "I'll take that as a yes. Okay, still six and a half minutes apart. Doin' good, babe. We're almost home, and the doula is already there waiting. You sure you don't want to go to the hospital ins—"

"Shut… up and… drive." She panted. This was their third child. How did he not know that he shouldn't speak to her during a contraction? When it passed, she said, "Okay. You can talk. Wait, why are you turning here?"

"Oh, I just want to drop this property listing off to Brandon. He's at the café for a family breakfast thing, so —"

Rosabelle glared at Miles. "Are you kidding me right now?"

"Babe, it'll just take a sec—" He took a quick glance at his wife. "But it can wait. You're totally right, babe. Look, see. I'm turning." Miles made a show of flicking on his blinker and turning the SUV onto Elm Street. He faced the road and exclaimed, "Shit," as he swerved hard to the left, then again to the right to avoid an oncoming car.

Rosabelle renewed her grip on the passenger door and looked to see what caused Miles' reaction. A stopped car sat angled out into the road. As they passed, she peered into the driver's window and saw a man who resembled William. Unlike everyone else who'd seen the man, Rosabelle had been prepared by Mae.

"Oh," she said. "It's William's long-lost brother. Should we stop to see if he's okay?"

It was Miles' turn to wear an incredulous expression. "No, babe. We should *not* stop. We should get you home to have this baby."

Rosabelle looked down at her massive stomach. "Right. Yes, we should. I'll text Mae." She hit the send button just as another contraction started.

Miles started to say something about a half-brother and Bruce. Rosabelle shushed him with a raised finger. They waited in their driveway until the contraction subsided, then Miles dashed around to Rosabelle's side and helped her out. In classic Miles fashion, he resumed the conversation as if nothing of higher importance was going on.

"So, according to Bruce, this dude—Jared—he's William's *half*-brother and isn't so much the dead ringer up close. Bruce says there's something not right with the guy, but I don't know. I think ole Moose is jealous, if you ask me. More importantly, though, is I've got the perfect house for him if he plans on sticking around."

"There's my Miles; always looking for—"

"A way to provide for my growing family," finished Miles.

Rosabelle mustered a smile. "Yes, that. Now help me upstairs and let's get this kid out of me."

"You swear you didn't find out what we're having without me?"

Rosabelle swore. "He or she will be as much a surprise to me as everyone else. Now go grab my phone."

Thanks to Nora, Rosabelle knew Miles had a gender betting pool going on at work *and* how much he had riding on his guess of baby Hannaford being a boy. For his sake, she hoped he was right. As for Rosabelle, she didn't care whether they had a boy or a girl—although another girl would be a financial win—and couldn't wait to meet their third child.

Miles rushed back into the room with her phone and their daughters skipping behind. "Baby time," exclaimed Fiona.

"Not yet, honey," said Miles.

Rosabelle patted the bed for them to sit with her. "I'm texting Bubbe now. She will come pick you up for ice cream and when you come back, your baby brother or sister will be here. Isn't that exciting?"

"Brother," said Poppy.

"*Or* sister," said Rosabelle.

Miles added, "Either way, we will love our new baby, right girls?" When they looked away, he mouthed to Rosabelle, "Brother," and crossed his fingers.

Rosabelle felt another contraction starting and gave Miles a warning look. Everyone claimed that the second and third babies came quicker than the first, and Rosabelle hoped it was true. As the contraction subsided, Ruth Waterman's voice rang through the house.

"I'm here. Bubbe is here," she called out. At the doorway, she grumbled, "Zayde is in the car, naturally. God forbid he come inside and help me." The girls ran to greet her and pulled her into the bedroom. "There's my darling girl. How far apart are your contractions? Should we go to the hospital?" To the doula, she said, "No offense, dear."

"None taken," said the doula in her soothing voice.

"I'm fine, Mom. Everything is fine. I told the girls you and Dad will take them for ice cream," said Rosabelle as she texted Mae.

"That sounds perfect, doesn't it girls? We can— wait. Are you *texting* right now?" Ruth's jaw dropped and her eyebrows lifted into her hairline.

Miles interjected. "Rosie's an old pro at this, Ruth. How about I walk you guys out?"

Her husband might be insensitive in some regards, but for playing the role of buffer, he won first prize every time. Rosabelle mouthed thank you to him, and he winked back at her. The girls gave their mother one more hug each and kissed her belly before dashing out and down the stairs. Ruth tried to fuss over her only daughter a moment longer, but Miles ushered her out using charm, cajoling, and bribery.

When the room fell silent enough to hear the classical music playing through their home system, Rosabelle and the doula exchanged knowing smiles. "Thank you, April."

The doula said, "No problem. Need anything?"

Rosabelle shook her head. "Just to finish this text before another contraction starts."

Amid everything, Rosabelle had a recurring image of the man in the car—William's brother—that she couldn't shake. When they swerved around him, she had thought little—there hadn't been time—but since then, the image had processed. A glimpse of open mouth, a red face flashed before her eyes. As they'd passed, the man flipped down the visor and smoothed his hair. His eyes slid to meet hers, and what she saw was... nothing. They were devoid of expression.

Maybe it was her heightened state at blame, maybe it was hearing about Bruce's misgivings, or a combination of both, but the man gave her the creeps, and that compelled her to tell Mae to be careful. If she was wrong, so be it. But if she was right...

Another contraction came, this one stronger than the others. She hit send and tossed the phone aside. A wave of intense pain blotted out all thoughts of Mae and the man with dead eyes. Rosabelle's sole focus for the next hour and seventeen minutes would revolve around bringing baby number three into the world.

32 Brianna

She had just enough time to jerk her steering wheel to the right as Miles the moron came at her. It all happened in a blink; no time to even mash her hand to her horn. Not for lack of trying, but for forgetting the horn's placement in the wheel. New car, new location.

At the stop sign, she jolted to a stop. "Fucking *idiot*." She slapped her palms against the leather wheel and found the horn by accident. A man, parked lopsidedly on the opposite side of the street, looked at her through his closed window. *He* was the fucking idiot. She powered down her window and yelled. "You can't park like that, asshole."

The man stared at her, his face red but impassive. Brianna corrected the impression. He didn't stare at her, he stared *through* her. She rolled up her window and elbowed the lock button. The man she recognized him now as thc stalkcrish guy claiming to be William Grant's long-lost brother—turned his head back toward his windshield and drove away. A chill crept up her spine.

"Creepy fucking asshole," muttered Brianna.

She drove off and vowed to call Mae as soon as she arrived at her appointment. Knowing her and her sappy sweet personality, she already considered this William knock-off as family and trusted him as such, too. If Brianna was in that situation, she'd bet her life she'd not be taken in easily. She could spot a snake from miles away.

Speaking of Miles.

Brianna acknowledged the one snake she'd let slither under her radar during one brief, regretful lapse in judgment years ago.

And morality, decency, self-respect, and—

She cranked the radio volume and blasted her thoughts away with Journey. Steve Perry's voice never failed to calm her nerves. As Brianna passed the café, she noted the closed sign with surprise. Then she remembered Brandon mentioning something about a family breakfast and sharing their big news with Mae and her ragtag crew of misfits. That thought led to the realization that someday, that ragtag crew could become *her* extended family by marriage if Brandon and Feather Anne ever tied the knot.

She turned the music up louder, but it still would not drown out her zig-zagging thoughts. They bounced from horror at calling Gina Byrd and no-longer-fat Fat Chris a relation, to visualizing a wedding—coordinated by her, naturally—and then back to Gina fricking Byrd and Fat Chris. At least she could say she liked Mae well enough. This brought her back full-circle to the creepy-ass William look-a-like.

"Oh, fuck it." She activated her Bluetooth, cutting off Steve Perry's exquisite vocals mid-note. "Call Mae Huxley." On the third ring, Mae's voicemail announced her unavailability to take the call. Brianna waited for the tone and cut right to the chase the second she could. "Mae. It's Brianna. I just saw that guy claiming to be your brother-in-law and there is something off about him. You should be careful. Anyhow, splendid news about the kids, right? Call me later so we can discuss the launch party. I hope Brandon mentioned it to you. Bye for now."

She ended the call and sat a little straighter. *There. Good deed, done.* Next, an appointment with a bride-to-be, and after that, she'd meet with Elise, Katie, Charlotte, and Brittany at the nail salon for mani-pedis, where she'd catch up on the latest gossip. And play referee for Elise and Brittany, who still could not let bygones be bygones.

Brianna minded none of it. Their fivesome, once fractured, was back together. Elise's jet-setting days were over now that she sold the spa franchise for a pretty penny—thanks to Brianna's suggestion and connections—and she had more time to hang out. Katie's obligations had lessened since Billy lost his run for reelection, leaving her free to become Brianna's assistant. Charlotte was the same old Charlotte; sappy sweet, hyper-involved in her children, her boring police chief husband, and bouncing back and forth between them and her *other* friends.

Brittany's return had served as the cherry on Brianna's ice cream sundae life. All it took was a few well-timed comments about Bart's new house, his flourishing dental practice, and his charming new wife to nudge her in the right direction. Three months after Brianna began her secret Brittany campaign, her easily influenced friend packed up her new husband—an oral surgeon—and her twins and returned to Chance, where they bought a bigger house than Bart's on the opposite side of town.

Sure, Elise would be furious when she found out she'd influenced Brittany's homecoming and yes, Ricky complained that Brianna manipulated the situation. But it was worth it to have her little crew back together again.

"This is home, Ricky. It's where they belong." She'd argued against his protestations.

"Bri, people can leave Chance, you know," he'd replied.

"But they always come back." Brianna dared him to dispute it.

"Come on. You can't be serious. Some people leave and don't come back."

"Name one." She'd rapped her nails on the kitchen island as she waited.

After a pause, Ricky blurted, "Kyle Hopeworth,"

She scoffed. "Kyle Hopeworth? He died in Iraq. Or maybe it was Afghanistan. Anyhow, *that's* why he didn't come back. Who else?"

He named three people she'd never heard of and dismissed them on the grounds of not existing. "It doesn't even matter, Ricky. Those people don't count because they aren't my friends. Brittany—despite being a pain in the ass—*is* my friend and I want her back in Chance."

Ricky huffed and sputtered and gave her his best *I can't believe you, Brianna* looks. "Bri? What else have you *influenced*? And don't say *nothing*. I heard you talking to Elise about selling the franchise." His eyes grew wide. "Please tell me you had nothing to do with Billy losing the election?"

"Oh, Ricky. Honestly. Do you think I have that much power? Don't be absurd."

They both knew it wasn't much of a denial. Still, Ricky let it drop. After all his years with Brianna, he understood which battles to fight and which to walk away from. Not that he could stop her, had he chosen to fight. Once Brianna Baker set her mind to something, it was as good as done.

At five of ten, Brianna valeted her car at the country club, tipped and threatened the attendant with instant death if he damaged her vehicle, and located the young woman who she already knew—sight unseen—would be a Bridezilla of epic proportions. She made the mental note to adjust her fee.

Forty-five minutes and a fat retainer later, Brianna made her way across town to the nail salon, where the others had already arrived according to the rapid-fire series of *get here now* texts from both Brittany and Elise. A glance at her screen told her Katie had added her pleading to the mix.

So many fires to put out in one day. My, my, my.

Brianna's grin widened. She lifted her insulated water bottle—a gift from Brandon, emblazoned with an image of a llama and captioned *No Drama For This Llama*—and sipped the still ice-cold water. The deliberate irony hadn't escaped her.

She dictated a list of topics she wanted to cover. "One, creepy William look-a-like. Who's seen him? Who's talked to him? Two, party for Brandon and company. Three, dinner on the eighteenth. Who's hosting? Four, Cassidy's birthday party."

Before she hit number five, her phone rang. The caller ID showed Elise's face, and Brianna tapped the ignore call icon. She was in the salon parking lot; Elise could wait the thirty seconds it would take Brianna to walk in and take her seat, for fuck's sake.

Instead of offering excuses why she was late, Brianna said, "Thanks for waiting, ladies. Lilly, I'd like Ravishing Red. It's number thirty-seven on the wall." She glided to the middle pedicure chair, sat on the edge, and removed her shoes. Next, Brianna extracted her phone and handed her purse to Lilly. Once settled, she adjusted the massage settings to her liking, accepted the complimentary mimosa, and found her topic list on her phone.

Elise spoke. "Bri, we—"

"After. First, I want to discuss a few topics before we go off course or Charlotte starts one of her interminable stories. Now, let's see. Ah, yes. Tell me what you know about this Jared guy. Who's seen him and have you spoken to him?"

Katie said, "Brianna, there's—"

"Ah, ah, ah, Katie. I see that look in your eye. No going off topic."

The four women exchanged glances. It was obvious they had their own little agenda—something cooking up in her absence—and for that, she'd make them wait longer.

Charlotte spoke up. "I-I know from Joel that Bruce wants him checked out. They think he might be a-a con man or something."

"He looks hot from afar, but up close," Brittany shrugged. "Not so much. Bruce has the right idea. Something's off."

Katie added, "I saw him from across the parking lot at the grocery store. I thought he looked handsome, just like poor Mae's William."

"She's not *poor* Mae anymore, Katie," said Brianna. "She's *successful, financially secure, likely future wife of Bruce Grady* Mae. Sorry, Elise," she added.

"All good," said Elise through tight lips. "Happily attached to Jeff, thank you."

"So why not move in together?" Brianna taunted her friend.

"Next topic," deadpanned Elise.

"Fine, but we will circle back to that one, sunshine," said Brianna.

"Girls?" Katie gave a pointed look to Elise, Charlotte, and Brittany. "Isn't there something…"

Charlotte shook her head and put her hands up in a *not me* gesture. Brittany found a deep interest in her cuticles. That left Katie and Elise arguing it out with exchanged glares and head nods in Brianna's direction.

"Oh, for fuck's sake. One of you spit it out already. Do I have something in my teeth? Is it my hair? I *told* Marisa just a few lowlights. But she—"

"Your father is back in town," blurted Elise.

Brianna blinked at her, then at Katie, Brittany, and Charlotte. She sipped her mimosa. Lifted her foot from the soaking tub and placed it on the footrest as Lilly requested. Looked back at Elise, and said, "I'm sorry, what now?"

Katie spoke as if to one of her children when they needed instruction; slow and deliberate. "Gordon is in town, Brianna. I ran into him this morning coming out of church. He said hello, I said hello, he kept walking, so did I."

"This morning? Here? In Chance?" She needed clarity, damn it. And to put down her drink. Her hand trembled, and the orange liquid sloshed inside the fluted glass. She finished it in one gulp and handed the glass off to Lilly. "Another, thank you."

The others had gone quiet, watchful of Brianna. It was obvious no one knew what to say or do. Brianna's history, subsequent hatred, and years of therapy because of Gordon Bourdreau's so-called parenting was long documented.

Katie waited until Lilly refilled Brianna's glass before continuing. "He looks about the same. Thinner, though. A lot thinner, actually."

"Well," said Brianna, "Good for him. Anyhow, what, uh, what were you doing at the church on a

Tuesday? That's odd, no?" She picked at an imaginary thread on her pants, then turned an attentive, cheerful smile to Katie. Brianna ignored the wide-eyed stares of the other three.

"I had to speak to Father Thomas about Regan's First Communion. Just finalizing a few things and… well, anyhow. Honey, are you… okay?"

"Y-you didn't know he was coming?" Charlotte found her voice.

"Duh," said Brittany with an eye roll. "Obviously not."

"Don't talk to her like that," snapped Elise.

"Girls, please," said Katie.

Brianna said nothing. Her vocal cords felt paralyzed. A loud hum filled her ears and her body felt numb. How many years had it been since she'd seen the man she almost shot? Her mind catapulted back to that day, still clear after all the time passed.

Gordon, on the floor of Brandon's bedroom. *You bitch, you stupid bitch*, he'd said, holding his blood-gushing nose. If she'd had the gun right then—as she'd almost done—she'd have shot him. Brianna knew it then and now. Instead, she'd kicked him in the balls, grabbed her mother off the floor and ran out.

That's where she'd met Officer Marlene Nikolopoulos for the first time. She spoke in a low tone to Brianna and Martha—whose battered face still appeared in Brianna's nightmares—and walked them away from the house. She stayed with them until an ambulance arrived. When lovable Denny Hammock—Ham Hock to his old high school friends—brought Gordon out in handcuffs, it was the first moment of genuine peace Brianna had ever known. Gordon's reign of terror and abuse met its end at last.

The emotional scars remained long after. Therapy had worked wonders, but so had her conversations with Marlene. Something she'd kept private from her other friendships. Brianna realized what she needed right then was not a pedicure, but Marlene.

"Stop." She jerked her foot back, startling poor Lilly. "I have to go. It's—I have an appointment I forgot about."

Lilly jumped up, grabbed a towel and blotted Brianna's feet while Brianna handed off her glass to a slack-jawed Elise and reached for her purse and shoes. She whipped out a twenty and slapped it on the tray beside the chair and strode out without a backward glance.

She'd already tapped out a message to Marlene before she reached her car. The reply came almost immediately.

Shift just ended. Meet me at my place in fifteen.

A second message followed.

Everything will be fine. Breathe.

Brianna did just that. In count to five, out count to five. Repeat. She could handle this. *Him*. Gordon Bourdreau had no power over her or her family anymore. Her family… Brandon. She needed to forewarn him that their father was in Chance. His phone went to voicemail, and she left him a message.

"Call me when you get this. We need to talk. It's important."

33 Brandon

"Sounding great, guys," said Brandon. Then he realized he hadn't stopped recording and hit the stop button. His gut reaction told him to panic, his rational side said, *calm down. It's a first run. We can edit it out of the recording.*

"Cool, let's hear it," said Nick.

He unstrapped his guitar and hopped off the stool. Feather Anne pushed her mic stand aside and followed him. She had a grin on her face, directed at Brandon. It was the happiest he'd seen her since she'd come home, and it reassured him on several levels. Now, he just had to not fuck anything up.

Once Nick and Feather Anne settled into what had become their spots in the recording booth—which was not yet an actual booth but would be soon—Brandon hit the play button. They laughed when they heard Brandon's voice at the end and teased him.

"Sorry, sorry, guys. Still learning. I'll cut it out later when—"

"Nah, keep it in there, man," said Nick.

"Yeah, Nick's right. Keep it. It's our very first recording at Loft. I want it as is, preserved forever." Feather Anne smiled. Brandon smiled back.

"No swoony eyes, you two. Back to work," said Nick. "Save a copy of that file. I want to try some shit." He pulled his chair up beside Brandon, and Feather Anne rolled hers on his other side.

"Yeah," agreed Feather Anne. "It needs *something*."

Brandon hit play and adjusted the controls. They listened. At the thirty-three second mark Nick said, "There. Right there. Drumbeat. Right?" He looked to Feather Anne for confirmation.

"Yeah." She nodded. "Nothing crazy. Just like—"

Brandon interjected. "Something like… this, maybe?"

With everyone pooling their money into the business, Brandon could afford some seriously good music programs. He'd learned and worked on them night and day, so he'd be an asset to the team. One of those programs allowed him to create simulated instrument tracks. He was no musician, but he thought he understood what Nick wanted. With a few clicks, he made the track, then added it to theirs. He held his breath and hit play.

"Holy shit, dude," said Nick. "Yeah. Kind of like that. I mean, we'd want a real drummer, though, right?"

"Oh, yeah, totally," said Brandon. "This is just so you can get an—"

"Brandon, can you duplicate that section there and, like, layer it? I want it to sound fuller."

"No need to duplicate. I just have to do this… and this… and this." He clicked more tabs as they watched over his shoulders. "How's this?" He hit play again and the new version of the song had a subtle drumbeat and sounded like it had back-up singers on the choruses.

They went on like that for another hour and only stopped when Kade showed up with a drum kit. He looked around and said, "Shit, you all are *legit*, huh?" He walked a slow circle, nodding his head as he did. "Damn, bro. You weren't fuckin' around when you said you guys were doing this. So, which one of you plays the drums?"

They exchanged sheepish glances, and Brandon confessed. "None of us do. We just want all the goods so that when we have other musicians come in, we've got everything."

Nick added, "Yeah, too bad we don't have a drummer right now to play."

Kade extended his arms wide and gave a curt bow. "Yeah, you do." He chuckled.

Brandon had been focused on the monitor, but at this, he jerked to attention. "What? You play drums, man?"

Kade clutched at his chest as if shot. "You wound me, bro. Did we not grow up together? Does my family not own a music store? Shit, yeah, I play drums. And rhythm guitar. And a little bass."

"Dude, why did you never mention this?" Kade blew Brandon away with this new-to-him information.

Feather Anne walked over and punched Kade's arm. "Dude, my sister is always looking for musicians for the open mic house band. Where the hell have you been?"

Kade shrugged. "Working for my dad, taking night classes, teaching piano to middle-age ladies."

"You play piano, too?" Nick had a Cheshire cat grin.

"Yeah. Did I not mention that one?" Kade affected a blasé attitude. "So, you know, if y'all ever need—"

"You're hired," blurted Feather Anne. She looked at the other two and said, "Sorry, but we need him."

Nick raised and dropped one shoulder. "No argument from me, dude."

Brandon thought of his bank account with a queasy stomach and in a less enthusiastic tone said, "Great. Awesome. Cool."

"Sweet," said Kade. "I'll set up the kit, then we'll talk money, honey."

When Kade and Nick retrieved and set up the kit, Feather Anne took Brandon's arm. "Hey. You okay? You looked tired. I hope you haven't been up all night with this stuff."

"All night, every night," said Brandon. He laughed to show he was joking, even though he was not. He kept his eyes on the monitor in front of him.

"Just… slow down, please? This is a work in progress, babe. It doesn't have to be perfect. Have fun with it, stay present." She took his face and turned to look in his eyes. "I-I know it sounds dorky, but I feel like we're making magic here. I want all of us to really, like, be *in* the moment. So we appreciate it. Some day we will look back at this and see how special it was."

He pressed his forehead to hers. "It's all good, babe. I'm here. One hundred percent."

Feather Anne pulled back and studied him. After a moment, she said, "Okay. Good."

Kade and Nick joined them. Nick said, "Yo, play that track for our boy, Kade."

Brandon did, and at the end, Kade clapped his hands together and said, "Well, God damn, that was good. What do you say we run it through with the real deal?"

"Well," said Brandon. "We still have to talk about—"

Kade dismissed him. "We'll worry about that shit later. Come on, man. I want to *play*."

The threesome ran to the recording area—not quite a room or booth yet—and set up. Three hours and twice as many songs later, they were back in the sound room area. They crowded around Brandon, which made his chest swell but also his hands shake.

Halfway through playback of the first song, Feather Anne announced, "I'm starving."

Nick and Kade chimed in. It was then that Brandon realized he'd be in charge of not two, but three overgrown children, all of which were off their ADD medication. One wanted wings, another wanted pizza, the third wanted Chinese. They mocked one another's choices, threw papers and random objects at each other, and generally annoyed the fuck out of Brandon, who was still trying to work.

He stood up and bellowed, "I'll go get the food."

They blinked at him, then resumed shouting their requests. He ignored them, fished around for his keys, and unlocked the cabinet holding all their cell phones. It was a rule he instituted after realizing neither Feather Anne nor Nick—and then Kade, also—could not stop texting, SnapChatting, or taking selfies for more than two minutes at a time.

Brandon shoved his phone into his back pocket and tossed them their phones. "Text me your order. I'll be back within the hour. In the meantime, you boneheads might clean up your mess out there." He gestured to the boxes and bubble wrap scattered around the room.

"Yes, Papa," said Nick.

"Sure thing, sir," said Kade.

"You got it, babe," said Feather Anne.

Brandon turned his back on the idiots and strode out to the sounds of their laughter. On the ride into town, he marveled again at how he'd somehow become the instant parent of the group. And how, just like that, they had a new musician.

Another mouth to feed.

This made Brandon chuckle. He really sounded like a dad. Not *his* dad. That thought dried the well of mirth. Fucking Gordon. Thank God that man at least had the decency to stay away. Decency? No. More like cowardice. Whatever the case, he was glad to never see that douchebag again.

He parked in the back lot of Lucky Loo's and hopped out of the truck. As he walked to the restaurant door, he snagged his phone from his back pocket and powered it on. He paused, one hand on the door handle, and waited for the screen to illuminate. If his merry band of musicians remembered to send their food requests, he'd be amazed.

Someone pushed the door from the inside, and Brandon stepped back and apologized. "Excuse—" he looked up from the phone and his heart lurched. "Dad?"

"Hello, son," said Gordon. He looked wary and tired.

Brandon's spine stiffened, and he forced his shocked face to appear unaffected. With ice in his tone, he asked, "What the hell are you doing here?" *And does Bri know*? He glanced down at his phone and saw the voicemail icon showed one message.

"I came to see you." After a pause, he added, "And your sister. If she'll allow it."

"You're kidding, right?" Brandon sneered. "There's nothing you could say she'd be interested in. I can guarantee you that."

Gordon came down the three steps and looked his son in the eyes. "Son, I know I don't deserve—"

"You don't deserve the right to call me son. I have no interest in what you have to say, either. So save it."

He brushed past his father, took the steps in one stretch, and swung open the door. He faced Gordon for what he hoped to be the last time. "Do us all a favor and go back to whatever hole you climbed out of, Gordon. We don't need you or want you in our lives."

He had one foot over the threshold when Gordon said flatly, "I'm dying, Brandon."

Brandon stopped, but didn't turn back. He waited.

Gordon said, "Pancreatic cancer. It's aggressive. Four months, if I'm lucky. I-I know I don't deserve your—or Brianna's, especially Brianna's—forgiveness, but I want to apologize for… for everything. I want to explain—not excuse—my behavior. So you can at least understand what made me such a-a monster."

Brandon stood on what felt more like a precipice than a doorway for a long moment. He hated this man. He hated everything he represented. Yet, something inside him needed to hear—needed to know—the *why*. At last, he spoke.

"Nine o'clock. Here, tonight. I can't promise Brianna will come, but I'll be here. After that, we're done with you."

"Fair enough, son—*Brandon*. See you then."

Brandon didn't bother with a response and went straight to the bar. He ordered a beer and requested a menu. After he placed his order and asked for a second beer, he played the voicemail. He knew already it would be from Brianna; she was his only missed call. The message was short and vague, but the tremor in the last words belied her attempt at calm. She knew about Gordon.

She answered on the first ring. "Where are you?"

"I saw him, Bri," said Brandon. Sibling verbal shorthand had benefits such as cutting right to the point.

"And?"

"And he wants to meet. He's dying, Bri."

"So? What does that have to do with us? Fuck him." Brianna spat a few more expletives.

When she finished, he said, "I'm meeting him at Lucky Loo's tonight at nine. Not for him, for me. I want—"

"Oh, for fuck's sake, do not say closure, Brandon. Closure is for television dramedies. Not real life. In real life, Brandon, there is no *closure*. There's moving on despite the fucking baggage."

He sighed and waited out the rest of her tirade, electing to not bring up her use of the same word not to long ago. When she took a breath, he said, "You may be right. I don't know, Bri. But I'm doing it anyway, and I'd feel a lot better if I had you with me. It's okay if you don't want to, I'll understand."

She swore some more, then huffed. "I've got to pick up Cassidy and Archer. I-I'll call you later."

He couldn't be positive she'd come, but his gut told him she couldn't resist an opportunity to tell Gordon to rot in hell. In the meantime, he had six hours and three musicians to survive before he had to referee that battle. He paid his tab, collected their food, and called Feather Anne.

She answered with, "Please say you're on your way. I'm about to die of starvation."

"I am on my way," confirmed Brandon. "So, you'll never guess who I just—"

The wail of an electric guitar pierced his eardrum and Feather Anne shouted, "Holy shit, dude. That sounds sick." To Brandon she said, "Hang on, babe."

He could make out the voices of Kade and Nick, the thumps of the bass drum, and muffled conversation. Then it sounded like Feather Anne dropped her phone. A second later, she was back. "Sorry dropped my—" The next words got drowned out by the sudden cacophony of instruments. She yelled louder, "I dropped my phone. What were you saying?"

He shouted too. "I said, you'll never guess who I—"

"I can't hear a word you're saying," hollered Feather Anne.

"Forget it, I'll tell you when I get there."

"Just tell me when you get here, okay?"

Brandon disconnected the call. No point in screaming it when he'd be back there in under fifteen minutes. He walked through the empty parking lot and climbed back into the truck cab. When the engine stuttered to life, music blared from the speakers, and he sprang forward to turn it off. He killed the engine and the weight of the silence enveloped him. Brandon stared out the windshield, seeing nothing. His gaze fell to a blank scrap of notepad paper on the dash. He slid it toward him, onto the center console, and grabbed a pen from the cupholder.

Without thinking, he wrote...

Empty parking lots. Empty soul. He's an empty man looking to come home.

Brandon stared at the words until they blurred. Then he crumpled the paper into a ball, tossed in in the back of the cab, and restarted the truck. *He* wasn't the empty man. He had a life and people who loved him, and his girl and her band waiting for him. Fuck Gordon Bourdreau. Fuck him.

34 Mae

It relieved Mae to see she'd arrived home before Jared. On the way, Lotus called and asked if the twins could join them for a kid's yoga class and dinner, which Mae agreed to. The further away from this strange situation, the better. At least for the time being.

She had a few things to prepare before Jared showed, one of which involved the envelope wedged in her mailbox, the other, William's office safe. It was a room she rarely entered after her husband died. The last time had been one week after William passed.

***

James—William's long-time friend and publisher—had spent a considerable length of time in William's home office in the dreadful days after he died. Mae had thought nothing of it, but about a week after the funeral, James asked her to join him.

They sat together on the old leather sofa nestled in the book alcove. "William had some instructions for me should he... pass unexpectedly. Mostly to do with manuscripts and his work in progress, that kind of thing. You can see any of it, any time you want. None of it is secret. Not from you, at least."

Mae listened without concern. She knew James as an honorable man and a loyal friend to both William and her, and a loving partner to her Aunt Katrina. He would do what was right and necessary with William's work.

She placed her hand over his. "I trust you to handle it, James."

He'd patted her hand and smiled. "Thank you, my dear. This has been... well, no need to tell you." He blinked away fresh tears.

"You said *mostly*. Is there something else I should know about?"

James looked out the window that overlooked the back yard. When he faced her again, his expression seemed apologetic. Mae's heart fluttered as her mind leaped to conclusions. William had a whole other life. A secret love child. An affair. James must have seen the alarm in her eyes and reassured her.

"It's nothing bad, Mae. At least, it's not likely to be. It's just something I can't figure out and I need your help."

"Okay," said Mae. "What is it?"

James pulled an envelope from his blazer pocket and handed it to her. On it, in William's neat script, the words, *"For J., if needed."* The flap of the envelope wasn't sealed, just folded into the pouch. Mae opened it and pulled out a rectangular slip of paper. It was a check. The amount written on the line widened her eyes.

"Do you know anything about it? It's signed, but not dated."

"And it's not made out to anyone," added Mae. "No, William never mentioned this. This isn't our regular account, either."

"So, you don't know who this *J* is, or why William would give him or her a ten-thousand-dollar check?"

Mae shook her head and peered inside the envelope for a note.

"There's nothing else. No letter or explanation anywhere," said James. "I found a file for the bank account in the safe; it has all the login information. I'm leaving it for you to investigate, so I have no idea what's in the account."

Mae said nothing. She could only stare dumbfounded and queasy at the check. Who could *J* be? A woman? Her mind raced back to impossible possibilities. Could her beloved husband... no, she would not believe it of him. Neither would James.

"Mae, I've never met a man more in love with his wife and children. He loved his life with you. He'd never, ever be unfaithful. I'd stake my life on it."

James spoke the truth she already knew in her heart. William Grant's love for her was unquestionable, as was his morality. Yet it still begged the questions. Who *was J, and why had her husband written an undated, signed check to them*?

As much a puzzle as the vague information was, Mae's grief pushed it aside for more pressing matters like her children and her own broken heart. She replaced the check in the envelope, the envelope back in the safe, and vowed she'd deal with it later. It turned out, later meant a year's time.

35 Bruce

"So, you talked to the guy? What's he like?" Nick tossed his father a beer from the fridge.

Bruce caught it and cracked the tab. "Damned if I know. Acted exhausted, so I set him up on the couch, and he was gone in the morning when I got up. Next time I saw him, it was with everybody else at breakfast." Bruce shook his head, took a sip of beer, and muttered, "Strutting into the café for breakfast with the family like he belonged there."

Nick leaned against the counter and shrugged. "I dunno, Pop. He seemed kinda, I don't know, shy or whatever."

"Whose side you on, dude?"

Nick spun a kitchen chair and straddled it. "Pop, c'mon. *Your* side, hundred percent. Just—you know—you might be over the top on this because it's Mae involved."

"Yeah, well—"

"Face it, man. You're jealous and freaking out that this dude is a clone of her dead husband. What, you think she's, like, going to fall for him, or something?"

"No," blurted Bruce. "Yes. Fuck, I don't know. All I know is, I don't trust him, and Mae shouldn't either."

Nick shook back his hair and grinned. "What's that saying? Something like, don't take kindness for weakness? Mae's a badass, Pop. She's a sweetheart, but she's never struck me a stupid."

Bruce had to agree. "Yeah. Yeah, you're right, kid. When the hell'd you get so smart?"

Nick brushed imaginary dirt from his shoulder and said, "What can I say? I'm a guy with beauty and brains."

He gave his son a Feather Anne worthy eye roll, then clacked his beer against Nick's. "Don't get carried away, Hollywood."

"It's Mr. Hollywood. No, actually, it's Mr. Nashville." He dropped his head in his hand and laughed. "What am I saying? I burned those bridges. Guess I'm Mr. Chance from here on out."

Bruce dismissed Nick's self-deprecated lament. "Bullshit, kid. You're talented as fuck. If anything, you'll put Chance on the music industry map. Listen, you took a risk and leap of faith here for all the right reasons. I'm proud of you."

Nick shrugged him off, but the smile on his face was enough to tell Bruce he appreciated the atta boy. Maybe Bruce didn't have the right—he'd only been in Nick's life a few years—but seeing the man he'd become made him damn proud. He'd come into Chance as a punk kid with a chip on his shoulder and grew into a thoughtful, caring, and immensely talented man. Sometimes Bruce wondered if Nick had a clue of how much he had to offer the world.

Like his father, Nick seemed to be unlucky in love—ironically falling for the sister of the woman Bruce loved—and he could only hope Nick accepted Feather Anne's choice as he'd accepted Mae's choice of William. The more he thought about it, the parallels were so obvious. Was it nature or nurture that his son ended up in a similar love triangle—for lack of a better term—as his father?

"Yo, earth to Pops. I'm going back to the studio in a few. I just needed to grab my spare amp from my room. You need anything before I go?"

"Sorry. Lost in thought. Nah, I'm good. Go do your thing," said Bruce.

When Nick left the kitchen, Bruce checked his phone for the umpteenth time. Still no message or calls from Mae. She wanted him to let her handle the Jared situation, and he was trying like hell to abide by her wishes even though it made him crazy. His phone rang in his hand and he answered it before seeing the caller ID.

"Mae?"

"Uh, hey, Bruce. It's Joel. Bad time?"

"Hey, yeah, no. I'm good, it's good. What's up?"

"Okay, so I'm not gonna beat around the bush here. This Jared? Bad news. No outstanding warrants—so my hands are tied—but he's got a record. Petty larceny, check fraud, few misdemeanors. Nothing too serious but enough to paint a picture and it ain't a pretty one."

Bruce's lips formed a tight line. He'd hoped for an outstanding warrant, so they could get rid of him, but the rap sheet should incriminate him enough to convince Mae to kick him to the curb. He prayed.

"So, do you think he's dangerous?" Being a criminal was bad enough, but if he represented a physical threat to Mae, Feather Anne, or the twins... well, it would be Bruce that Joel would be arresting before the day's end.

Joel hedged. "Hard to say, Bruce. He's obviously not averse to illegal activity, but that doesn't make him violent, you know?"

"That's Chief Joel talking. What does my friend of over twenty years have to say?" Bruce waited; confident he'd get real talk from his buddy.

Joel exhaled hard against the receiver. "My opinion—off the record—is you need to get that shitbag away from Mae." He added, "And don't do it illegally, my friend."

"Well, I'm sure I can do it in a way that can't be proven by—"

"Stop. Don't say another word, Grady. Any issues you call me direct. You hear?"

"Yes, sir, Chief," said Bruce.

"Dickhead," laughed Joel. "Talk to you later."

Bruce laughed as he disconnected, but the laughter dried up as he imagined Mae alone with Jared. He looked at the time. The twins would be home from school unless she had Gina or Chris pick them up. He hoped to hell that's what she'd done. The thought of that creep around Evvie and TK made him want to punch a wall. The thought of him laying a hand on Mae made him want to rip the hinges off the door, grab him by the throat, and...

"Fuck this. I'm going over there."

36 Miles

Miles stared into his newborn's puffy but alert eyes for the first time and let the tears from his own eyes fall unchecked. Before any of his children were born, he'd have sworn love at first sight didn't exist. Now, he'd tell that past version of himself to wait until he met his children, and he'd realize love at first sight absolutely existed.

"So, Mr. Hannaford, what are we naming our son?" Rosabelle lay exhausted but more beautiful than ever against the pillows propped behind her.

"Our son," repeated Miles. "Our *son.*" Miles wasn't often speechless, but he had no words worthy of the magnitude of his love for his family. Nor did he have a name in mind for his son.

He sat on the edge of the bed beside Rosie and positioned their swaddled boy so they both could gaze at his tiny face. The handful of names they'd bantered over the months all seemed wrong suddenly. *Nathaniel. Nicholas. Shawn. Michael. Evan.* None of them fit their son. They'd done the same with their girls—made a short list of possibilities and chose what they felt suited them best on the day of their births—but it had been easy; they just *knew.*

Miles had never cared much for his own name— a moniker passed through the generations on his mother's side—and decided long before this baby that, if he had a son, he would not carry on the tradition. He wanted his son to have a strong name; that much he felt certain about.

Rosie stared at them, father and son, with a thoughtful smile. She caressed the baby's cheek. "What about..." She tilted her head. "What about Max? It's simple, I know. But he just—"

"He looks like a Max. You're right. *Max,*" repeated Miles twice more. On the third time, he smiled and said, "Hi, Max. Welcome to the world."

"Welcome to the world, Max," echoed Rosie. "Can you call my mom for me? Let her know her new grandson is here."

Miles reached in his pocket for his phone with his free hand and saw a text from Nora. A quick glance told him it was about Brianna Baker's kid brother and the prospective property deal. He didn't need to read it; it didn't matter anymore. Specifically, his desire to one up Brianna Baker didn't matter anymore.

"Everything all right, Miles?" Rosie watched him, a small crease in the center of her brow.

He swiped the message away and grinned at his wife. "Better than all right. Everything is perfect, and I plan on keeping it that way. No more looking for trouble where there isn't any."

"Well, if you're referring to what I think you're referring to, then good. I'm glad."

Miles had no doubt his wife knew exactly what he was talking about. Rosie always could see right inside his brain. He didn't mind it one bit, either. She had a way of making his life easier and his worries fewer. The least he could do was reciprocate.

He also didn't mind the amusing fact that the self-proclaimed onetime wallflower had tamed the often-proclaimed perpetual playboy with little more than a smile... and perhaps some patience. A lot of patience. This was his life, his everything. Wife, children, crazy dog, crazier in-laws, house... *home*. It was more than enough to keep him occupied for the rest of his life. The future he envisioned wasn't guaranteed, but that only made the goal more precious.

Miles wanted to say all of this to Rosie, but the words balled into a lump in his throat. He looked into her eyes, and Rosie took his hand. She nodded, and said, "Me, too." And that, to Miles, was everything.

37 Brianna

She left Marlene's house lighter than how she'd gone in. No surprise. Marlene had a knack for knowing what to say... and what *not* to say. For instance, when Brianna told her Gordon was in town, Marlene did not say, "You should talk to him, get closure." Nor did she say, "Don't see him, he's a piece of shit."

Marlene instead made her a cup of strong coffee and sat at the opposite end from her on the couch. She folded one leg under her bottom, slung an arm over the couch back, and said, "So, if you were to meet with him, what would you say?"

Brianna blurted the first words that came to mind. "I'd tell him to go fuck himself. Then I'd tell him to get the fuck out of Chance."

"Fair enough. Will that satisfy you?" Marlene sipped her coffee and gazed at Brianna with her no-nonsense eyes.

"Yes. No. I don't know," admitted Brianna.

Marlene warmed her hands around the mug and seemed to consider for a moment. "Okay. Let me ask you this—and you don't have to answer, just think about it—if he's giving you this opportunity to tell him off, maybe it's worth hearing what *he's* got to say." She held out a hand. "I'm not saying he deserves it. In fact, this isn't about him, and what he needs or wants. It's about you and Brandon."

"Yeah, but if I—we—give him a shot at telling his side of things, it's like..." Brianna struggled for the words.

Marlene helped. "It's like you're giving him a pass. I get it. Listen, do what feels right to you. I'm not encouraging or discouraging this powwow. All I'm saying is, if you meet with him, you're doing it for yourself, not him."

Brianna frowned but nodded. "I suppose I *am* curious how he became such a pile of human waste."

"You hold all the power here, Bri. Don't like the direction it's going? Walk away. Any control he had over you and your family is long gone. From the sounds of it, he's in no condition to put up much of a fight."

Brianna's gaze narrowed. "So, you think I should talk to him."

Marlene leaned toward the coffee table and set her mug down. Then she folded her arms, tucked her chin to her chest, and looked at Brianna from beneath her dark lashes. "I am saying no such thing, and you know it. Pros and cons. That's all I got for you." She sat up and ticked off her two lists. "Pro. You get to tell him to fuck off once and for all. Pro. You maybe find out what the hell his deal was. Pro—and I know you hate the word—closure. Con. You get upset or pissed off. Con. You don't get the answers you were hoping for. Con. No closure."

She spread her hands out, palms up, and shrugged. Classic Marlene. She'd make an excellent hostage negotiator if cause ever came her way. Being in Chance, the odds stacked against it. Even though it might be selfish of her, Brianna hoped Marlene never left her job in their quaint, mostly crime free town for the excitement of a city police department.

Brianna next said something that rarely came out of her mouth. "Enough about me. Tell me what's new with you. How are things going with Joanne?"

A smile lit Marlene's serious face. "Things are good. Very good, actually. She's moving in."

Brianna clapped her hands together. "It's about damn time. When you two get married, I happen to know of a *phenomenal* event coordinator."

"Whoa, whoa. Slow down, crazy. Let's see how this goes first. And yes, I wouldn't dream of using anyone other than B. Baker Events for our special day."

"Excellent. I really need to expand my clientele. I've had three gay weddings, but not one lesbian."

Marlene had been about to take a sip of her coffee and almost spilled it. She shook her head, laughing. "Well, glad to be your token lesbian couple, I guess."

"Oh, don't pretend you're offended. But just so you know, I refuse any décor involving flannel. And don't you dare go cutting off all your hair." Brianna smirked, knowing this would get a mock rise out of her friend.

"Oh, come on," said Marlene. "I could be Ellen to Joanne's Portia. Isn't that, like, you're only lesbian couple point of reference, anyhow?"

Brianna shrugged one shoulder. "I know of several lesbian couples."

One of Marlene's eyebrows arched. "Oh, yeah? Name one."

Brianna couldn't. After much teasing from Marlene, the two women stood and walked to the door. "Well, as usual, you set my mind straight. Thank you."

Marlene leaned against the frame and looked at her unexpected friend. "So, what's the verdict? You meeting him tonight or what?"

Brianna gazed out at the blue sky for a long moment. "Yeah. I think I am."

As she drove through town toward home—where her husband and children awaited—Brianna came to some conclusions about herself. She was not the forgive and forget type, but *might* she be the give a chance type?

For so long, Gordon Bourdreau had been the proverbial monster under the bed and source of her real nightmares. Had that become an excuse or a crutch for her to continue the unending blame laying? And by doing so, had she allowed herself to be a victim of circumstance, rather than her own destiny master as she claimed to be?

She allowed herself to consider a time where she could let go of that heavy weight and just live her life. Logic told her the only way to do that was to—it boggled her mind to think it—to forgive.

Was it so simple a matter as that stupid meme she saw on Facebook suggested? *Forgive, not for those who hurt you, but for your own peace*. She'd rolled her eyes when she saw it—Charlotte posted it—and dismissed it. She could not dismiss the irony of its timing. Did that mean it served as a sign? Her practical nature rejected such folly.

Brianna's other internal voice spoke up to say, *there's no such thing as coincidences*. Reading a quote about forgiveness on the morning her dead-to-her father returned to Chance *could* be viewed as no coincidence… if Brianna allowed the notion. But then she'd have to allow for a higher power. Wouldn't she?

Her hypocrite father's zealous faith had pushed her away from church as much as his abuse had. She blamed it as much as him for every awful thing that ever happened. Then, out of nowhere, a faint childhood memory squeezed its way through the cracks.

The empty church. Her ballet flats soft tip-tap on the gleaming plank floor between the pews. The warm, breathy, undulating melody of the organ in the church loft. The smell of lemon wax and snuffed candles. The beautiful stained glass.

Yes, there *had* been a time when she'd loved it. How had she forgotten such a beloved memory? Every week, in the hour after the last mass, Father Thomas tasked her with replacing the candles in the devotional alcove while he and her father talked church business in his office. Often, the church organist, Lydia, practiced while Brianna carried out her work.

In that one brief hour, with the still church all hers, she felt closer to God than during any sermon. But the many prayers she'd sent up to Him had gone unanswered and her love turned to disappointment, then resentment. She long ago rejected the promise that prayers were answered in mysterious ways, but now—all these years later—Brianna wondered if Ricky had been one of those mysterious ways.

They'd known one another their whole lives, but when exactly was it they developed feelings for each other? With a jolt, Brianna realized it was in the same year she'd given up on God.

No, it was the same day.

Even as she doubted it, she knew it to be true. It was the night of her thirteenth birthday. Earlier in the day, her parents had thrown a party. All her friends had come, including Ricky Baker. Like every other girl, she thought Ricky was cute. *Un*like every other girl, she hadn't the same reaction to Bruce Grady. For her, it had always been Ricky.

Brianna never knew if Gordon had overheard the girls talking about the boys, or whether he'd seen or imagined something between them, but when the party ended and all the guests went home, the jovial demeanor fell away and the real Gordon emerged.

"Did you have a good time, Brianna?"

He smiled at her from the doorway, but his eyes were cold with fury. Brianna backed up into the kitchen. It was no use; in three swift steps Gordon had a fistful of her hair and had dragged her down the basement stairs by it. She struggled against him, but silently, so as not to alarm her baby brother.

Hours later, when the house fell even more silent than usual, and her parents and brother slept, Brianna heard tapping on the small basement window. Her head jerked up and her eyes met Ricky's through the glass. She froze in disbelief, then fear made her shush him as she scurried to the window, grabbing a footstool on the way across the dim basement.

She cranked open the cobwebbed casement and hissed, "What are you doing here?"

Ricky grinned and ducked his head. "I didn't get to give you this." He held up a square box. The wrapping was silver, the bow black. She liked him infinitely more for the black bow. Everyone else had used pink. She hated pink.

Brianna smiled despite her many aches from her father's punishment. Being locked in the basement overnight only served as part two of her penance for having the audacity to talk to boys under his roof.

Ricky stared at her funny. "Bri? It's after midnight. What are you doing in the basement?"

Brianna stammered. "I—it's—I thought I heard a noise, so I came down to look." He looked down at her clothes; she still wore her party outfit. To distract him, she blurted, "Well, give me the box, dummy."

Together, they worked the screen up enough to slip their hands through. As Brianna took the box from Ricky, her sleeve fell back and exposed the angry bruises. An unmistakable handprint ringed her forearm.

Ricky's eyes bulged. "Bri, what the—"

"It's nothing. I fell." She yanked her arm back and fixed her sleeve. So she wouldn't have to see his expression, Brianna made a fuss of opening the box, being careful not to tear the paper or wreck the bow.

Inside was a delicate silver chain with a lock pendant. She looked up at Ricky, her brow drawn together, and head tilted. Ricky reached inside the collar of his shirt and extracted a thick silver chain. Hanging from it, a small silver key. Slow smiles spread across both faces.

"Bri, I've liked you since fourth grade. Only you. Will you be my girlfriend?"

Brianna had said yes, and from that night until all the years later, he'd been her champion, confidante, and protector. He'd stayed at that basement window until the sun crept over the horizon, so she wouldn't be alone. She told him everything, and he never gave her cause to regret it.

Brianna dabbed the corner of her eye and her hand instinctively felt at her throat for the little lock that wasn't there, but kept safe in her jewelry box beside Ricky's chain and key. She looked out her windshield, then out her driver's and passenger side windows in wonder.

So lost in her memories she'd been, that her subconscious led her to the least likely place of all. St. Paul's church stood before her; its ornate arched doors propped open as it if knew she was coming.

"All right, then. Message received. I guess it's time to say thank you, isn't it?"

As if by answer, Father Thomas appeared. His hands rested clasped in front of him, and he seemed to be looking at Brianna, a gentle smile on his lips. If the signs weren't clear enough, the sun broke through the clouds and cast a beam of light on him and the stairs.

"Yeah, yeah. You've made your point. I'm coming, show off." She grumbled, but she also smiled as she turned off the ignition and climbed out of her car.

At the foot of the stairs, she squinted up at Father Thomas. "It's been a while, Father."

Father Thomas's smile widened. "It's never too late to come home."

38 Feather Anne

She could see it the moment he walked in; something was wrong. Brandon waved the bags in the air at them and called out with a convincing cheer, "Come an' get it, you animals," but he made eye contact with no one. Not even her.

Feather Anne attacked the contents of the bags with no less enthusiasm than Kade or Nick, but she also tried to get Brandon's attention. It was to no avail. He went straight to the soundboard and dicked around with the knobs as if he were performing surgery. With burger in hand, she made her way around the two resident idiots wrestling over a container of onion rings and sidled next to Brandon.

"What's up?" She took a bite then waved it at him. "You eat?"

He glanced at the burger, shook his head, and said, "Nah. All good. You guys eat." More messing around with the buttons and levers.

"Dude, what's going on?" Feather Anne stuck her face in front of his, so he'd be forced to look at her. That's when she smelled the beer on him. "Have you been drinking?"

"Easy, killer. It was one beer, maybe two while I waited for the food."

"Hey, I was just asking. God. So, you gonna tell me what's wrong? And don't say nothing. I know you, Brandon. I can tell when something is wrong, okay?"

He raked back his hair and exhaled through his mouth. "Sorry, yeah. I, uh, ran into—"

"Dude, check out this sick riff," yelled Nick. He'd scarfed down his meal and already had his guitar slung in front of him.

Kade jumped up, tossed his wrapper over his shoulder and yelled, "Fuckin' sweet. But you need a kick ass beat to follow. Yo, Feather Anne, come on. Grab the mic."

"Hang on a sec," said Feather Anne over the racket. She returned her attention to Brandon, but he'd already gone back to adjusting the levels.

"Go on," he said, "It's not important."

"Are you sure? You seem—"

"I'm fine, babe. Let's get some more tracks down."

Part of her said to stay right there and force him to talk. But the music beckoned her like a lover, and she'd never been able to say no to that call. Feather Anne dropped the hardly eaten burger back into the bag, wiped her mouth, and grabbed a tambourine.

It was hours and night had fallen before she realized that Brandon had snuck out somewhere during the session. "Hey, did you guys see Brandon leave? He say anything to you?"

Kade and Nick both shrugged and shook their heads. "Chill. He'll be back," said Kade.

"I'm gonna run back to my place for my other guitar. You guys keep working."

She and Kade gave a go at songwriting, but their styles didn't mesh, and they soon gave up in favor of the acoustic guitars. They picked and strummed a while, but mostly they talked.

"So, tell me—honestly—you think this," he gestured around them, "is something? Like, I mean, going to be something?"

Without hesitation, Feather Anne said, "Yeah, Kade. I do. I think it—we're—going to be something big. Everyone just has to keep their shit straight, though."

Kade said nothing for a long while and kept strumming. Then he surprised her. "It's our boy Brandon we gotta watch. You feel me?"

Feather Anne bristled. "No. Why would you say that? Brandon is the most solid, dependable, honest, giving, good man I know. He cares more about this than any of us."

Kade looked her dead in the eyes, his trademark Cheshire grin smile absent, and said, "Exactly my point, m'lady. He ain't like us scrappers. Doesn't have the thick skin." He rubbed his thumb and forefinger together to emphasize.

It was Feather Anne's turn to fall silent. She wanted to argue; tell Kade he had no idea what he was talking about. But something in her knew it was true. And it wasn't a weakness in Brandon, but a gentleness.

She gave Kade a hard look. "Then it's our job to protect him. We protect each other. All of us. Are you cool with that? Because it can't be any other way, Kade. I've seen what this business does to people."

Kade held her gaze, reached out his fist, and said, "All in, baby."

Feather Anne bumped her fist against his and nodded. "All in."

Nick strolled through the open garage door, guitar on his shoulder and a six pack of beer dangling from his fingers. "Yo, people. The life of the party is back." He looked around. "Where's our sound guy?"

Feather Anne said, "Dunno." She checked her phone. "No text, no message. Did he seem weird to you guys before?"

Kade and Nick exchanged baffled looks. Nick said, "Seemed fine to me. Shit, maybe he, like, told us he had to go somewhere, and we forgot."

Kade said, "We *were* playing pretty loud earlier. Let's just keep playing until he comes back."

Feather Anne looked at the time and debated. "All right. For a little while longer." Before she joined them, she texted Brandon one more time. Maybe Kade and Nick were right, and she read too much into things. But then the echoes of her and Kade's conversation came back.

It's our boy Brandon we gotta watch. He ain't like us scrappers. Doesn't have the thick skin.

She reached for her phone again to call him.

"Dude, come one," called Kade. "We need our female lead."

"We're dying over here. Save us, Byrd." Nick made his guitar whine.

"Idiots. You're both idiots. I'm coming, Jesus."

Feather Anne pushed her unease to the back of her mind. Not because Kade and Nick called to her, but because the music did. It was her drug of choice, and she was its addict. Music had saved her from an ordinary life. A sneaky voice in the recess of her mind whispered one question before she drowned it out with song. *Would music be Brandon's salvation... or his downfall?*

39 Gina

"She's a smart girl, Chris. I'm not worried. Much, I mean." Gina paced their kitchen, a cup of black coffee and a stirrer pinched between her fingers. A phantom cigarette.

"Yeah, I can see you're not worried. Can you sit, please? You're making me dizzy."

Gina didn't sit. Not right away, at least. She hated being told what to do. She also hated not feeling in control. That was the thing about recovery; feeling out of control led to *being* out of control.

Once she refilled her coffee mug, she sat across from Chris. He watched her with a mix of amusement, understanding, and his unending patience. "You saw it, too, right? The guy isn't right. Those eyes. Right? But Mae's no sucker. She won't fall for the sob story. Right? Maybe we should go over there. Or call. Right?"

Chris sipped his tea.

"Jesus, I hope she's not letting him meet the twins. Do you think she is? Should I say something or just keep my mouth shut? I should stay out of it. Mae's got more mother's instinct on her worst day than I've ever had on my best."

Here, Chris spoke up. "Past is the past, Gi. You're a great mom to both your girls and they love you." Gina grunted and raised her mug to hide her grin. He saw it, but whatever. He continued. "And I'd say your mom instincts are spot on. That Jared dude is a creep, all right. And you know me, babe. I like to see the best in everyone. I see nothing good in him."

"So, you think I should call? Or go over? Maybe I should just, like, pop by or... no, *you* should go over the house. Yeah. Bring your toolbox and say, I don't know, you wanted to fix the dryer for her."

Chris scratched his chin and looked at the ceiling. "Well, she did say it was making a funny sound the other day. I guess I—"

"Perfect," said Gina. She jumped up and dashed to the counter. "Here are your keys. Call me when you get there. No, text me and tell me what's going on. That way you can say more."

Chris caught the keys against his chest and stammered. "Oh, I, uh, now?"

"Yes, *now*, Chris. They're alone in that house. I can't believe Bruce has just dropped the ball on this. How is he not over there right now?"

"Maybe he is. Have you—"

"Obviously, I texted him. He is home, wallowing in self-pity. God damn man-child. Why are you still here? Go, Chris." Gina shoved him toward the door.

She watched him back out of the driveway, then took the dog out back with her. "Go on, Rutger. Run, enjoy being a dog with no worries. Must be nice." Rutger whined and wagged his tail, staring up at her with doleful eyes. "Okay, fine. Come back inside with me. We'll pace together."

Instead of pacing, Gina took out her mixing bowls and ingredients for Feather Anne's favorite cookies. White chocolate macadamia. She and Brandon were coming over in the morning. Maybe she'd invite Mae and Bruce, too. With any luck, the William wanna-be would be gone. She could only hope.

It seemed like every time life settled down, some new catastrophe came up to shake her world. It wasn't fair. Gina paused mid-stir to appreciate the childish irony of her thoughts. Since when did she think life was *fair*? Damn, she'd gotten soft over the years.

To Rutger, she said, "That's what happens when you have a family to give a shit about. And family who gives a shit about *you*." Rutger licked his chops and wiggled his butt against the floor. "No, you can't have any of this, old boy. You're fat enough."

Rutger snuffed and snorted, then sprawled out on the living room floor. Gina resumed her baking... and thinking. Even though the dog showed his disinterest, she mused out loud. Silence still irked her.

"I've got both my girls home. Two gorgeous grandkids. A man who loves the shit out of me. And I even have my own business. What the fuck am I bitching about, then? Huh, Rutger? Why do I have to look for trouble?"

Gina deepened her voice. "Well, Gina, it's probably because until these last half-dozen years or so, your life was shit, and now you're terrified of it ever going back that way. Oh and woof."

She resumed her normal voice. "Gee, thanks, Rutger. You're pretty insightful for a dog. Do you have any advice for me to help manage those fears?"

"Sure, Gina," she said in her Rutger voice, "you should probably just calm the fuck down and enjoy this good time in life instead of worrying about shit you can't control. And we're almost out of dog food, FYI."

Gina chuckled at her own silliness. Her Rutger voice—okay, fine, her subconscious—was right, she had to calm the fuck down and live in the present. She also had to stop walking on eggshells around her daughters. They'd both told her repeatedly they would not toss her aside at the first sign of trouble, and they'd both proven themselves good on their word.

Even when Feather Anne was pissed off at her for accidentally talking to the press, she'd said, "I can't talk to you right now. And don't freak out, I just need time to calm down." Gina *had* freaked out and fallen off the wagon—albeit briefly—before pulling herself back together with the help of Chris and Mae.

Gina Byrd—onetime town loser—was now Gina Byrd, loved and accepted, faults, flaws, and all. Her only job was to not self-sabotage. For the first time, she was ready to let the past be the past—as Chris reminded her—and live in the present.

40 Mae

Mae filled the teapot with enough tea for two cups. She set the pot and cups on a tray along with a dainty sugar bowl, creamer, and spoons. Jared didn't strike her as a dainty tea man, but there was a psychology to setting a particular tone. Here, Mae set the tone for civility, gentility, and a not-so-subtle aloofness.

From the living room, Jared cleared his throat and asked, "Is there—can I help you with anything?"

"Thank you, no. All set," said Mae as she walked in with the tray.

She positioned it between them on the coffee table and sat an arm's length away from Jared. Without asking if he wanted any, Mae poured him a cup. Her father, Keith, had taught her this. *"When someone comes into your home serve tea. Theirs power and magic in that simple act. I can't explain it, it just is."* She couldn't explain it either, but it proved true.

Jared accepted the offered cup. A smile wavered on his lips and his eyes darted to and away from Mae's face.

He rarely makes eye contact.

Keith had also taught her to be wary of anyone who can't look others in the eye... unless they have a valid reason. Mae had no cause to think Jared had Asperger's or another condition that made eye contact a challenge, but Mae attempted to excuse it as shyness until she had more information.

Now she had confirmation Jared Simon was of questionable character. And yet, it pained her to send him away. Of the little he told; he spoke the truth. His biological mother gave him up soon after birth, grew up in the foster care system, and had no familial connections. Most importantly, he *was* William's half-brother. For this alone, she'd been compelled to act.

After everyone had left the night before, Mae found herself unable to sleep. Something nagged at her; a memory danced in the edges of her mind. She climbed out of bed to start a pot of coffee, but gravitated toward William's office.

The door had been shut for some time, and when she opened it, William's familiar scent embraced her. She sat behind his desk and touched the objects on it. Pens and notepad, his closed laptop, the picture frames of them and the children. They all bore a fine film of dust. Her attention drifted about the room—the bookcase alcove with the worn leather sofa, the framed art on the walls, the reading lamp—until it landed and stayed on William's safe. A fragment of a memory surfaced.

... who was J, and why had her husband written an undated, signed check to them?

Mae sprang from the chair and kneeled before the square steel box. William had given her the combination—the date they met—on the same day he'd brought it home. She extracted the envelope and the bank account record. Clipped to the second page was a business card. The backside faced out, showing a phone number and the words *Stan, Bank.* No extension number followed, so Mae suspected it to be a personal number. She flipped it to read the front, which stated: Stan Vincelette, Investment Banker. First Premier Bank. Mae stared at the number on the back again.

One glance at the time told her not to call, her impatience commanded otherwise. A man—

sounding wide awake—picked up on the first ring. "Hello. Stan Vincelette speaking."

"Good morning. I-I'm sorry to call so early, but... did you know William Grant?"

The man's tone warmed. He'd said, "Hello, Mae. I wondered if I'd ever hear from you. Yes, I knew your William. Sorry for your loss. He was an exceptional guy."

"Oh," was all she'd managed around the lump lodged in her throat.

He'd continued. "I take it you've found the letter, then?"

Mae's brow creased. "Letter? No, I—there was only a signed, blank check for ten-thousand dollars. Oh, and the bank info with your number. I'm sorry, but how did you know my husband?"

Stan Vincelette explained how he and William had met in New York many years ago at an author convention—William had been promoting a recent release, Stan had just started writing his first novel— and become friendly. They exchanged contact information—Stan had given him his business card with his personal number—and confessed William's request surprised him.

"I'm an investment banker, so this was out of my lane. But because of your husband's advice and help with my novel—for free and on his own time, mind you—I felt compelled to pay him back somehow. I don't know if I'd have completed it without him."

Mae had smiled as she walked to the bookcase and found the spine bearing the name Stan Vincelette. The book title—*The Banker's Tale*—gave Mae a chuckle. The inscription inside read, "*To William. Without your help, this book would've never seen the light of day.*"

"We *have* met. I remember now," said Mae. "The gala thrown by James McKenna a few years ago."

They'd mused over the meeting for a few minutes, then Mae turned the subject back to William's check. Stan picked back up where he'd left off. "About six months of corresponding—book stuff, mostly—William called with his unusual request. He said he discovered he had a half-brother—sorry, I don't know the specific details on that part—and after some research, decided not to reach out to the man."

"How long ago was this?" Mae's puzzled why William chose not to mention his finding.

"About a year and a half ago. He said he didn't expect the guy—the half-brother—ever reaching out, but he wanted to be prepared. A-actually, his words were, *If I'm gone, I want Mae to get rid of him without too much production.*"

There'd been a rustling of papers and muffled sounds on Stan's end for a moment, then he exclaimed, "Ah-ha. Mystery solved. I have the letter,

Mae. He must've sent it by accident when he sent me the other form."

Mae asked, "Other form?"

"Yes. He stipulated that if this Jared fellow accepted the check, he had to sign an agreement to never contact you or your family again. We meant to get together again—so I could give him back the papers after the lawyer looked at them—but then..."

"Then William died," finished Mae.

"Listen, I've got to pass through Chance today anyhow. How about I drop these off to you and you can read the letter for yourself?"

Mae had thanked him for his help, and they'd ended the call. Stan was true to his word, and the envelope in her mailbox had come from him. In it, a folder holding William's letter of explanation and the agreement form. A quick read told her what she'd needed to know.

William had discovered a correspondence between his father and a mystery woman about a child born out of their affair. His disgust and embarrassment over the discovery kept him from bringing it up to Mae, but his curiosity made him seek information on the child who by blood was his half-brother. Once he learned the whereabouts and lifestyle of his younger half-sibling, he decided not to facilitate a relationship.

Knowing his wife's love of family and welcoming nature as he did, William elected to spare

Mae the story. Or so he stated in the letter. To Mae's mind, he meant sparing himself her incessant pleas to reach out to the man. The next line had caused her to laugh out loud...

"I confess, my reasons for not telling you about Jared have more to do with knowing how you love to collect strays more than anything else."

She rolled her eyes but grinned, too. It wouldn't have surprised William that she now owned six orphaned ducks and two new goats. The rest took a more somber tone. He warned against allowing sympathy to overrule sensibility, yet acknowledged his own sympathetic thoughts and a desire to right the wrong done to him by their father somehow.

"If you're reading this, it's for the obvious reasons, and I'm sorry for that. I'd hoped to spare you and the children of this... association. I trust your judgment, Mae. If you wish to allow this troubled man into your life, I'm sure you'll do so with caution. The second letter is for him. Jared. This, too, I leave to your discretion."

Mae had so little time in between opening the letter and Jared's arrival, that she hadn't a proper chance to absorb this one unexpected gift of William's return to her, even if just in letter form. The silence between her and Jared grew. Hers was of contemplation. His? Nerves, she guessed by how his leg bounced. That's what decided it for her. The leg bounce.

Whatever this man was—be it con man or not—he'd been given a raw deal in life. Even though Mae believed people had a choice in how they handled their burdens, there still lie truth in the unfairness of his past.

"I have something for you," said Mae at last.

Jared's eyebrows—so like William's—furrowed before they lifted. "Y-you do?"

She handed him the envelope with the check with his name now on the 'to' line. He placed his teacup on the tray and opened the seal. Mae watched and waited as he stared at the check. He looked at her, back at the check, and at her again.

Jared licked his lips and wiped one hand on his pants. The one holding the check trembled. "I-I don't understand." The laugh that followed sounded nervous. "Is this a joke, or something?"

"Not at all. Let me explain." Mae told him the whole story, less the assessment of his character by William and any other hurtful details.

Jared read between the lines. "So, what this is, is a payoff to go away. Basically, another blood relative saying they don't want me. Great." He stood and stalked to the door.

Mae called out to him. "Originally, yes. The decision was made to protect us, Jared. I won't lie. William learned of your... your criminal history. He suspected you might come looking for money and feared that you might scam us somehow if he..." She trailed off, cleared her throat, and restarted. "That was the original idea, yes. But *I* feel differently."

Jared paused. "What are you saying?"

"I'm saying I'm not sure I trust you, but I am sure you are family. You have a family, Jared. Here, in Chance, if you choose to be a part of it. But it's conditional."

Jared sneered. "Yeah? Let me guess. If I don't cash the check, I'm in and if I cash it, I'm out?"

Mae blinked in surprise. "Oh. No, Jared. That's yours, free and clear." She had not mentioned the form William had drawn up. "The condition is honesty. I need to know I can trust you."

"Okay." He drew the word out and studied her.

"Good. You can start by telling me what your actual plan was."

It was Mae's turn to study him. She had a good enough idea what his intentions had been. Now here was his chance to own it. He looked down at the check—still in his hand—then out the open door. Without glancing back, he walked out. Mae let out her held breath and waited until the sound of his car faded. She finished her tea before carrying the tray back to the kitchen.

Well, that's that, I suppose.

Any time Mae had ever felt out of sorts, she turned to cooking. This time was no different, and by the time she remembered Feather Anne wouldn't be home to eat, it was too late. A knock at the front door startled her.

"Knock, knock," said Chris, poking his head in.

"Come on in, Chris," said Mae.

"Oh, hey. I just, uh, came by to, uh, fix your—"

"He's gone, Chris. Text Gina and tell her before she has a fit."

Chris slumped in relief. "Oh, thank God. Your mother was making me crazy with all this. So he's gone, huh?"

Mae gestured for him to sit at the island while she opened the cupboard for plates. "Tell her I'm feeding you, too. Yes, he's gone."

She considered whether to elaborate, but the front door opened yet again. This time it was Bruce storming in. He stopped short at the sight of Mae and Chris. He spun a half circle. "Where is he?"

"Gee, I don't know, Bruce. Maybe he's out having dinner with an old flame. Oh, wait, sorry. No, that was you the other night. You know, the day you kissed me, and then—"

Chris stood up and inched toward the back doors. "Okay, well, it looks like everything is all set—"

"Sit down, Chris," said Mae.

Bruce said, "See ya later, bud."

"No, he can stay, Bruce. It's *my* house. Why don't you see what *Ophelia* is doing tonight?" She said Ophelia in a whiny, childish voice.

Bruce shoved his hands in his pockets only to yank them out and rake back his hair. He took a step toward her and stopped. Mae could see he was near bursting with wanting to say whatever it was he had to say, so she goaded him more. Mostly because she'd pent up all her feelings for days and she'd had enough.

Chris stammered behind them. "Yeah, so I'll just—"

"Fine, bye Chris," spat Mae.

"You can stay, Chris," said Bruce.

The pair glared at one another. Bruce found his words and shouted them at her. "You—no, I—this is... God damn it, Mae. I love you. *You*, okay? No one else. Just you. I haven't stopped thinking about that kiss since it happened, and I only left because I was afraid *you* regretted it."

"Oh, yeah?" Mae shouted back. "Well, I-I love you, too. So, there. And for your information, I did *not* regret that kiss at all until I found out you went on a date with your ex the same night." It took her a moment to realize that Bruce no longer looked angry. A big, dopey grin spread across his face. "Why are you smiling, weirdo?"

He stepped closer. "Because you said you love me. Technically, you yelled it at me, but I'm not complaining. Mae—just so I'm clear here—you love me like... a friend, or like a..."

Mae smiled, too. "Like the second choice." She stepped closer to him. There was a vague awareness of Chris in the background, but not enough to distract them.

"I only went out to dinner with Effie as friends. Nothing more, nothing else. I'm sorry I missed your text about meeting up. I'd left my phone at home, and—"

"It's fine. I'm sorry I—"

"You have nothing to apologize for, Mae. I'm a big idiot. I overreacted to that Jared guy, and—wait. We still need to talk about him. He's a real—"

"I know, Bruce. Give me a little of credit, huh? It's a bit of a long story. Wanna have dinner with me and—hey, where's Chris?"

"He snuck out somewhere in the middle of our conversation," said Bruce.

"You mean our fight," corrected Mae.

They'd taken a step closer with each exchange and now stood mere inches apart. Bruce smiled down at her, and Mae's heart knocked against her chest. Why had she held him at bay for so long—way before William had come into her life—and denied her feelings for him?

Everyone else had known what she'd been oblivious of. She and Bruce belonged together. Maybe not always—to think it would negate the wonderful years she'd had with William and the children their love created—but their time had come.

Memories flooded her mind. Bruce fixing her café roof in the rain. Their one-night stand. Him showing up at her door, drunk and professing his feelings for her. All the years after of him always being there for her, Feather Anne, and the twins.

"I never want to fight with you again, Mae." Bruce stroked her cheek and slipped his fingers through her hair.

"Well, just do everything I say, Grady, and we'll have no troubles," said Mae. She wrapped her arms around his waist.

He pulled her closer. His head bend toward hers. "Fair enough, Huxley."

Before she could reply, Bruce kissed her, and kissed him back. For once, nothing and no one interrupted them. It was Bruce who broke their embrace. He looked at her a long moment, as if trying to decide if she was real. He brushed her hair back and held her by her shoulders.

"I want to do this right, Mae. Like, with you, the kids… everything."

"Yes, of course." Her smirk belied her serious tone. "What do you propose we do, Grady?"

He nudged her. "Come on, now. I mean it."

She laughed and led him to the sofa. "Yes, yes. I know. And I agree. Bruce, I'm ready for this… for *us*. I want you to know that."

"But what about TK and Evvie? Will they be okay with this? I don't want them to be, like, freaked out or anything."

Mae squeezed his knee. "I love you for saying that, for *thinking* like that. You won't believe this, but they brought this topic up not too long ago. It was after William's memorial service, to be exact." She shifted to face him. "Evvie asked if you were my boyfriend, and when I said no, we're best friends, TK announced, *well, then he should be your boyfriend.*" She imitated his little gruff boy voice. "And Evvie chimed in with, *yeah, we already love Brucie, so he should be your boyfriend.*"

Bruce looked stunned, but he couldn't stop the huge grin from spreading across his handsome face.

God, is he handsome.

Mae had a notion to attack him right there on the sofa, but a glance at the time told her Lotus and Dylan would drop the kids off at any moment. As if her thoughts had summoned them, Evvie and TK burst through the door at full steam.

TK's casual, "Hi, Mom," turned into a whoop when he saw Bruce, and the six-year-old dove over the back of the sofa to tackle him. Evvie behaved only slightly more civilized and came around the sofa before jumping on top of the pair.

Mae extracted herself from under the flying limbs and went to greet Lotus at the door. The second Mae got close enough, Lotus grabbed her arm and tipped her head at Bruce while raising her eyebrows. Mae bobbed her head. Then she did something she hadn't done since… ever. She giggled.

This caused Lotus to do something she probably hadn't done in ages. She squealed… but quietly. The two women clasped each other's arms and stamped their feet while grinning maniacally. When they stopped, they realized Evvie, TK, and Bruce stared at them with open mouths.

"Why is Mom and Mrs. Davidson being so weird?" TK scrunched his nose at them.

"Cause they're girls," said Bruce.

Evvie punched him in the arm. "Hey, watch it, Mister."

"You tell them, honey," said Mae. "I'll walk you out," she said to Lotus.

Outside, Lotus said, "Well? Are you two, like, official?"

Mae bowed her head into her hand. "Oh, my God. I feel like… like a teenager. Yes, yes. We're… official. Whatever that means. There's still a lot to figure out, I guess. It's all brand new. I-I haven't even wrapped my brain around it yet."

"Sure, sure. But are you happy, Mae? That's what matters here."

Mae released a content sigh and nodded. "Yeah, I am. Happiest I've been since… since William died."

Lotus hugged her tight. When she stepped back, she said, "Okay, all the ladies, tomorrow, Rosabelle's house, yes?"

"Yes," exclaimed Mae. "Oh, my God, the baby. I've been so caught up with all my craziness, I haven't had a chance to do more than message her."

"Yeah, speaking of crazy, what happened with that Jared guy? It's all anyone has talked about all week."

"I'll fill everyone in tomorrow. It's a long story."

Mae thanked Lotus and went back inside. The trio still formed a tangled, laughing, shouting heap on her sofa. She clapped and called over the din. "All right, enough. You two take your bath or shower and hop in bed. I'll be in to read the next chapter in our book."

"Aw, Mom. Can Bruce read it?" TK gave Mae a hopeful, pleading look.

Evvie said, "Brucie, we're reading The Narnia Chronicles. We're on Prince Caspian. Do you know the books?"

Bruce widened his eyes. "Do I know the books? Heck, ya, I do. It's only one of the greatest series of all time." He looked at Mae, mirroring TK's expression. Evvie joined them.

"Wow. Seriously? All three of you with the puppy eyes? Fine. Take your showers and get in your jammies. *Bruce* will be in to read the next chapter."

After they'd run off, Bruce shrugged an apology. "Hope you don't mind."

"No, it's sweet."

It was more than sweet. It also made her heart hurt a little, too. The twins craved a father figure. She forgot that sometimes. But when Bruce came around, they lit up and became another version of themselves; ones more animated, physical, and exuberant.

Bruce didn't feel like a replacement for William; yes, they shared core traits like inherent goodness, integrity, and strength. Bruce added a physical energy to the equation that neither she nor William had. She didn't want to consider him their missing link; their family unit had been built on solid ground, but he most definitely made a welcome addition.

"Whatcha thinking, Mae? Are you having—"

Mae took his hand and kissed his palm before pressing it to her cheek. "No doubts. The opposite, in fact. You are one of the things in my life I feel most certain about."

The tension lines around his eyes smoothed and his shoulders dropped. "Okay. Good. I mean—"

"Shut up and kiss me, will you?"

She felt his smile against her lips. A few seconds later came the sounds of two little voices from the hall. "I told you so," loud-whispered Evvie.

"Ew, gross, kissing," loud-whispered TK.

"Shut up, it's romantical," hissed Evvie.

Bruce and Mae broke apart and faced the duo. "Sorry, guys. Are you... okay with... this?" Mae held her breath.

"Uh, yeah, Mom. Duh," said Evvie.

"Yeah, duh. It's about time," added TK. "But kissing is gross, so don't do that. You'll get germs."

"Thanks, bud. Solid advice," said Bruce.

Evvie stomped forward and grabbed Bruce's hand. "Come on, Brucie. We're ready for our book."

Bruce let her tug him down the hall, but he called over his shoulder. "I still want to hear about that other thing, you know."

She waved him off, laughing. "Yes, I know. Lots to talk about, plenty of time to do it. Go on, now."

Mae returned to the kitchen and set the forgotten dinner on the warmer. Bruce would be in there for a half hour, maybe more if the twins suckered him into a second chapter. Instead of tea, she reached for the bottle of wine and poured a generous glass.

At last, she had time to digest the rapid-fire events of the past month. William's memorial. Feather Anne's homecoming. The shocking discovery of Jared's existence. This one gave her a sad pause. He'd disappointed her by leaving, but he hadn't surprised her. Still, she'd tried, and that was all she could have done. William would have been proud, if not wary.

Her thoughts rested on Bruce. Or rather, her and Bruce. Were they an instant couple? How were they supposed to do this? They knew everything about each other already; there could be no *getting to know you* phase. Or could there be? They knew one another as friends, not lovers. Their one-night stand didn't count. Or did it? She needed to talk to someone objective.

Katrina? No. I love my aunt, but she is the farthest thing from objective. Rosabelle.

Mae reached for her phone to send a text and remembered her best friend just had a baby and Mae's latest life event might not be high on her list of interests. A new baby in their lives, how exciting. She would go through her baby clothes from TK to pass down. Unless...

A new thought dawned on her—premature as it was—would Bruce want children? If so, would *she* want another child? Her childbearing years weren't past her yet. It could happen. She wouldn't want to wait long though. Was that crazy to even think so early? They'd just professed their love less than an hour before, and her mind had traveled to babies in a blink. Ridiculous. And yet, she couldn't stop smiling.

Epilogue

One year later...

The much-anticipated wedding day arrived at long last. Some—like Georgie and Charles Brightsider—equated it with a royal wedding, much to Mae and Bruce's embarrassment. The sun broke through the clouds a few hours before the guests filled the rows of white chairs on either side of the grassy aisle. The town green's gazebo—where the vows would be taken—had been decorated with wildflower garlands.

Brianna Baker, in all her dictator glory, ordered her staff around via Bluetooth or by snapping of her fingers at whoever dared appear without a task. Mae peeked out from the bridal tent with a champagne flute clenched in her hand. It wasn't marrying Bruce that gave her anxiety.

"It's tripping down the aisle in front of everyone."

Katrina snorted, "Oh, please do."

Georgie *tsked* at Mae's aunt and patted Mae's arm. "Every bride's great fear."

"I say go barefoot," said Lotus.

"Mae, you could fall, run, or do cartwheels and no one will care so long as you two say I do," deadpanned Feather Anne.

Rosabelle gave each a withering look before using her gentle mom voice on Mae. "Sweetie, everything will go perfectly. I promise. Just breathe and remember we are all here with you to celebrate."

"Exactly," said Marisol. "Just breathe, relax, and enjoy."

Charlotte swiped a tear from her cheek, and Lotus admonished her. "Don't you dare start. If you start, I'll start."

Rosabelle said, "And if you two start, I'll start."

They laughed, and when Charlotte hiccupped, they all laughed harder. Mae joined in, dabbing at the corner of her eye. Gina walked in with the twins in the middle of their cry-laugh and rolled her eyes at them.

TK crinkled his nose. "Why are they crying?"

Gina replied, "Because they're happy."

"But then—"

Evvie, in a tone that called to Mae's mind a younger version of Feather Anne, said, "You wouldn't understand. You're a *boy*."

TK stared at all the women a moment longer, then he shrugged and said, "I'm going to hang out with the guys." He turned to leave but spun around and ran to Mae. He kissed her cheek and said, "You look pretty."

A chorus of *aw*'s chased him out. He sped past Brandon as he came in. "Sorry to interrupt. Feather Anne? Anytime you're ready."

"Okay," said Feather Anne. "Be right out." To Mae, she said, "Nick and I—and Brandon—have a surprise for you guys."

Before Mae could respond, Feather Anne slipped out of the tent. Brianna entered next. "Places, ladies. Look sharp. Charlotte, stand straighter, for fuck's sake." Everyone, including Mae, stood taller. "You, little one. Your brother will be right outside the tent. You can walk—do not run—down the aisle. Remember to smile."

Brianna aimed her laser beam gaze on Gina. "Mother of the bride can go out now and sit up front with..." She trailed off as if she'd forgotten Chris's name or role. "After the music starts, my assistant will cue the rest of you. Charlotte, Marisol, Lotus, Rosa… *belle*, Katrina, then you, Mae. The timing is very specific. Don't mess it up."

After she strode out, they all let out a collective exhalation. The first notes played. Mae recognized it immediately. *Lucky*, by Jason Mraz and Colbie Callait. When Feather Anne sang the line about being *in love with my best friend*, Mae took her spot beside Bruce.

The ceremony passed in a blur, as did most of the reception. The food, dancing, and drinks flowed throughout the night, and by the end of the evening, they all felt the effects of the alcohol. All except Mae, who discretely abstained. Mae passed off the secret smile she'd been wearing for days as pre-wedding joy. She would tell Bruce that night once they were alone.

"Best wedding ever, sis," said Feather Anne. She sank into the chair beside Mae and they watched Marisol and Pedro dance slow circles around the dance floor.

"It was pretty great, wasn't it?" Mae briefly rested her head on her sister's shoulder.

Brianna swept by, pulling Ricky onto the dance floor, and said, "You're welcome. Feather Anne, don't let my idiot brother drive, please."

Feather Anne raised a thumbs up. The sisters glanced over at the cluster of friends and family at the bar. All but Bruce—who looked back at them and grimaced good-naturedly—were well lit.

Mae asked, "So, are you all set in the house?"

Feather Anne shrugged. "It's still weird. I'm not used to you guys not being there all the time. The studio is totally fucking awesome, though."

Mae elbowed her. "Language. Yeah, it's weird for me, too. Don't get me wrong, I love the Victorian. The kids especially love it. But yeah. Not living in the house I grew up in and made a life in… so weird. Brianna seems to have chilled out. Has she forgiven you guys for relocating the studio?"

"Mostly. That's thanks to you though. Letting her plan the wedding took a lot of the heat off us. I love her to pieces, man, but she stresses Brandon out too much."

Mae bend her head to get another look at Brandon. He seemed the most inebriated of all. Feather Anne had only alluded to his drinking, so she tried not to say too much. "Well, hopefully the change will help his… help him. All of you. You excited for the album release?"

"Yeah, we're pretty stoked. It's good, Mae. Like, really, really good. I've got a feeling about it, you know? Maybe I'm crazy, but—"

"Feather Anne, I've heard it, remember? It *is* that good. John St. James thinks it's good."

Feather Anne snorted. "Yeah, who'd have thought it a year ago that St. James would end up back in our corner?"

"Time is funny that way. So much can happen in so little of it. You know, after William died, I couldn't fathom loving anyone again, let alone remarrying. But he knew."

"What do you mean?" Feather Anne slipped her arm through her sister's.

"It was in his letter. He wanted me to end up with Bruce. I think part of him somehow knew it would end up this way. That sounds crazy, huh?"

Feather Anne squeezed Mae's arm. "No. Not crazy. Sweet is more like it." From across the hall came the sound of shattered glass. They sprang forward to see Brandon swaying and slurring an apology. "And on that note, I'd better sit him down," sighed Feather Anne. She walked over to Brandon and the group, but turned back and mouthed, "Congratulations," and pointed to Mae's still flat belly.

Mae glanced down and realized she'd probably had her hand there for some time. She grinned back and winked at Feather Anne. She stood, intending to join the group by the bar when something—or rather, someone—caught her eye by the side doors. Someone had propped them open during the reception and now a man stood in the light.

She walked toward him. Up close, she saw the changes. He no longer parted his hair like William, and he dressed in jeans, t-shirt, and blazer. After a pause, he said, "I was at the wedding. You looked beautiful."

"Hello, Jared. I'm glad you came," said Mae with warmth.

"I-I almost didn't. But… well, I don't know. It felt like maybe it was time." He ducked his head and rubbed at the back of his neck.

"I'm glad. Won't you come in? Have a drink?"

Jared shot a nervous glance inside and stepped backward. "I don't think so, Mae. I-I just wanted to say thank you. For, you know, the letters and pictures, all the updates. I'm sorry I didn't start answering them until lately."

"It's okay, Jared. It's all new for you. I'm so proud of what you've accomplished since we last met."

A shy head shake preceded his words. "Ah, it's not that impressive, Mae. I got a regular job and a small apartment. I'm just, you know, trying to do right. I, uh, see a therapist."

"Good for you, Jared. You know the offer stands. When you're ready, okay?"

An unexpected smile transformed his face. "Okay. That'd be—I appreciate that, Mae. Someday, I hope to be the kind of guy your kids would be proud to call uncle."

"They'll be lucky to know you, Jared." He bobbed his head once, then turned to leave. Before he did, Mae said, "Jared? You'll always be welcome here."

She watched until he faded into the night. Bruce joined her. "Everything all right?"

Mae faced her husband and best friend. "Everything is better than all right."

They watched their friends and family laughing and talking at the bar, and nearly fell over at the sight of Miles and Brianna clinking their shot glasses together. Gina and Chris sat off to the side, each holding a nearly asleep twin on their laps. Feather Anne, Brandon, Nick, and Kade posed for a picture taken by Rosabelle. Pedro and Marisol joined the group, and another round of shots were ordered by Bruce's father. On the dance floor, one couple—Georgie and Charles—swayed under the chandelier.

Bruce wrapped his arms around his wife. "Are you sure you don't want to go away for a honeymoon?"

Mae leaned against him. "I'm sure. This is the only place I want to be. Here, with you, our friends, our family." She looked up at Bruce. "Are you okay with that? I know staying home isn't the most romantic thing. If you want to go away—"

He kissed her. "Home, it is. And there's no place I'd rather be."

About The Author

Elsa Kurt is the author of over a dozen novels, as well as numerous short stories, children's books, and guides for new and aspiring authors. She began her Path To Authorship© coaching program for writers in 2018, where she helps aspiring authors navigate their journey through the writing, publishing, and promoting process. She is a married mother of two grown daughters. Elsa loves to hear from her readers at authorelsakurt@gmail.com & you can also connect with her on social media @authorelsakurt.

If you've enjoyed this book, please consider leaving a rating or review on Amazon!

COMING HOME